Praise for Stuart M. Kaminsky

"Pacing a series is a tricky maintenance job. Move too fast, your hero loses credibility. Move too slowly, your readers get bored. Move just right, you produce *Denial*."
—*The New York Times Book Review*

"Kaminsky's distinguished series is always worth your time."
—*Kirkus Reviews* on *A Whisper to the Living*

"Kaminsky takes the reader on a great, wild ride with a couple of sudden, surprising twists. . . . It's great fun to watch a master at work, and Kaminsky fits the bill."
—*Sarasota Herald-Tribune* on *Terror Town*

"Edgar Award–winner Kaminsky renders characters so vivid you can nearly hear them breathe."   —*Mystery Scene* on *Denial*

"There are three things we've come to expect from a Kaminsky story: superb plotting, real-world dialogue, and character development. He doesn't place a foot wrong in any of these departments in *Midnight Pass*."   —*Sarasota Herald-Tribune*

"Jam-packed with the stuff of good crime fiction—character, style, place, recognizable human conflict."
—*The Washington Post* on *The Big Silence*

BY STUART M. KAMINSKY

Porfiry Rostnikov Novels

Death of a Dissident
Black Knight in Red Square
Red Chameleon
A Cold Red Sunrise
A Fine Red Rain
Rostnikov's Vacation
The Man Who Walked Like a Bear
Death of a Russian Priest
Hard Currency
Blood and Rubles
Tarnished Icons
The Dog Who Bit a Policeman
Fall of a Cosmonaut
Murder on the Trans-Siberian Express
People Who Walk in Darkness
A Whisper to the Living

Abe Lieberman Mysteries

Lieberman's Folly
Lieberman's Choice
Lieberman's Day
Lieberman's Thief
Lieberman's Law
The Big Silence
Not Quite Kosher
The Last Dark Place
Terror Town
The Dead Don't Lie

Lew Fonesca Mysteries

Vengeance
Retribution
Midnight Pass
Denial
Always Say Goodbye
Bright Futures

Toby Peters Mysteries

Bullet for a Star
Murder on the Yellow Brick Road
You Bet Your Life
The Howard Hughes Affair

Never Cross a Vampire
High Midnight
Catch a Falling Clown
He Done Her Wrong
The Fala Factor
Down for the Count
The Man Who Shot Lewis Vance
Smart Moves
Think Fast, Mr. Peters
Buried Caesars
Poor Butterfly
The Melting Clock
The Devil Met a Lady
Tomorrow Is Another Day
Dancing in the Dark
A Fatal Glass of Beer
A Few Minutes Past Midnight
To Catch a Spy
Mildred Pierced
Now You See It

Nonseries Novels

When the Dark Man Calls
Exercise in Terror

Short Story Collections

Opening Shots
Hidden and Other Stories

Biographies

Don Siegel: Director
Clint Eastwood
John Huston, Maker of Magic
Coop: The Life and Legend of Gary Cooper

Other Nonfiction

American Film Genres
American Television Genres
   (with Jeffrey Mahan)
Basic Filmmaking
   (with Dana Hodgdon)
Writing for Television
   (with Mark Walker)

Stuart M. Kaminsky

A Whisper to the Living

A TOM DOHERTY ASSOCIATES BOOK
NEW YORK

A WHISPER TO THE LIVING

A Forge Book
Published by Tom Doherty Associates, LLC
175 Fifth Avenue
New York, NY 10010

www.tor-forge.com

Forge® is a registered trademark of Tom Doherty Associates, LLC.

The Library of Congress has cataloged the hardcover edition as follows:

Kaminsky, Stuart M.
    A whisper to the living / Stuart M. Kaminsky.—1st ed.
        p. cm.
    "A Tom Doherty Associates book."
    ISBN 978-0-7653-1888-6
    1. Rostnikov, Porfiry Petrovich (Fictitious character)—Fiction. 2. Police—Russia—
Fiction. 3. Serial murders—Fiction. I. Title.
    813'.6—dc22

                                                                                    2010279772

ISBN 978-0-7653-1889-3 (trade paperback)

First Edition: January 2010
First Trade Paperback Edition: January 2011

Printed in the United States of America

P1

For my grandchildren:
Molly, Nicholas, and Chloe
and those to come

A Whisper to the Living

1

The Boy in Bitsevsky Park

It was cold.

Not so cold that Yuri Platkov would not do that which he had promised himself to do if the man was still sitting on the bench in front of the path into Bitsevsky Park. It was cold, but the boy could detect a faint drifting fall of moisture from the dark sky.

The man was still sitting there.

Was this the fifth day in a row? Yuri counted backward and decided that it was. It had snowed three days earlier, putting another white layer on the park. The man had been there before and during the snow.

Every afternoon as Yuri walked home from school the man had been sitting there. Sometimes he was reading a paperback. Sometimes he seemed to be just thinking. He was a block of a man made even bulkier by the thick coat and fur hat he wore.

The man with a broad face similar to that of hundreds of thousands of Russians did not look up from his book. Yuri approached and sat at the end of the bench away from the man, who turned a page slowly.

Darkness was no more than an hour away and people were trudging or scurrying home from work after emerging from the Bitsevsky Park Metro station at the end of the Kaluzhsko-Rizhskaya Line, the orange line.

Yuri, eleven years old and supremely confident, felt safe enough. The man was old and certainly slow, his left leg oddly still. Yuri could run with confidence if he felt the need. He was the fastest boy in his form at school. Thin, pale-skinned with blond hair under his earflapped wool hat, he had nothing much to look forward to when he got to the apartment where his mother might be home and his father certainly would not be yet. His grandfather would be in front of the television, whatever he was watching the enemy. They would be having a dinner of salad with the vegetables chopped into little pieces, leftover bean soup with sour cream, and sautéed mushroom stew with onions and sour cream served over mashed potatoes. The mushroom stew was also left over and stored in those plastic see-through containers with blue plastic tops.

Yuri's mother worked in the Coca-Cola bottling plant in Solnovo, seventeen miles outside of Moscow. Her job was quality control, watching the bottles fill with syrup, water, and carbonation, looking for even the slightest imperfections. She was well paid. She had frequent headaches. On headache days, Yuri sometimes prepared simple dinners or at least opened the plastic containers, heated the contents, and set the table.

Yuri's father was a bartender in Vodka Bar near the Park Kulutry Metro stop. His father, if he were still home, would leave for work shortly after Yuri came home. Though Yuri was sure his father loved him and his mother, he did a poor job of hiding his desire to get away from his father-in-law each night.

And so Yuri sat on the bench.

The man read on.

"Why are you sitting here?" Yuri said after a minute or two.

"I am waiting," said the man.

"For whom?"

"You," said the man, still not looking at the boy.

"Me?"

"Or someone who would be curious enough to wonder who I might be and why I was sitting here on an early winter day."

Yuri didn't understand, but he was curious.

"What are you reading?"

The man held up his ragged paperback. Yuri looked at the cover. The title was in English, a language Yuri was slowly and painfully learning in school.

"*Ice?*"

"*Da,* yes."

"You are reading an English book about small rodents?"

"Not 'mice,'" said the man. "Ice. Frozen water. It's a story. I would offer you a Red October chocolate, but you might think I was a dirty old man."

"Are you?"

"No," said the man.

"Then you can offer me a chocolate."

"What makes you think you can trust me?"

"You have been coming here for five days. You are slow. I think I can trust you. At least I can get away if you try to do something. People are passing and I am sure I am faster than you are."

The man shifted his weight and with a grunt reached into his coat pocket and came up with a brown see-through bag, which crinkled invitingly. Yuri had a near passion for chocolate. The man reached into the already open bag and fished out a wrapped candy. Yuri could see the familiar image of the woman *marioshki* figure on the wrapper.

"Throw it," Yuri said.

The man threw the candy and Yuri caught it. Yuri could catch almost anything thrown to him. He fully expected to be the goalkeeper on his lower school team next year. Yuri pocketed his candy.

The man opened a second one and popped it into his mouth, stuffing the wrapper into his pocket.

"You want another for here?"

Yuri shrugged. The man came up with another wrapped chocolate and threw it to the boy, who caught it.

"You are a goalkeeper," the man said.

"Yes," said Yuri, this time unwrapping the chocolate and taking a small bite from the end. The candy cracked between his teeth and spread its taste as he chewed it.

"My son is a goalkeeper," the man said. "He was a goalkeeper. He's old enough to be your father."

Yuri wondered how old this man must then be, but he was too polite to ask. "What position did you play?"

In answer the man leaned forward and rapped his knuckles against his leg. It sounded like a knock at Yuri's front door.

"No position," said the man. "My leg was lost when I was your age. So you see that there is no way I could chase a ten-year-old goalkeeper down the street."

"I am eleven and I wasn't worried," said Yuri, popping the last tidbit of candy into his mouth.

"It is probably a good thing to worry when you are near the park and nightfall is approaching."

Two women passed them by with barely a glance. The women were both carrying their string grocery bags weighted down with the night's dinner. Both women were fat, possibly sisters. The fatter of the two kept shaking her head as the other woman raised her voice higher and higher. Yuri caught the word *baranina*. Lamb.

Yuri and the man watched the two women until they were far down the street and the loud voice was lost in a riff of the wind.

The man shifted again, holding the candy in his right hand and fishing his wallet out of an inner pocket with his left.

If he offers lots of money to do some unspeakable thing, I will go find a police car. There is always a police car roaming near the park. This is because . . .

The man held open the wallet to show a police badge.

"I am a policeman," said the man. "My name is Porfiry Petrovich Rostnikov."

"My name is Yuri Platkov. I know why you are sitting here." Porfiry Petrovich nodded.

"Him," said Yuri. "The Bitsevsky Maniac."

"You know about him?"

"Everyone who lives near the park knows about him. He attacks the old people who hang out around the park. He beats their heads in with a hammer and hides their bodies in the bushes. Some say he has killed fifty or more. You expect him to walk up to you and confess?"

"It has happened in the past, but I do not expect it."

"How would he even know you were a policeman?"

"He would know," said Porfiry Petrovich.

"So, you thought someone would just come and sit down and tell you that they knew who the Maniac was?"

"No, but that would be very nice, nicer even if the murderer himself were to sit where you are and confess. I do not expect it, but it would be nice."

"Then why sit here if you do not expect someone to come to you?"

"You came," said the policeman.

Cars were moving cautiously in front of them, windshield wipers rubbing faster than was called for by the falling cold mist. Both Yuri and Porfiry Petrovich watched a large white Chaika stretch limousine with tinted windows come by.

"We don't see cars like that here very much," said Yuri. "There's no place a car like that could be going."

"There's a big dinner at the Posvit Hotel on the other side of the park," said Porfiry Petrovich. "Our government is trying to convince a Japanese investment group to develop an area called Gargarin Street."

"How many has he killed now?" asked the boy.

"Many," said the policeman. "I can't tell anyone because the number might be important when we catch him."

The official internal number of victims, Porfiry Petrovich knew, was nineteen. The unreported number of victims was fifty-one. It was assumed that there were other bodies to be found.

"You are not hoping he will come out of the woods to confess?" Yuri said.

"No, I am not."

"Maybe you are hoping he will come by and try to kill you?"

"I have considered that possibility," said Porfiry Petrovich. "I expect that at some point he will come and sit down as you have. Or perhaps he will pass by letting our eyes make contact."

"Will you be here tomorrow?" Yuri asked.

"Perhaps," said Porfiry Petrovich, urging his plastic and metal leg to allow him to rise with some dignity.

Now that he was standing, Yuri could see that the man was neither tall nor short. He stood with his legs apart, reminding the boy of a cylindrical box of kasha on the kitchen shelf.

"Shall we shake hands, Yuri Platkov?" Porfiry Petrovich said, holding out a thick right hand.

Foot traffic had grown heavier. People streamed from the direction of the subway. It was safe enough. He placed his hand in that of the policeman. Yuri steeled himself to squeeze, but it wasn't necessary. The policeman's grip was firm but gentle.

"The Maniac has moved the bird feeders," said the boy.

The policeman knew the makeshift bird feeders made of shoe boxes or cereal containers. The feeders, tied by string or ribbon, were hung from the low branches of trees with piles of seed inside left by bird lovers. They existed in almost all parks within the city.

"Moved them where?" asked the policeman.

"Farther from the path, deeper into the trees," said the boy. "People have to move away from the eyes of others to put in seeds or watch the birds feed. And some of the old men with no home eat the seeds."

No further clarification was necessary.

"I will look at the bird feeders," said the policeman.

"*Paka*, good-bye," the boy said.

"*Paka*, Yuri Platkov," said Porfiry Petrovich.

Yuri started to move away and then turned to face the standing man.

"Are you important?"

"I am Chief Inspector in the Office of Special Investigations."

"I have never heard of such an office."

"Good. That is as it should be."

Yuri turned and hurried away adjusting the scarf around his neck as he followed the jumble of icy footprints in the thin layer of snow that crackled under his feet.

Porfiry Petrovich Rostnikov had been handed the case of the Bitsevksy Maniac only six days earlier. For the past two years, the murders had been under the jurisdiction of the MVD, Ministerstvo Vnutrennikh Del, the Ministry of Internal Affairs.

The existence of the murderer had been kept a secret. But the public began to learn of the Maniac through word of mouth, surviving relatives, and newspapers and small magazines that couldn't be silenced. They learned of it long before Rostnikov was handed the case. The MVD was embarrassed and the way out of the embarrassment was to issue an internal document, which they were certain would be leaked, stating that their resources had to be concentrated on terrorist threats and that the Office of Special Investigations was

ready to take on principal responsibility for finding "the murders in
and around Bitsevsky Park."

Fortunately, Igor Yaklovev, Director of the Office of Special
Investigations, was quite willing to take on the high-profile case.
The Yak was always willing to take on cases that no one else wanted
provided there was a payoff in the end, be it an acknowledgment of
his skills as an investigator, the possibility of a promotion, or the likelihood of an opportunity to blackmail a government official or a
wealthy citizen.

The Yak, lean and always impeccably dressed in a dark suit and
tie, seldom left his office in Petrovka, Moscow's police headquarters,
though it was rumored that he engaged in regular martial-arts exercises with Vladimir Putin, with whom he had served in the KGB
in St. Petersburg. The Yak relied completely on Rostnikov and his
team to successfully take care of the investigations for which the
Yak took credit. In turn, Colonel Yaklovev did his best to protect
Rostnikov and his team when trouble arose.

Now in his own office down the hall from the Yak's, Rostnikov
continued to go over the MVD reports on the investigation. The
stack was at least three inches high, and he was sure that everything
had not been turned over to him. It was only natural that MVD officers and the Yak would pull out possibly vital documents to hold
for possible gain or simply to hamper the investigation in the hope
of failure.

Still, there was much in the pile of folders and reports, including
the photographs of all the victims and the autopsy reports. Rostnikov had divided the pile of reports in two and given one stack to
Emil Karpo, the gaunt, almost cadaverous inspector who would certainly read every word placed in his hands. Rostnikov, however,
would move through instinctively, catching a word here, something
in the corner of a photograph there. Sometimes he knew what to
look for, but more often he would simply sense what he needed to
know, though he would acknowledge there were times in the past

when he missed some vital piece of information. In a few days, he would switch piles with Karpo and go through the same process again. They were a good team. Karpo was an analyst of fact with no imagination. Rostnikov trusted his imagination and doubted facts.

The others on his team who shared an office with Karpo were on other cases. Rostnikov's son, Iosef, mistakenly named for Stalin when the Man of Steel was still considered the savior of the Soviet Union, was investigating the death of a professional boxer and the wife of a giant of a man who was on the verge of becoming heavyweight champion of the world. That investigation had just begun. Iosef was assisted by Akardy Zelach, the Slouch, a lumbering man of no great investigative skills but often surprising talents.

Zelach's mother was in the hospital almost certainly dying from an ailment that the doctors could not identify. Zelach, who was forty-one years old, lived with and listened to his mother. He could not even imagine what life might be like without her. On the other hand, Sasha Tkach dreamt of living without the daily unannounced appearances of his mother.

Sasha's mother, Lydia Tkach, was a retired government *apparachnik* who was given to shouting directions to her son about how to live, what to eat, and what he could do to try to win back his wife and Lydia's two grandchildren. Lydia was nearly deaf. Lydia had a pair of very effective hearing aids. Lydia refused to wear them. Sasha was sure this was because she had no interest in hearing what anyone else had to say.

Sasha was still morose and not a joy to be with since his wife, Maya, had moved to Kiev with their two children. Sasha had willingly fallen victim to one woman too many.

Elena Timofeyeva had her own concerns, primarily the coming wedding to Iosef Rostnikov, son of Porfiry Petrovich to whom she was to be married in five days. It was required that they were to be wed exactly thirty-two days from the time that they registered with ZAGS, the all-powerful office that controlled marriages. At the moment, however, Elena and Sasha were assigned to protect a British journalist about to look at organized prostitution in Moscow.

Any of them could be pulled from there to concentrate on the Maniac if and when they were needed.

Rostnikov looked at his watch. It was growing late, but he had one important stop to make before heading home. He had removed his leg and massaged the stump when he had sat back behind his desk. He had no recollection of the time when he was a child and had a functioning left leg. He well remembered his atrophied leg, a burden he had grown accustomed to. He missed the leg, which resided in a large jar in the underground laboratory of the possibly mad scientist Paulinin, who claimed to engage in conversations with the dead. Now Porfiry Petrovich faced the prospect of allowing the never-fully-welcome device to take on much of the weight of his considerable bulk.

It couldn't be helped. He picked up the phone on his desk, pushed a button, and told Karpo to meet him two levels below Petrovka.

Rostnikov knew that the Yak's assistant Pankov listened to all conversations in both Rostnikov's office and the shared office of his team from a trio of hidden microphones. Rostnikov took some pleasure in sometimes leading the often-perspiring little man astray. This time, however, there was no deceit.

It was time to pay a visit to the dark labyrinth of a laboratory on the second level below the ground floor of Petrovka where the bespectacled Paulinin worked on and talked to the dead amid chards, fragments, books, and jars of formerly living parts and tissue of man and animal.

In one of the larger jars on a shelf not far from the two autopsy tables, Rostnikov's shriveled left leg floated languidly.

———

"I will need to see them all," Paulinin said, looking over the top of his rimless glasses.

He wore off-white latex gloves and a wrinkled but clean laboratory coat with only a few stains of plum-colored blood on the left arm and a small dark ochre splatter on his chest.

Neither Karpo, who was generally regarded as the closest thing Paulinin had to a friend, nor Rostnikov reminded Paulinin that there were at least fifteen bodies of the Maniac's victims, two of which now lay naked in front of them.

Rostnikov nodded his agreement. The MVD would resist. They had no desire to open the door to evidence of any more victims. Rostnikov would need intervention from the Yak, but he was sure he could get it. Karpo did not nod. He would check the reports and notes on his desk to determine where they might seek additional victims.

Meanwhile, on the two tables in front of them lay the nearly white corpse of an old man with a chest covered by wiry black-and-white hair. The other corpse was of a man about forty-five or fifty who had the dark cast and looks of a person whose ancestry hinted at Mongol. The corpses lay on their sides facing away from each other. Paulinin stood between them, a proprietary hand on the shoulder of each as if he were trying to mediate a dispute between the dead.

Rostnikov and Karpo could see the back of the head of each corpse. The skulls, shaved by Paulinin and the hair carefully placed in Ziploc bags, were crushed, revealing dark jagged wounds of deep red and black.

"My friend here," said the scientist, patting the arm of the old man on his right, "was homeless before I took him in. He washed frequently but without soap. He cut his own hair. You can see that here. He could not reach all the way back, which suggests arthritis.

"He had a place in the park near a large oak tree. There are traces of leaf and root fragments of oak in his hair where he ran his fingers through like a brush. Wait. The traces are also on his quite filthy clothing, and some of those traces go back at least a month."

Paulinin moved around the tables and into the darkness next to a desk overflowing with books and reports, with barely enough room for the computer. Paulinin used the mouse and scroll and music began.

"Schumann. Piano. My guests will be more comfortable with Schumann, don't you think?"

"How could they not be?" asked Rostnikov.

With the sound of Schumann behind him, Paulinin returned to the corpses and whispered to the younger dead man, the one who looked like a Mongol, "You have not been forgotten."

The scientist continued, "These new friends were killed by the same person. Wounds are so similar that even those idiots who have been looking at the other corpses could see that. What may be even more consequential is that the same weapon was used, a claw hammer, first the blunt end and then the claw. From behind. The killer is strong, probably young. I will know after examining the other corpses if all were murdered by the same person and with the same hammer.

"If so . . . ," he continued, looking at Karpo and Rostnikov to complete his thought.

"If so," said Karpo, "he has the hammer, and if we find one where he lives or works you can tell if it is the murder weapon."

"I can," said Paulinin with a grin of satisfaction. "But there is more. The dolts who wrote reports on previous victims noted that there was evidence that they had been drinking shortly before they died. They were correct. It takes no great forensic skill to open a stomach and find alcohol, but . . ."

He paused again for his students to finish the sentence.

". . . but what kind of alcohol?" asked Rostnikov.

He could have used a chair at this point. His left leg was beginning to feel irritation in its mooring.

"Precisely," said Paulinin. "The alcohol was a cheap off-the-shelf wine called Nitin from Greece. Cheap though it may be, it is not usually the first choice of the homeless. There are cheaper ways to get drunk."

Paulinin paused again, waiting.

Rostnikov felt like raising his hand as he had done almost half a century ago in school. Instead, he looked at Karpo, who nodded and said, "Therefore it is possible the wine belonged to the killer."

"Right. It is too late to be sure it was drunk by any of the victims except, perhaps, for these two and the two or three before them. The autopsy reports on the previous victims mention nothing about the brand of wine. The dolts missed it," said Paulinin.

"So," said Rostnikov, "we check with the shops in a five-mile radius of the park for ones that carry Nitin and see if they can think of any customers who have been buying Nitin at least since the days of the first murder."

"Assuming, of course," said Paulinin, "that he has been using the same wine since he started."

There was a soft ripple of the piano and rapid rise to a near-frenzied crescendo.

"You disabled the microphones?" asked Rostnikov under the frantic pianist.

"Moments before you arrived."

Paulinin's laboratory was bugged not by Pankov but by some department of the former KGB. It was to be expected, as whoever was listening accepted the likelihood of being discovered. Once disabled, someone would come in when Paulinin was not there and move the microphone or microphones. Then the game of Find-the-Bug would begin again. In spite of the clutter, the size of the laboratory, the ones who were doing the listening were having trouble finding a new location for their devices.

"When you have the next victim," Paulinin said, "do not let anyone but your people touch it. Bring them exactly as you find them. These two here have been hosed down. They were delivered nice and clean. I want them dirty if dirt was their destiny. I had to look harder than necessary for evidence traces. You understand?"

"Perfectly," said Rostnikov.

"Fortunately, their hosing down was as inept as the examination of the content of the stomachs," Paulinin continued. "Look."

The scientist turned the body of the older man farther on his side, holding him in place and reaching down with his gloved hand to push the dead man's ear forward.

"See?"

Rostnikov and Karpo moved forward to look. Rostnikov saw nothing.

Karpo said, "A small green spot."

"A stain," said Paulinin with a smile.

"What is it?" asked Rostnikov.

"Juice. Guava juice," the beaming scientist said, still holding up the body.

"You analyzed it?" asked Rostnikov.

"I tasted it," said Paulinin.

The image of Paulinin touching his finger to his tongue after pressing it, probably moist, against the tiny dot was less than tantalizing to Porfiry Petrovich.

"Would you like to try?"

"I don't care for guava juice," said Rostnikov.

Karpo declined with a nod.

"Suit yourselves," said Paulinin, easing the body down. "It is a distinctive taste. In any case, I shall see if there is a trace of guava juice in our silent friend's stomach. If not . . ."

"Then the killer may have been the one drinking guava juice," said Karpo. "The wine was for the victims."

"Precisely, but in fact he did not have to drink the wine or the juice," said Paulinin. "Just touch them."

"Who," asked Rostnikov, looking down at the dead man, "would have guava juice on his fingers without having drunk it?"

"How should I know?" asked Paulinin impatiently. "Maybe someone who works with guava juice. Moscow cannot be crowded with purchasers of guava juice and Nitin wine. You are the detective. You find out."

"We will," said Rostnikov.

"You want to see your leg?" asked Paulinin.

"Why not?" asked Rostnikov with a shrug. "Why not."

Aleksandr Chenko carefully removed the cans of sweet potatoes and lined them up on the shelf, labels facing forward, after carefully and quickly examining each can for rust or dents or torn labels.

He had been refilling the shelves of the Volga Supermarket II for the past nineteen years. He was good at it. No, he was perfect at it. It was taken for granted that Aleksandr would have the shelves full, report low inventory or damaged or no-longer-fresh produce, help customers find what they were looking for. Six store managers had come and gone in the past nineteen years while Aleksandr never missed a day, was never sick, never late for work. His reward for this was that he was almost completely unnoticed. It was easy to go unnoticed among the seventy employees in the hypermodern twenty-four-hour supermarket. He could lose himself among the shopping carts and the high metal shelving in the huge storeroom at the back of the store. He could report various damaged cans of juice and take them home. Nitin wine he had to pay for.

Aleksandr had the face of a forty-year-old Russian, smooth shaven, brown hair evenly cut. He was not handsome, but neither was he homely. His face was without blemish, his body neither heavy nor thin, and he was a few inches under six feet tall.

He was paid every two weeks. He never asked for a raise, though he had received four since he had taken the job. Assistant managers rose from the ranks between the many brightly lit aisles under twenty-five-foot-high ceilings and in the dank, dull light of the back rooms. That was fine with Aleksandr, who now backed up to examine the line of asparagus cans in even rows, close together but not quite touching one another.

Aleksandr Chenko believed in setting goals for himself and working to achieve them. The goals could even be arbitrary. Any set of goals worked to give meaning to life. As it happened, Aleksandr's goals were meaningful. When he completed his quest, he would be famous. That would be good, but the discipline of working toward his goal would be more rewarding.

Aleksandr lifted the empty box and carried it through the door to the rear of the store. The smell of fresh-cut meat greeted him. That was good, one of the many smells he enjoyed: fresh meat, fresh fish, particularly salmon, fruit, vegetables, strong cheese. He placed the box on the floor, took out his cardboard cutter, and gracefully and efficiently broke down the box.

When the day's work was done, he would take off his always clean apron and place it on the hook behind the door next to Max's always dirty apron. He wondered how a slacker like Max could do so little work and make his apron so filthy. Aleksandr would select a few items for his dinner and say good night to all. He would smile. They would smile back. He was liked, perhaps not well liked because of his reclusive ways, but liked nonetheless.

He would walk through Bitsevsky Park as he always did, barely looking into the snow-covered trees. He would pass close to where his two latest victims had been found only two days ago.

Aleksandr Chenko wondered if the police would figure out what he had been doing for the past two years. He wanted to tell them, but he was no fool. There would be no phone calls, no e-mails, and no notes to the media.

Once in the one-room, always neat apartment in which he lived alone, he would put away his groceries, prepare a small meal,

have a half glass of nearly black Georgian dry Saperavi. Working in
a supermarket had advantages. There was still a boycott of Georgian and Moldavian wines, a punishment for dealing with the West.
However, various products, like Georgian wine, could always be obtained from longtime suppliers. Aleks would drink the wine after
dinner and then sit back and wait an hour or so to see if the feeling
would come. If it did, he would retrieve the hammer, go to the
park, and kill someone. It really didn't matter who. It was neither
"the who" nor "the when" that mattered; it was "the how many."

Yes, he wished to succeed in his goal, but he was not, as the
frightened public or the police certainly believed, insane. He could
wait for the feeling, wait indefinitely. It was not a compulsion, barely
an urge. He made no plans to kill but would strike when the feeling
was upon him.

There was a problem. He was never certain about how many
of those he killed had been found by the police. It was essential
that they be found. He did not bury them and did not really hide
them. He did not go into the depths of the park dragging the dead
and bleeding.

It was incredible that so many police regularly searching the
park were unable to find the dead.

Aleksandr waited awhile and then said, "Not tonight. Not
yet."

After eating a hot pork sandwich, Aleks got undressed, removing all his clothing, and then moved to his bed in the corner with
the book he had been reading. He put an arm behind his head atop
the two pillows, placed the book on a third pillow on his stomach,
and began to read.

He did not turn on the radio or listen to music. He had never
understood the lure or pleasure of music. The instruments that created these sounds had struck him since early boyhood as ridiculous
toys. He preferred silence.

Later he would turn out the light, put the bookmark in the page, and place the book on the floor. Finally, in the darkness, he would reach down and gently fondle his testicles. There was nothing consciously sexual in his doing this. It was comforting and helped him fall asleep.

"Perhaps tomorrow," he would tell the darkness. "Perhaps tomorrow."

2
Where Does a Giant Hide?

Ivan Mediukin was a giant.

Not a literal giant, but at six-foot-ten and weighing 310 pounds, he qualified in the eyes of most people. Ivan's face was slightly contorted and his head shaved. He could charitably be called homely. Those with less charity called him ugly.

Everything about Ivan was a bit off, even his smile, which came out as a horrific grin. He did have strong, white, and even teeth, though most were not his own. When he removed them, even he beheld himself in the mirror as incredibly homely.

However, Ivan was admired throughout Russia. People came to see him, wish him well, give him advice, ask for his autograph, or have a photograph taken with him. Ivan always obliged and tried not to grin when he heard the click of the camera button.

Ivan was a boxer, a very good boxer whose record as a professional was twenty-nine wins and no losses, with eighteen knockouts. He was not only powerful—his right hand was compared to a triphammer—but he was also a surprisingly agile boxer who used his long arms to fend off jabs and tie up opponents who tried to get in close to throw a desperate punch.

It had happened by chance. First, in the small town of Galich where he was born. He was recruited to play basketball. He had no talent for it. His parents were a midwife and a postal clerk of average height and no great skills. And then he had been discovered by Klaus Agrinkov, who was visiting his sister in Galich. Klaus had been a middleweight until age and a soft belly had ended his career. Klaus had achieved world-class rating and even fought his way into contention before being knocked out and suffering a dangerous concussion at the hands of a promising Kenyan who went on to the championship. Klaus jokingly sparred with Ivan for a photo in the Galich newspaper. Klaus was impressed by the big man's natural ability.

And so it began.

And now five years later Ivan the Terrible was scheduled to fight in New York for the championship of the world. But an adjustment, postponement, or cancellation of the bout would have to be announced because Ivan Medivkin was being sought for the murder of his wife and his sparring partner, both of whom had been furiously beaten to death in a room in the Golden Apple Boutique Hotel.

Some of this Inspectors Iosef Rostnikov and Akardy Zelach knew before they entered the Moscow Circle Health and Gymnasium, not inside the Inner or Outer Ring but on a run-down street in an eastern Moscow suburb.

"Have you ever boxed, Akardy?" asked Iosef.

Iosef was a good-looking man of average height, with the first signs of gray in his short sideburns. He was not as broad as his father, but time was slowly changing that. Iosef was scheduled to be married in less than a week to Elena Timofeyeva. He had evaded the inevitable far too long, and so had she. Love was undeniable, but so was apprehension and even fear.

"I boxed in school, a little," said Akardy, whose nickname, the Slouch, was almost inevitable.

Akardy Zelach, slightly taller than Iosef and about the same weight, walked and stood with an unconfident slouch. At the age of forty-one, Zelach lived with his mother and took care of her. There was almost nothing he thought that he did not share with her, including the way she looked and walked. There was something almost benevolently bovine in their looks. This was mitigated by the glasses Akardy had been forced to wear in the past year. He now had the look of a cloddish university professor who specialized in something vaguely arcane, like plant life in the mountains or literature of the Inuit. This was a false impression. Akardy was, in fact, not very bright. He was a man of many small talents and a wide range of interests, but a stunning intellect was not one of them.

The two inspectors worked well together and enjoyed each other's company. Iosef was a born leader, ready to confront authority. Zelach was a follower.

They mounted the narrow stairs accompanied by the smell of sweat and tobacco. Iosef went first. Above them was the sound of a man shouting. The door at the top of the stairs was marked only with the crude and faded drawing of a boxing glove.

When the two detectives entered, they could both see and hear the shouting man who paced alongside a floor-level boxing ring. Inside the ring two small men in sweatpants, T-shirts, and headgear were trading punches with oversized boxing gloves.

There were dirty wall-to-ceiling square windows on one wall and posters announcing old fights, many with renderings of real boxers. The newest posters were of Ivan Medivkin, "the Giant."

The room was decidedly cold. The cold did not seem to affect the shouting man who wore trousers and no shirt. A white towel was draped over his left shoulder.

Iosef and Zelach approached. The man's hoarse voice vibrated through the room, which was lit only by the morning sun that managed to make its way through the dirty windows.

"Drop your right one more time and I climb in there and show you what can happen to you," the man shouted.

One of the two boxers touched his thumb to his forehead to signal that he understood, and the young men in the ring went at it again.

"Better. Better, but don't drop it."

"Klaus Agrinkov?" Iosef said.

The shouting man held up a hand without looking. The movement was designed to stave off for a minute or two whoever had called his name.

"What happened to your left hand? Are you suddenly paralyzed? Should I call a doctor? Use the damn thing!"

Klaus Agrinkov turned his head now and looked at the two visitors.

"Police?"

Iosef nodded. Zelach adjusted his glasses.

"You found him?" asked Agrinkov.

"No, not yet," said Iosef.

Agrinkov wiped his face with the towel, looked at Iosef, and said, "I know you."

Iosef had seen the man before him fight at the end of his career. It had been a bizarre spectacle in which the six-round boxing match was held after the presentation of a play Iosef had written before he had become a policeman. Agrinkov, paunch already showing and hair already graying, had handily beaten the twenty-year-old sailor who had won the fleet middleweight championship the previous year. It had been no real contest. It had looked to Iosef like a father beating his son in a fury for showing a lack of respect.

"Gronsky Theater eight years ago. I wrote the play that was presented before your fight."

"I remember you, but I never saw your play. I don't have the patience for plays or movies or books."

"That night your patience was rewarded," said Iosef. "The play was a misconceived effort, a didactic ramble. The audience was wrong, but even so the play should have been staged after the fight. Actually, it should not have been staged at all. The people of Moscow do not need to be lectured about Chechnya."

The punches, grunts, and footsteps of the men in the ring punctuated the conversation.

"Is there somewhere quiet where we can talk?" asked Iosef.

Agrinkov shrugged and said, "This way."

And then back at the men in the ring he shouted, "Take a break. No, do not take a break. Go work on the bags."

As they walked across the gym, Agrinkov exchanged the towel for a blue sweatshirt on a folding chair standing lonely, facing nothing.

"I'd be better off going into the ring myself next week. In here."

He held open a windowless door to let the policemen walk in. He followed and closed the door on a large room with a cluttered desk and what looked like a massage table covered with a thin white mattress. The walls were covered with framed photographs of boxers and unframed posters from past battles. There were five chairs scattered around the room in no pattern. Agrinkov slipped on his sweatshirt and sat behind the desk. Iosef and Akardy both found chairs and turned them toward the desk. They sat.

"We looked for you at the Novotny Gymnasium," Iosef said. "They sent us here."

"Here," Agrinkov said with a sigh as he looked around the room. "This is where I started managing eight years ago, picking up promising thugs, like the ones you saw out there sparring, from the streets. Booking whole cards in neighborhood clubhouses that used to be Communist meeting halls. Now I'm here again, hiding from reporters and Ivan's fans. I may never get out of here again. All I need are bars on the windows. Can you believe this place used to be a chop shop?"

"*Da.* It's a bit surprising that you are back at work a day after your biggest boxer became a fugitive in a murder investigation," said Iosef.

"I needed the distraction. Work is the best mask for a broken heart."

"You read poetry?" asked Iosef.

"No, but I'm of a poetic bent. All I have remaining is that talented but stupid lightweight out there. He has heart. His only problems are he drops his hands and won't let his jab lash out."

"He lets his right hand go off the wrong foot," said Zelach.

Agrinkov looked at the policeman, who adjusted his glasses yet again.

"No," said Agrinkov. "He never . . ."

"Slight shuffle just before he jabs when he is punching for power," said Zelach.

Agrinkov looked at Iosef, who held up his hands and said, "If Inspector Zelach says he punches off the wrong foot, you can be sure he does. My partner never fails to amaze me with his talents."

Agrinkov said nothing but nodded to show that he was taking the assessment of his boxer seriously.

"What do you think happened?" asked Iosef.

"The same question reporters from all over the world have been asking on the phone for the last day. I unplugged the phone. The ones who come here are turned away. I'll probably have to sleep here tonight. What do I think happened? I think Ivan married a very beautiful woman with not enough meat on her bones. I think I made a mistake in hiring a sparring partner for him who was good-looking and had a reputation for bedding down ladies young and old, married and single, willing and coaxable. I think Ivan, who is a trusting fool, found them in the hotel room, lost his temper, and . . ."

He let the sentence trail off.

"How did he know they were at the hotel?" asked Iosef.

"I don't know."

"Where do you think he might be?"

"Where do you hide a famous ugly giant? I don't know."

The three-room apartment on Leninsky Prospekt had two great virtues and many drawbacks for Ivan Medivkin.

The three rooms on the fourth floor of the Stalin-era building were all small. He had nowhere to pace. The ceilings were all so low that he had to bend forward slightly when he walked. Vera Korstov had given her bed and bedroom to him while she slept on the small sofa in the minute living room. The problem was that Vera's bed in the narrow cell-sized bedroom was not long enough for him. Add to this the thin walls that required him to speak softly and the need to stay away from the windows.

The two great merits of the apartment were that he was relatively safe and Vera was completely trustworthy and willing to help.

On this morning following the death of his wife, Lena, and his sparring partner Fedot Babinski, Ivan sat in his undershorts and a red sweatshirt that he had left in this same apartment when he first came to Moscow four years ago and he and Vera had been lovers.

He had not seen her in more than three years. She had not changed. She was a tall woman of thirty-one with short black hair and a pleasant face. She was firmly built, with breasts that Ivan had always thought adequate, though nothing like those of his wife, Lena, Lena who was beautiful, tall, twenty-five, with long, always-shining straight hair that touched her creamy shoulders.

Four years ago Vera had taken him in when he knew no one in Moscow but his manager and was considered an ugly curiosity by those who passed him on the street. When he began to box in

Moscow, that changed. He no longer looked ugly to the fans, nor, apparently, to Lena Golumbievski, who asked him for his autograph following his sixth knockout.

Now she was dead and he had sought refuge with Vera, who snuck him into her apartment when he called her at two o'clock in the morning.

The day was overcast. Vera had not turned on the lights. She poured him more coffee.

"I did not kill them," Ivan said, holding the bloodstained towel to his nose.

The towel was wrapped around ice, and the pack seemed to have stopped the bleeding.

"I know," she said.

It was at least the tenth time he and she had said this.

"Your clothes will be dry in a few more hours," Vera said, getting up to retrieve the bread from the toaster.

Ivan looked up at the clothes on hangers over the door to the kitchen. Vera had to duck to get under them.

"No blood?" he asked as she returned and placed a plate of six pieces of toast and a jar of English lemon curd in front of him.

"Clean," she said. "It is easy to get blood out of clothing."

"No," he said, reaching for toast and a knife. "I do not think it is."

She took the wet blood-soaked towel from him. Ivan's nose was still red and bruised, but the bleeding had stopped. He had explained that he had tripped and fallen when he left the hotel room.

"I'm sorry for your trouble," she said.

He nodded and said, *"Da."*

They were silent for almost a minute while they ate and drank their coffee.

"I called in," she said. "Sick. Lots of people have the flu. I'm never sick. I won't have to go to work for at least a few days. They can shoot around me."

Vera had been a talented high jumper who had made it to the Olympics in 1996. She had not won a medal though she leaped a personal best of six-foot-four. Then, in need of an athletic type, a producer cast her in a movie, and she proved to be a consummate actor, moving on to a series of movie roles, generally playing the strong-willed and supportive best friend of the female star.

And now she was ready to support her downcast former lover.

"What will you do?" she asked.

"Think," he said.

"About?"

"Killing the person who murdered my wife and my friend."

"The police think you did it. Maybe you should just tell them what—"

"I ran away. I hit a policeman. They wouldn't believe me."

"You have a plan?" she asked.

He shook his head and said, "No."

"I have," she said.

Ivan looked up, coffee in one hand, toast in the other.

"What?"

"You tell me all the people in Moscow who your wife knew and all the people your sparring partner . . ."

"Fedot, Fedot Babinski."

". . . knew. And I'll question them."

"Why should they tell you anything? What if you question the killer?"

"I can be very persuasive," she said.

"I've lost everything," he said.

"Not quite," said Vera. "Not quite."

She smiled and reached out to touch his massive hands on the table.

"After we've made the list, I have a question for you?"

"Ask it now."

"Why did you go to the hotel room?"

"I got a call. A man at the hotel said I should come right away, that he was calling me because he was a fan, that he thought I should know what was going on in the room, that Lena was there."

"And when you got there . . . ?"

"The door was unlocked. I went in. They were dead. I went to Lena, picked her up. Her face . . . She was covered with blood."

"And the police came through the door how long after?"

"A few minutes. Before I could call them or the hotel desk."

"I think your fan called them," said Vera. "I think your fan wanted the police to find you in that room with your dead wife and sparring partner."

"Why?"

"Let's make that list."

3

An Englishwoman in the Jungle

The Zaray Hotel on Gostinichnaya Street was Iris Templeton's favorite hotel in Moscow. It was a short walk to both the Main Botanical Garden of the Russian Academy of Sciences and the Vladykino Metro station. Iris knew her way around Moscow.

The last time she had been here Iris had done a freelance story for *The Globe* on Putin's tightening of the flow of gas through the Ukraine. She had interviewed the managing director of Gasprom, the largest natural gas company in the world and possibly the largest corporation in the world. The story had earned her two prizes, one in England and one in Denmark. It had also earned her several enemies in Moscow.

This time Iris was on her own, fully freelance. She intended to do a story on the wealthy and powerful of Moscow who take advantage of and are even complicit in the beatings and deaths of prostitutes. Iris had already done much of the groundwork and probably could have enough information from the Internet to do a satisfactory job, but that wasn't the way of Iris Templeton, armed with her compact computer in a briefcase that never left her side when she was in any country other than her own.

She did, however, frequently leave Philip, her husband, who was a quite successful London barrister. They were good friends, and occasional lovers and independent souls.

Iris was not a fool. That there was some degree of danger in her pursuit was without question. Therefore, she did not reject the offer of police protection, though she decided that she would examine those assigned to guard her to be sure that they did not simply offer another possible danger. She didn't really think the Moscow mafia or the government would risk killing her and setting off a new international outrage. Better to let her probe, see to it that she obtained nothing too embarrassing, and let her sell her tale. Besides, she could use a chauffeured ride in her pursuit.

She sat in the bar of the Zaray Hotel drinking coffee, computer in its case on the table, while she waited for the arrival of her promised protectors.

Sasha and Elena had not spoken all the way from Petrovka to the Zaray Hotel. She had driven. They were not arguing. They simply had nothing more to say right now. Sasha was, as he had been for months, lost in thought about Maya, his wife, who now lived in Kiev and showed no signs of wanting to return to him or to Moscow. He had tried, but his frequent infidelities had been too much for her. Now she said she wanted a divorce and had a good man who wanted to marry her. When Sasha went to Kiev to try to retrieve his family he had met the man. Sasha had liked the man. Sasha had admitted to himself that Maya would be better off with the man. But still Sasha had hoped that would not be dashed by his mother, who haunted his apartment and shouted the shouts of the deaf.

Elena had a wedding to worry about and something Iosef had to be told. It was time to tell Iosef.

"Yes," she said emphatically.

"What?" asked Sasha.

"Nothing. Just thinking aloud."

"Dangerous."

Elena parked in front of the hotel, adjusted the police identification on the dashboard, and got out, locking the doors after Sasha.

She wore a clean dark suit and white blouse. He wore trousers and a jacket neatly ironed by his mother. His tie was unwrinkled, his face shaved, and his hair trimmed. He had been warned gently but firmly by Rostnikov that he must overcome his brooding or risk the ever-present possibility for any policeman that he would not be ready when the need arose. Sasha made a very conscious effort to heed the warning. To lose his family was a tragedy. To lose his job would be a horror.

They entered the lobby and strode side by side to the bar where they had agreed to meet the English journalist.

Only one person sat in the bar at this morning hour, a woman of about forty in a black dress with a jacket draped over the chair next to her and a computer on the table.

The woman was dark with very pale, clear skin and blue-gray eyes. She was also decidedly pretty. She looked up at the detectives as they approached and removed her glasses. At first her look was probing and cautious, and then she examined Sasha Tkach and smiled.

"Iris Templeton?" asked Elena.

"Yes," answered Iris, holding out her hand.

"Inspector Elena Timofeyeva."

Elena took the hand, relinquished it, and watched as the woman extended it to Sasha. She gripped his hand firmly and looked directly into his eyes.

"Inspector Sasha Tkach," he said, and added in halting English, "We have been assigned to serve as your escorts."

"I speak your language," Iris said in only slightly accented Russian.

Much might come of this visit besides another prizewinning story.

The decision to kill Iris Templeton was not arrived at lightly. No vote was taken by the three men in the office of Daniel Volkovich overlooking Red Square. It was one of three offices in which he worked throughout Moscow. This office was in the center of the city and was intended to impress visitors and business associates.

The second office was in a rotting neighborhood beyond the Outer Ring Circle surrounding the city. This office was used for dealing with the sordid but necessary day-to-day running of Daniel's less-than-legal businesses, primary among which was the running of the prostitution ring. This was not a simple matter. Locations had to be procured and maintained. Bribes and threats had to be made. Street pimps had to be kept in line and paid and watched carefully and punished for theft if necessary. Bookkeeping was a nightmare. The easy part was finding and keeping the girls. Once they were recruited they were kept in line with threats of disfigurement or death.

The third office was not really an office at all but a three-room apartment not far from the Moscow river. It was in this office that prostitutes were lured, secured, tried out, and rated after undergoing a complete physical examination, including X-rays and blood work. Only then did Daniel try them out, rate them, and assign them to a pimp. The best of these women and girls went onto the list of those catering to visiting and domestic diplomats, businessmen, military, MVD, and high-ranking drug dealers.

The next level down catered to tourists and out-of-town Russians who stayed in the second-level hotels and were directed to the prostitutes by desk clerks, cabdrivers, and policemen, all of whom also had to be paid. The lowest level of prostitutes simply stood in groups in tunnels and basements in lineups for street trade.

Most girls came willingly offering their bodies readily hoping to make a good living for five years or so and return to the towns and farms far from Moscow.

Daniel prided himself on his principles. The girls had to be examined every two weeks by a physician who was also on the payroll. If one was found to be ill or have a disease, she was given a bonus commensurate with her level and sent home, never to return. If a client abused a girl, he would, depending on his station in life, be warned or punished. Street trade customers were beaten and warned. Upper-level customers were informed that their abuse had been recorded on tape, which it had.

Daniel Volkovich was very successful at his profession, and at the age of forty-two he was a very wealthy and important man. Daniel was a tall man with the smiling clean-shaven face of the kind of movie or television actor who plays a policeman or an earnest politician. His well-groomed prematurely white hair was brushed back. Daniel always wore a knowing smile that suggested he could read your thoughts. Daniel's mother had been a prostitute, as had his grandmother. He learned the business as he learned to walk and talk.

Now, his enterprise and his good name were threatened by the Englishwoman. It was not the first time a reporter or the representatives of some international do-good organization had posed a threat. Such people from the West were not easily dissuaded or deceived. Such people on occasion had to be eliminated.

"I can discern no pattern," said Emil Karpo.

He and Porfiry Petrovich Rostnikov were seated in the Chief Inspector's office in Petrovka and had been for the past five hours.

Records, forensic reports, calendars, weather reports, a chart of phases of the moon, photographs of the Maniac's victims, and much more were piled in front of them.

"Review," said Rostnikov reaching for the tea in his Eighty-seventh Precinct mug. It would be their third review of the morning, none of which had suggested a new approach. They spoke slowly so that Pankov or the Yak, who would be listening either now or to the tape, could take notes.

The dogs in the kennel across the courtyard were barking. In the years of listening to them, Porfiry Petrovich had learned to discern the different barks. There was a slow bark with a slight catch deep in the throat that indicated hunger. A rapid higher-pitched bark indicated tedium. A moaning bark suggested that someone had hit one of the dogs who had called out in fear and sympathy. Later in the day the dogs would not be barking as they sniffed through Bitsevsky Park pulling a uniformed officer behind, searching for the dead.

"He kills on any day of the week," said Rostnikov. "No pattern. It might be two Tuesdays in a row and then a Saturday and then a Friday. He can kill for three straight days and then wait a month before taking another victim. Phases of the moon show no consistency. There is no pattern of holidays or birthdays or days of historical or newsworthy significance."

He leaned back and took a sip of his no-longer-hot tea.

"The positions of the bodies seem random," Karpo went on. "Nothing about the clothing of the victims or their health informs us. He seems to prefer men over the age of fifty-eight, but he has also killed two young women."

"One of whom he decorated with wooden spikes in her eyes," said Rostnikov, holding up a photograph to look at the grisly work of the Maniac.

"All of the killings seem to have been done at night, and he is drawn to Bitsevsky Park."

"Emil Karpo, are we missing something?"

"Yes."

"What?"

"I don't know."

Rostnikov scratched the stump of his leg thoughtfully. Then he turned his chair and looked out the window.

"The weather is breaking," he said. "The temperature is supposed to reach forty-five degrees."

Karpo nodded.

Rostnikov reached into the top drawer of his desk.

"I have never heard you whistle, Emil Karpo."

"I have never felt the need."

"To make music," said Rostnikov, gently placing an odd squash-shaped instrument on the desk in front of him.

"The appeal of music is unknown to me. I feel no need for it. It is a functionless distraction."

"You are a true romantic," said Rostnikov.

"I do not believe I am."

"I was engaging in irony."

"I see."

Rostnikov picked up the ocarina he had taken from his desk drawer, placed it to his lips, and blew, slowly working his fingers over a line of small holes. A piping of music emerged.

"Here," said Rostnikov, handing it across the desk. "It is yours. When you feel the inclination, make music."

Karpo took the ocarina and placed it in front of him.

"Now I think I will take a walk in the park," said Rostnikov.

"**He is** going for a walk in the park," said Pankov.

Colonel Igor Yaklovev, sitting at his desk under the framed discreetly sized print of the face of Lenin, looked up at his short, always nervous assistant. One of the many reasons Pankov was perspiring was that the Yak looked very much like the Lenin in the print above Yaklovev's head. He had cultivated the resemblance decades earlier and maintained it throughout the fall of the Soviet Union and the fickle changes in the government. It was a safe resemblance. Were it not, the Yak would see to it that he bore no similarity to the founder of the Revolution.

"Did he say why?" asked the Yak.

"No."

"Did he say which park?"

"No, he did not," said Pankov.

"Guess."

"Bitsevsky."

"Good."

Pankov went silent, anxious to get away from the Yak. Pankov did not do well in the presence of power, which was, as even he knew, an irony, because few in the government were as fervently but patiently seeking power as the Yak. On several dozen occasions, Pankov had taken phone calls directly from one of the assistants of Vladimir Putin himself. This caused near panic in Pankov, but once, and he was certain of this, Putin himself had come on the line, thinking that he would be speaking directly to Yaklovev. Pankov had almost passed out as he identified himself and transferred the call. His hands had trembled. Perspiration on his forehead had beaded, and his underwear had tightened with moisture.

"The journalist?" asked the Yak, folding his hands in front of him on the desk.

"Tkach and Timofeyeva are taking Iris Templeton to talk to people for her story."

"I want a list of everyone she talks to."

"Yes."

Yaklovev made a note. This information might prove useful, especially if one of the supposedly tough mafiosi in the prostitution business was potentially compromised or embarrassed and the Yak could help him in exchange for future considerations.

"The boxer has not yet been found," Pankov added.

Yaklovev cared little about that. Rostnikov's annoying son and the slouching Zelach would find Medivkin, though that might not in any way add to the popularity or power of the Office of Special Investigations. Taking on such no-win cases was the price one sometimes had to pay for ultimate success.

"Go home, Pankov," Yaklovev said.

"I still—"

"Go home," the Yak repeated with a smile his assistant would have preferred not to see.

"Yes, thank you," Pankov said.

The sun would be going down within the hour. This early release would give Pankov time to pick up a few groceries, particularly a few more boxes of oatmeal. Pankov almost lived on oatmeal made with water and artificial maple syrup. Boxes of oatmeal lined his small shelves, and his small refrigerator held three bottles of syrup. Still, one could never be sure when one might run out.

In the outer office, Pankov put on his coat and pressed the button that activated the recording of not only the mocking conversations in Rostnikov's office but also the conversations in the outer office across the hall where the other inspectors had desks and conversation.

Both the Yak and Pankov had been invited to the wedding of Elena and Iosef. Both had accepted. The Yak was well aware that his presence would make everyone uncomfortable. That did not bother him.

Pankov gladly accepted when he knew that the Yak was going to attend. Pankov had never been to a wedding. Never. He had no friends outside of the thirteen members of the Monocle Club, the group of ten men and three women who not only collected the ocular affectations of the obliterated aristocracy but also knew everything worth knowing and even more not worth knowing about the lenses. Strictly speaking, the members of the Monocle

Club were not his friends, but they shared a common, if arcane, interest. They met every two weeks in a small room of the Budapest Hotel, a hundred meters from the Bolshoi Theatre.

As he stepped out of the office, closing the door quietly behind him, Pankov remembered to turn on the cell phone in his pocket. He hated the phone, but the Yak insisted that Pankov keep it charged and in his pocket where he could hear it. There was no place he could be comfortably alone and really no place where he could feel comfortable among people.

It was his life. He accepted it. It did keep him on the fringes of power. He was the assistant and secretary, really, of a very powerful man who would only grow more powerful. This was not bad for a man whose father had been a sub-foreman in a government uniform-manufacturing factory and whose mother had been a sewing machine operator in the same factory.

Behind Pankov as he left Petrovka he could hear a single dog wail. The sun was dropping in the west, and the temperature seemed to be rising.

He headed for the Metro station willing his cell phone not to ring. He would ask his neighbor Mrs. Olga Ferinova what gift he should bring to the wedding and how he should dress and behave.

Vera Korstov was a highly methodical and determined woman. She had left her apartment with a neatly printed list of six names carefully coaxed out of Ivan Medivkin. She had expected more, but this, she had been sure, would be a good start. At the top of her list was Albina Babinski, the widow of Fedot Babinski, the murdered sparring partner.

The police, Vera was certain, would have a similar list of names with at least several duplicates. They would be looking for Ivan as she would be looking for the murderer who had set Ivan up for the crime.

It was unlikely the police would be in a hurry to talk to Albina Babinski. They had no reason to think that she might know where Ivan was hiding.

The apartment building, in one of the many four-, five-, and six-story concrete Stalin-era complexes throughout the city was a river map of cracks and fissures. Three men huddled in the demi-warmth of the tobacco-fouled entryway. They took some notice of her but were more interested in arguing about what they thought of the latest Russian rage against Georgia.

Vera walked up the staircase lit only on the landings by dim yellow bulbs. She tried not to touch the walls, which were dappled with stains and graffiti, most of which brightly extolled the virtues of one gang over another.

She found the apartment on the second floor where two women stood in opposite open doors talking. A child of no more than two clung to the dress of one of the women.

Vera knocked at the door and prepared herself, got into character. She held her purse protectively in two hands against her stomach. She let her shoulders drop and pinched the flesh under each eye to make them moist. She knocked again, and this time the door opened a crack.

The two women in the hall stopped talking to hear what would be said.

"Albina Babinski?"

Vera could see little of the woman who replied with a tentative "Da."

"I am sorry, so sorry, to bother you," Vera said nervously. "I am . . . was a cousin of your husband from Odessa. I happened to be in Moscow with a meeting of raw sewage engineers and I heard . . . I'm so sorry. I haven't seen Fedot since we were about twelve. He was always so . . . I shouldn't have come. I'm sorry."

"Come in, Countess," said the woman on the other side of

the door. "And I shall endeavor to snatch from you the halo you have been imagining about your cousin's head."

Vera could smell the alcohol on the woman's breath as the door opened. Sunlight illuminated the small, disheveled room. A dark brown sofa sat heavily across from two chrome and plastic chairs that had probably been considered modern in the seventies. A bottle with three glasses stood on a glass-and-steel table the size of a bicycle tire. The table had chosen to side with the two chairs, but the large sofa with obviously soft pillows had a distinct magnetic attraction for objects in the room that stood in deference to the largest piece of furniture.

Albina Babinski was a mess. Her dyed blond hair was losing its color, and its loose strands were held tentatively in place with five little red plastic clips. Her brown dress was draped over her commodious frame like a Roman toga. Albina Babinski's face was round, very round, with pink cheeks punctuated by two small pimples on her left cheek and three on her right. Thick, unflattering makeup covered her face, neck, and even the backs of her hands. Vera did, however, give the widow credit for her bright blue eyes and the look of something painful, likely the death of her husband.

"Would you like a drink?" Albina said, motioning toward both sofa and chairs to give her visitor a choice of discomforts.

"Yes, thank you," said Vera, sitting on one of the chairs, which proved to be just as uncomfortable as it looked.

Albina poured vodka into two glasses, handed one glass to her guest, and clutched the other in her hand as she plopped into the sofa, spilling a few drops of her drink in the process.

"You may return to Odessa to spread the news that Fedot the cousin of fond memory was a walking blind erection that managed to be unable to locate me for the past four years. He was, however, more successful in locating a colorful array of other willing, waiting receptacles."

Vera looked down.

"I shock you, you who deal in sewage?"

"No."

"He found the wrong vessel in that giant's wife," said Albina, holding up her drink and looking at it as if it were a masterpiece.

"Were there other wives, other women?" Vera asked as if amazed at the possibility.

Albina drank, held her glass to one side, leaned over toward Vera, and whispered, "Dozens. I do not know why women were attracted to him. Fedot was a decent-looking man with a scarred body, but he was hardly a Michael Clooney."

"I think the actor's name is George," said Vera softly.

"Who gives a shit?" said Albina even more softly. "What's your name, Countess?"

"Vera Egorovna."

Albina pursed her lips, thought, and said, "Who are you?"

"Vera Egorovna, Fedot's cousin from Odessa."

"Bullshit. Fedot was taken from Riga to Moscow when he was a baby. He liked to tell people that he was from Odessa, that he had family there, but he did not. So who are you besides Countess of the sewers?"

Vera sat up straight, put down her purse, and smiled.

"I am a reporter for *The Moscow Times*."

"And you are going to write an article about the giant and his slut and Fedot?"

"Yes."

"How much are you willing to pay for my undivided and truthful story?"

"If there is a story, I am authorized to pay either five thousand rubles or two hundred euros."

"I'll take the euros. Can you pay me now? In cash? I have bills to pay, a future to consider."

"I can give you one thousand rubles today and have the rest in euros delivered by two this afternoon."

It was, of course, a lie, but the thousand rubles would be a reasonable price for an expanded list of suspects.

"In advance," said Albina.

"On the table," said Vera. "The rest tomorrow. Before ten in the morning."

Albina nodded agreement and said, "What would you like to know?"

It was almost six. There was still enough daylight for the chess players in Bitsevsky Park to see the pieces on the wooden tables. The day had grown warmer, almost fifty degrees Fahrenheit, with only a mild wind, warm enough to draw out what appeared to be the usual regulars, all of them men, most of them retirees, the out-of-work, and those who had hurried over after work. There was also a trio of what appeared to be homeless men wrapped in whatever coats and hats might come close to fitting. When the weather really broke, the present number of sixteen would double and be added to by visitors to the park who had not come to play chess.

Rostnikov paused at the first table, where a thin, bespectacled old man stroked his white beard as he considered his next move. His opponent was an impatient bulky man in his fifties whose left leg bounced rapidly as his fingers tapped on the plank of the bench on which he sat.

Rostnikov had been picked up in front of Petrovka by a black ZiL belonging to the MVD, the Ministry of Internal Affairs. Seated in the back was a man with military-cut steel gray hair and eyes to match.

Aloyosha Tarasov had held out his hand to shake once Rostnikov maneuvered in next to him in the backseat.

"Porfiry Petrovich, how fares the appendage?" said the Major, glancing at the extended left leg.

"The leg and I are not yet friends, but we are making headway."

Rostnikov had known Major Aloyosha Tarasov through decades of change in the MVD. Departments had been eliminated. Others had sprung up as the tides of political opinion changed. It was difficult to determine sometimes which department had responsibility for specific tasks. What was certain was that Tarasov had been assigned the task of finding the Maniac. It was also certain that Tarasov had not succeeded. They drove in silence for a minute or so looking out the window.

"You are welcome to the case," said Tarasov. "My superiors, including the Deputy Director, were more annoyed that the murders took so much of their time and budget. Murder has been relegated to a very low level in the MVD. The military branches of our organization take most of our resources and present the best opportunities for high-profile success."

"Or failure?" said Rostnikov.

"Or failure," Tarasov agreed. "You have all of our files, with the exception of those that demonstrate the fallibility of many of the staff I was given for the search."

Pause in the conversation and then Tarasov sighed.

"You have questions for me," he said. "First I have one for you. Why do you want me to go to the park with you?"

"You have been to the sites where the bodies were found. You have seen the bodies. You have done the investigation. The files show the facts. I would like your impressions."

"For all the good they will do you," Tarasov said.

"What did you feel when you looked down at the bodies?" asked Rostnikov.

"What did I feel? As if I would get little sleep that night. Let me see. Neatness. They were all laid out on their backs, hands at their sides, faces forward. Their wounds could not be seen, though some had blood on their faces from the attack. Indifference. They were not the objects of hatred. The killer didn't care about them as people. It was all very efficient. Those were impressions. They are not in the report. Our killer is intelligent. You were in the park this morning again."

"Yes."

Though responsibility for the serial killer had been passed onto Rostnikov, Tarasov would continue to monitor progress or failure from a distance. Rostnikov had assumed at least one of Tarasov's people would be lurking in the wind.

"He will not attack you."

Rostnikov shrugged.

"We had people posing as homeless or pensioners for weeks. He never struck. He seems to know when we placed a decoy in the park. Add to that the fact that no one of reasonable interest ever appeared more than once in the hundreds of photographs we took with a telephoto lens. The Maniac struck quickly each time at various places both inside the park and on the walks around it. He will not strike at you."

"He might come and talk to me," Rostnikov said.

"Why would he do that?"

"Curiosity, a desire to talk to someone about what he has done and why he has done it."

"He never spoke to any of my undercover men."

"Would you have?"

"No," said Tarasov. "Good luck."

Except for having murdered his wife, Aloyosha Tarasov was a law-abiding Russian. He took no bribes, played no favorites, kept the secrets of his superiors, and always did what he was told. He was considered a highly competent investigator, and rightly so. He wanted nothing more than to survive, do the work he loved, and be respected. His wife had never understood that. She had wanted to get out of Russia, with or without her husband. Were she to leave, his career would be in jeopardy.

Olga had never been the object of his love. He needed a wife for appearances and a reputation for normalcy. One morning eleven years ago, he had stopped at home after having been at a crime scene nearby. He had found Olga standing in the living room with a suitcase in her hand. She told him that she had arranged passage to Poland and was leaving immediately. He had calmly struck her with his fist and thrown her out of the window of their eighth-floor apartment on Kolinsky Street. A passing pedestrian was slightly injured by the falling body.

Olga had cooperated in death as she never had in life. She had left a good-bye note that could easily be interpreted as a confession of suicide. Tarasov had unpacked her bag, called in the demise of Olga, and sat down to wait for the arrival of an investigator who was dutifully uncomfortable in the presence of an MVD major.

Aloyosha Tarasov did not have pangs of guilt, did not experience bad dreams, and spent almost no time remembering his dead wife or his deed.

Years later Rostnikov had read the supposed suicide note and concluded that it was just what it had been, a statement of her decision to leave. Though it had all taken place years earlier, Rostnikov had asked Emil Karpo to dig into the evidence. He had found airline bookings and discovered that Olga Tarasov had a ticket to Warsaw on Aeroflot the day of her death. He pursued the matter no further. Not yet, perhaps never.

Rostnikov liked his MVD counterpart. They weren't quite friends, but they were a bit more than acquaintances. From time to time they had lunch together or met to keep each other informed. Rostnikov knew that if the opportunity presented itself, he would have no trouble launching a full investigation into the death of Olga Tarasov.

"Anyplace particular in the park?" asked Tarasov.

"Where they play chess."

Tarasov leaned forward to tell the uniformed driver where to take them and then turned back to Rostnikov.

"We checked all the chess-playing regulars. They are mostly

old men, and the younger ones all have alibis for at least three or four of the murders."

Rostnikov nodded and said nothing.

"None of them remember seeing anything or anyone suspicious."

Rostnikov nodded again.

They were silent for most of the rest of the drive.

And now they stood side by side next to a table on the end.

The playing was quick. The small-timers were not necessary.

A skinny, shivering old man at their side glanced at them and whispered, "The sun is going down. Games have to be finished. A game unfinished is a game that gnaws at the heart and mind. Better to lose than to leave a game unfinished. You understand?"

"Yes," said Rostnikov. "Yes, but there are unfinished games that cannot be abandoned with the setting of the sun."

"You are the police," the man said.

"Yes," said Tarasov.

"I have seen you here before."

"Yes," said Tarasov.

"You asked me about suspicious strangers and I told you I had seen nothing."

"Yes," Tarasov said once more.

"Even if they finish now," the man said, "I don't think I'll play."

"Avoid the unfinished game," said Rostnikov.

"Yes."

The old man smiled, showing uneven brown Russian teeth.

The policemen walked away, leaving the thin man alone in front of the coveted table and game.

"They would not notice if our killer came up behind one of them, caved in his skull as he sat considering his next move, and dragged the body away," said Tarasov.

"They would notice a new player who sat down."

"Yes," said Tarasov. "But they would not notice a missing player. One of your victims may well have played here a few times. They seem to show no curiosity about regulars who do not show up one day and never appear again."

"Maybe I'll have Emil Karpo play tomorrow," said Rostnikov. "He plays chess?"

"He is quite good, but he shows no enthusiasm for the game."

"And do you?" asked Tarasov.

"Not for the game of chess," said Rostnikov, taking in the area while still looking at Tarasov.

Aleksandr Chenko, string shopping bag in hand, hurried down the path about fifty yards from the chess tables. The bag was heavy with milk, bread, vegetables, and cans of sardines and a large box of kasha. His prize purchase that day at the Volga Grocery had been a bunch of large nearly perfect radishes. He had brought the radishes out and placed them in the bin, spreading them to give their best effect. To ensure that this bunch would still be available, he had placed it gently in a corner of the bin and covered it with ice. He would clean them and admire them before slicing a few of the larger ones and putting them on a sandwich with the sardines.

He did not look directly toward the chess tables, nor at the two who were obviously policemen. Yet he saw them. One had been here several times before. The one with the bad left leg had only begun to come over the past week. At odd hours he would sit on a bench and read a book.

There was something intriguing about the man with the bad leg who was built somewhat like a large brick. It would be interesting to get close and see what he was reading, perhaps even to talk to him. At some point Aleksandr knew he might be caught, but it was essential that this not happen before he had reached his mark. If he chose to go on killing, every victim after that would be a bonus.

At that moment he decided that the policeman with the bad

leg would be the one with whom Aleksandr made the record. That would happen soon. Then he would celebrate. Tonight, after eating his sandwich of radishes and sardines, he would call both *The Moscow News* and *The Moscow Times* and give them an accurate count of the dead. Since the police were not letting people know, he would tell them. It was essential that people around the world knew.

Just before turning to the left at the point where the path divided, Aleksandr allowed himself one quick glance at his next victim.

The policeman with the bad leg was looking back at him.

4

The Scientist in the Cellar

"**This is** foolish," Elena Timofeyeva said, peering through the window of the bistro on Kalinin Street.

Elena looked at Sasha for support. He intended to give it, but a look from Iris Templeton tempted his resolve. He had not been with a woman for almost five months and here was a pretty, smart, famous woman regarding him with obvious intent.

"It is not a good idea," he said in compromise.

Iris Templeton smiled at Sasha and said, "Perhaps not, but I've made my career by doing foolish things that others were afraid to do. You are police officers. There must be many times when you tread when there might be danger."

The meaning of her words was not lost on either Elena or Sasha.

"Besides, you will be right behind me."

"But—" Elena began.

"But," Iris Templeton continued, "your orders are not to give me advice, but to provide me with protection. Is that him?"

Iris nodded at a lone man who sat drinking from a coffee cup at a small, round table against the far wall of the crowded bistro.

"Yes," said Elena.

The man they were looking at was well built, fair skinned, with prematurely white hair. He could not have been more than forty years old. He wore a blue button-down shirt and on his chair was draped a leather jacket so fine that it shined with the reflection of the overhead lights.

"I'm going in. Stay here," said Iris, examining her reflection in the window.

"We are not under your orders," said Elena. "We decide where we must be to protect you."

"It would be better if we were friends," said Iris. "Sasha and I are going to be friends."

Sasha resisted the urge to brush back the unruly lock of hair that dangled down his forehead.

Iris Templeton entered the bistro. When the door opened, the two police officers could hear the sound of music from a CD player inside. As the door closed, they heard the somewhat familiar sound of some popular singer shouting loudly. Neither Elena nor Sasha recognized the performer. Both knew that Zelach could immediately identify the song, the performer, and his complete discography.

"It is not a good idea," Elena said with mocking sarcasm as the door closed. "If something happens to her, we will be held responsible."

Sasha did not respond.

He watched Iris Templeton move to the table of Daniel Volkovich, who half-stood in greeting. He was smiling as he took Iris Templeton's hand and held it for a few seconds longer than Sasha thought necessary.

Iris Templeton sat across from the pimp. She was in profile.

White light danced on her face. It was a cameo that attracted Sasha, who well knew the danger of responding to what he was feeling. Yet he could not control it.

"Let's go in," said Elena, pulling the collar of her jacket around her neck. "I'm cold."

Sasha felt neither hot nor cold. He felt bewildered.

"Yes," he said.

The two entered the bistro. There were two empty tables, only one of which had a clear view of where Iris and Daniel sat talking. A fat man with a red face had to move in tightly to allow Sasha to sit. The fat man looked annoyed. He was about to speak, but something in the near baby face of the man who had forced him to move warned him that it would not be a good idea.

The police officers were too far away and the music too loud to let them hear what was happening at the table where the reporter and the pimp were sitting. What Sasha could see was that the two of them were getting along very nicely, with smiles, words, and nods of agreement.

Elena wanted to say, *You are jealous, Sasha Tkach. How many times must you be misled by your sex? This woman plans to use you.*

"Jealousy and love are sisters," Sasha said as if reading her mind.

Elena knew the proverb. It did not impress her. She had experienced jealousy with Iosef, but it had been under her control and did not deter her from the wedding. Was it really only two days away?

Daniel Volkovich leaned across the table and rested his hand over that of Iris Templeton.

The familiar demon within Sasha banged at his chest and in his brain. It took a great effort to control it, to keep from walking over to the table and sitting next to Iris. He had only known the woman for hours, but there were factors that made her difficult to resist. Perhaps the most important factor was that she was definitely interested

in him. Next, she was pretty. Next, she was smart. He was not looking for love or even for sex, but when it presented itself so openly
he knew resistance was impossible.

Elena saw no waiter moving from table to table, nor did she
see anyone behind the bar who might be a waiter.

"You want a drink?" Elena asked, rising.

"Beer. American or German," he said, his eyes fixed on the
couple at the table against the wall.

He willed Iris to pull her hand from under that of the charming seducer. She did not move it.

Elena had no need to tell Sasha to keep a close watch on Iris.
She moved through the random harvest of crowded tables to the
bar determined not to drink anything that might blur her senses
or add unneeded calories. Iosef said that he liked her the way she
was. She was sure he would like her even more if there were less
of her.

Ten minutes later Daniel Volkovich took a cell phone from a
pocket of his leather jacket and punched in a number. He did it
all with one hand so he would not have to relinquish Iris's hand.
Daniel spoke briefly and put the cell phone back in his pocket.

During the phone conversation, Volkovich had glanced at
Sasha and nodded. Sasha averted his eyes.

Both Sasha's beer and Elena's coffee were long finished when
there was a noise at the table of the fat man behind them. The fat
man shouted. A chair was pushed into Elena, who stood facing the
disruptive table. The fat man stood on unsteady feet and toppled
against Sasha, who struggled not to be blown from his chair.

Sasha pushed the man away.

"Not your business," the fat man said, his large red nose inches
from Sasha's face.

Sasha threw an elbow into the man's face. The fat man tumbled backward into his already-overturned table. A pair of men,

one with a bald head and large, bushy mustache, came to calm things down and usher the fat man and his party out the front door.

It was only after some sense of order had been restored that Sasha looked toward the table in the corner. Elena did the same.

Iris Templeton and Daniel Volkovich were gone.

This is what it comes to," Paulinin said, changing his gloves.

On the two tables deep below Petrovka lay the bodies of Lena Medivkin and Fedot Babinski.

"Comely in life, serene in death," Paulinin said, scalpel in hand as he looked down at the naked bodies that lay side by side on their backs only a few feet from each other.

Paulinin had the urge to help them reach out and clasp each other's hands. They made an interesting couple. She was young, dark, and when the blood was cleansed quite beautiful except for the bruises on her face and the crushed right cheekbone. He was a man of no more than forty-five. His was a muscular body with no chest hair. There were a few scars, one on his stomach, another on his forehead. His face was roughly handsome, with a much-broken nose that made him more interesting than he might otherwise have been. The blood had also been cleansed from his face, but the man's fists and knuckles were quite bloody. He must, Paulinin tentatively concluded, have fought back and done some damage to whoever had beaten him to death. Paulinin did not clean the knuckles. The blood of the killer might still be on them.

"Do you have secrets, my pair of lovers? Secrets that you will share with me as we talk?"

Paulinin reached for the cup and drank lukewarm coffee. He had been working for more than forty hours straight, taking time off only to eat, shower, change his bloody and fluid-stained whites. He could have taken pills that would guarantee that he would stay awake, but it wasn't necessary, at least not yet. The sight of this pair in front of him woke him with great interest.

"What shall it be?" he said, addressing the man and woman whose eyes were closed. "What have I not listened to yet in the last days? Ah, Mussogorsky, *Night on Bald Mountain*. Perhaps *Pictures at an Exhibition*. Yes? Good."

Paulinin put down his coffee cup and, scalpel still held up high, moved to the new CD player on the cluttered desk a dozen paces away.

As the first eerie strains of *Bald Mountain* came through the speaker on the shelf just beyond the heads of his guests, Paulinin tried to decide with whom he would begin. He turned the woman's head to her right and the man's head to his left. They were now facing away from each other as if to hide the shame of the desecration to their skulls.

Paulinin leaned forward under the strong light looking first at the woman and then at the man. He repeated the look at each leaning closer, this time with a magnifying glass. He began to hum along with the music as he leaned ever closer.

He did not know how long he moved from one body to the other, but when he did stand upright his back signaled a familiar ache.

"Thank you," he said to the pair. "I shall wake the Chief Inspector and Emil Karpo in the morning with the news you have given me. I admit that I am rather given to professional surprises when I am the one presenting them and not the one receiving. I would prefer you not pass on that truth. I am trusting you not to do so."

He did not remind them that they were dead. It would spoil the mood.

Now, with music around him and the smell of alcohol and blood to give him encouragement, Paulinin began his work.

———

"The girls are sleeping over tomorrow night," Sara Rostnikov said as she watched her husband eat the Zharkoe pork she had prepared for him.

The dish was one of Porfiry Petrovich's favorites, pieces of pork sautéed with onions, mushrooms, potatoes, herbs, and pickles. Tonight it tasted particularly good and the news of the two girls was welcome.

"Galina has the opportunity to work the night shift at the bakery. She will make double her salary."

Laura, now eleven, and her sister, Nina, now nine, lived in an apartment with their grandmother Galina, one floor below the Rostnikovs. Until a few months ago, the three had lived with Sara and Porfiry Petrovich in their one-bedroom apartment.

The girls' mother, Marina, had run off with a petty crook after trying to sell them. And then Galina herself had spent time in prison after shooting her abusive boss at another bakery. It had been his gun. She had wrestled it from him. In the struggle, he had been shot. Galina spent almost a year in prison. Without Rostnikov's intervention, she might yet be working in the bakery of the women's prison. During her imprisonment, the Rostnikovs had gladly taken in the two girls.

There were days like today that Sara and Porfiry Petrovich missed having the girls from early morning until they fell asleep on makeshift bedding on the floor of the living room only a dozen feet from where Rostnikov now sat.

"Good," he said.

"The news or the food?"

"Both. How are you feeling?"

He paused in his eating and looked at his wife. It had been the crucial nightly question in their lives for years, particularly since the successful surgery to remove a tumor from her brain three years ago. The wound had healed, but her once vibrant red hair had quickly lost its flare and settled for a more subdued hue. Her face

was still round and pretty. Her lips were full and her voice was still
as husky as when he had first heard it almost forty years ago.

"I have an appointment with Leon tomorrow," she said.

Leon was her doctor and Porfiry Petrovich's. Leon was also
her cousin.

"The headaches?" Rostnikov asked.

"Yes, but they could be caused by many things."

Rostnikov nodded and resumed eating. They both feared the
return of the tumor or a new one, but there was nothing to say
that would enlighten them or give them hope.

It was almost midnight. Rostnikov would have to be up early
and he had yet to do his weights, remove his leg, and quite liter-
ally hop into the shower to shave and wash. He hoped the water
would at least be tepid. He had done his best to ease the flow of
heating gas. His efforts had proved to have dubious success.

Rostnikov's hobby was plumbing. Plumbing fascinated him.
The pipes in the wall, the sinks, were all part of a system not unlike that of the human body that disposed of waste. Pipes and
sinks were things that he could repair. There were many things he
as a policeman dealt with every day that he could not repair.

The entire building in which the Rostnikovs lived counted
on him and not the post-Soviet owners to take care of everything
from leaking faucets to major assaults on the rusting system.

When they could, the two little girls accompanied him in his
efforts. Nina was particularly fascinated by his efforts and tools.
The older sister, Laura, joined them when she had nothing else
to do.

He finished the food in his bowl and wiped it clean with a
piece of heavy grain-filled bread.

"More?" Sara asked.

"Yes, please."

She brought him more and smiled as he began working on
another bowl.

"You are a great cook," he said.

"When we first married, I believed that, but I have learned that you will eat almost anything and declare that it is delicious."

"Your cooking is special," he said. "Your chicken *tabak* is so good it would even make Vladimir Putin smile with gastronomical delight. Ask Iosef."

"Our son is as undiscerning about food as you are. Almost every morning when he still lived with us he had the same breakfast as you, a large bowl of hot kasha with milk and sugar, and declared it delicious."

Rostnikov said nothing. She was right. He too thought the morning bowl of kasha was delicious. He had thought so since childhood.

"Finished," he said with a grin. "It was delicious."

"And I am a great cook."

"The greatest in all of Russia and all the former member states of the Soviet Union."

Getting up took great effort. It was not just his leg but also a weariness in his bones. For some reason he thought of the boy on the bench that afternoon. What was his name? Yes, Yuri Platkov. He wondered if the boy would be back the coming afternoon. Rostnikov had enjoyed their conversation. The coming day was supposed to be mild, without either rain or snow. Trusting forecasts could be disappointing in Moscow.

He still had the chance of six hours' sleep if he moved quickly and efficiently. Six hours would be fine. He would be one hour short of that goal. At 5:00 A.M. the phone would ring to inform him that the Maniac had struck again.

Aleksandr Chenko had eaten not one but two sandwiches of radishes and sardines. He had turned on the television when he came home but absorbed almost nothing that passed in front of him.

Aleksandr could not stop thinking of the man, the barrel of a detective who had looked right at him in Bitsevsky Park. It would be right to make him the next victim, but when would that be? The need was there and the passion was in him. He needed to kill again soon. His chessboard called to him. He needed it as others might need a third sandwich. He felt the need in his stomach, his heart, his throbbing head.

If he was to make a place for himself in history, he would have to act quickly. The policeman would have to wait. Aleksandr's watch told him it was almost midnight. He moved with certainty to the hook on the wall near the door to the hall. He removed his jacket from the hook and put the jacket on.

Aleksandr locked his door behind him and moved down the silent stairwell to the basement. He encountered no one. He wouldn't have been surprised to run into one of the other tenants in the building wandering in drunk and loud. There were several who would have made excellent additions to his list, but he did not want the police to be this close, not yet.

Aleksandr turned on the light. Behind a pile of boxes against the wall was a loose brick. He flattened himself between boxes and wall and removed the brick, first with the tips of his fingers and then with his hand. He reached into the now-open space and found the handle of the hammer. He closed his eyes as the familiar feeling of almost sexual pleasure electrified his hand and moved over his entire body. He shuddered as he carefully withdrew the hammer and placed it on top of the boxes. It took him only seconds to put back the brick and slither back into the light.

As he stepped toward the light, he looked back knowing that he would see his shadow, bent in half by the juncture of floor and ceiling, clutching the hammer.

It was midnight now. He turned off the light and headed up the stairs and out the building to head for the park to find a stranger to murder.

Taras Ignakou was content, as content as a homeless man in the park could be on a cold day in Moscow. He wore a brown sweatshirt that had the words "Property of the Cleveland Browns" written across the front. Over the brown sweatshirt he wore a heavy black wool coat two sizes too large for him. He had gotten the sweatshirt and coat by telling the rabbi in the little black Jew cap at the synagogue on Poklonnaya Gora that he was a Jew. Maybe the man was not a rabbi. He had no beard. It did not matter. The man told Taras he did not have to be a Jew to get used clothing that had been donated by the small congregation. The Jew had looked at him carefully when he came to the door. Synagogues had been bombed and attacked in the past year. Taras had learned that from an overheard conversation.

Nonetheless, Taras had wandered around wondering if he could or should trade the very nice coat to the fake Catholic priest who was always willing to look at decent clothing, jewelry, shoes. The coat would surely be worth a bottle of vodka. The one thing Taras would not trade was the watch in his pocket. It was the vestige of humanity to which he clung. When he had sunk so low that he had to exchange it for vodka, he would no longer have the right to think of himself as anything but an animal. He was reasonably sure that day would eventually come, eventually, but not tonight.

Taras had for the moment forgotten where to find the man who pretended to be a Catholic priest. It would come to him. Yes, in the bar off the Arbat. The pretend Catholic priest would not be there at this hour. Besides, it was too far a journey for tonight. Now Taras needed a place to sleep.

Taras walked, walked in thick socks and heavy army boots. He could not remember where he had found the boots. There was a hole the size of a large coin in the toe of the left boot. Taras had filled it in from the inside with newspaper. He had wrapped both feet in newspaper. The boots, like the coat, were too large.

But Taras had hope. With three newspapers, fished from the garbage behind a restaurant where he sometimes delved into the garbage for something edible, he walked. His boots sloshed through shallow puddles made by melted snow.

The reason Taras Ignakov was filled with hope as he trudged through the night was the bottle in his coat pocket. Luck had been with him. A parked car. The door open. The almost full bottle on the floor. And it was Putinka vodka, the vodka claimed to be good for relaxing and overcoming fatigue. Good. He had drunk most of it while standing in the doorway of a bookstore far from the car. There was still a lot of vodka remaining in the bottle.

He touched the watch in one pocket and then caressed the bottle with his hand in the other pocket. He decided he would drink half of the remaining contents slowly and save the rest for to-morrow. He would do this when he got to a spot where he could sleep for the night without being disturbed by the police.

Normally, Taras walked with his shoulders slumped and head facing down. Now he looked up, wondering where he was. He had walked for hours, many hours. He needed to abandon his plan and drink the rest of the vodka.

He found himself in front of a vaguely familiar park. The wind was blowing, but not hard. The leaves of the many trees were whispering to him to stop.

Taras moved into the park but did not use the path just beyond the bench. He walked into what seemed like total darkness. He stopped, almost fell, put a hand on a tree to balance himself. It took a long time for his eyes to adjust.

Taras reached up to pull his hat down and discovered that he had no hat. He knew several others who endlessly roamed the streets and had lost ears to frostbite. Taras touched his ears to see if they were still there.

"They are intact," he told the darkness.

He tried to remember the name of the park he had entered. He could not. It would come to him.

He trudged on, his eyes now capable of seeing outlines and shadows. Trees, bushes, a fence, a man.

The man was in front of him. Taras could not judge how far away the man was. The man was not moving. Taras took a step to his left and began walking away from the man.

"Wait," the man said.

Taras waited.

The man approached and said, "I did not think I would find anyone in the park this late."

The man looked neither old nor young from what Taras could see in the dark.

Taras began walking again. The man kept pace with him.

"I often come to the park at night just to get out, sit on a bench, and drink a bottle of wine. Sometimes I find someone with whom I can share it. Do you like wine?"

"Do I look as if I would turn down wine?" asked Taras. "Where is a bench?"

"This way," said the man, walking just a bit ahead of Taras on his left.

"I really do not feel like drinking wine tonight. Here, you take the bottle. I have brought some juice for me."

"Please yourself," Taras said, taking the bottle.

The cork was already halfway out. Taras pulled it the rest of the way out and dropped the cork. No matter. He had every expectation of drinking the entire bottle. It continued to be a very good day.

The stone bench was cold against his rear end even through two layers of pants.

"I am fifty-nine years old. I was born in Omsk. I was a dealer in expensive watches, a writer for a newspaper, a tire thief. I had a wife and two daughters. I have not seen them for a very long time."

"You miss them," the man said sympathetically.

"No," said Taras, taking a long drink from the bottle. The wine was not bad. It was not vodka, but it would do.

Taras held out the bottle with little enthusiasm.

The young man declined, saying, "Maybe I will take it later."

"Must I tell you more of my biography?"

"No," said the man.

"My health history? I have but one tooth left. It will not last much longer. I am fond of it. I wiggle it a great deal with my finger. I shall miss it when it is gone. My heart functions adequately, as do my other organs, with the likely exception of my liver. My right arm does not rise above my waist. An accident when I was stealing tires in Omsk . . . Is that enough for you?"

"I said I did not want to hear any more about your life."

Taras shrugged his shoulders and stopped talking.

It was then that the young man lifted his hand from his jacket pocket and showed Taras a hammer.

"I am in Bitsevsky Park," said Taras.

"You are."

"And you are the Maniac?"

The man did not answer.

"Once, not many years ago, I was tall and strong and I would have taken that hammer from you and shoved the handle down your throat. Now I am shorter and weak. And I am drunk, but I will fight you."

"You think you can beat me?"

"There is not a chance that I could, but I want to live."

Taras pulled the coat around him. A cold wind had suddenly been brought to life to dance through him.

"You are very drunk," the man confirmed.

"Well, I will still fight you and try to get that hammer from you. This is probably the last few minutes of my soul in this almost worthless body. Until my death this had been a very good day for me."

Taras lunged toward the man, swinging the wine bottle at his head. He missed by at least two feet and landed facedown on the cold, wet grass. He thought about crawling away, but he knew that effort would be of no use. Instead, he reached into his coat pocket and managed to touch the watch.

Akardy Zelach lay on his bed in the living room. In the lone bedroom of the apartment he could hear his mother cough, a moist, rattling cough. She had gotten home from the hospital that morning. He was afraid, afraid of losing her, afraid of being alone. There was nothing he could do. He did not know if she was awake and he did not want to wake her at this hour to offer her tea or medicine.

She coughed again and again, and through the door he could hear her sitting up. He got out of his bed and went to her bedroom. He knocked gently.

"Yes, come in," his mother said hoarsely.

Akardy entered.

"Would you like some tea?" he asked.

"Do we have any brandy left?" she asked.

"I think so."

"Raspberry tea?"

"Yes."

"Tea with a little brandy," she said.

"Yes," he said. "Anything else?"

"Are you tired, Akardy?"

"No," he lied.

"You could perhaps read to me a little while."

"Yes," he said. "Tea with brandy and a book. Which book would you like?"

"I'll get it. You make the tea. Make a cup for yourself. I'll read the leaves."

When he had finished making the tea, Akardy Zelach carefully brought it to his mother on a wooden tray. He had also made himself a cup of tea, but he had added no brandy to his.

Her eyes were closed, but when she sensed him in the room they opened. He placed the tray carefully on the table next to her bed.

"Thank you."

She touched his cheek when he sat on the bed next to her.

"Don't look so frightened. I'm going to be fine."

He nodded and smiled, not knowing what to say. He had no gift for words and he knew it. This may have been the reason he was so drawn to those who could create words, poets, novelists, politicians, rock musicians, and rappers. He took the book she held out and he opened it to a place she had marked with a red feather, all that remained of a hat she had worn once almost thirty years ago.

Zelach read the poem by Anna Akhmatova she had marked.

> *He loved these three things.*
> *White peacocks, evening songs,*
> *And worn-out maps of America.*
> *No crying of children,*
> *No raspberry tea,*
> *No women's hysterics.*
> *I was married to him.*

"The tea is good," she said, patting his hand.

"I'm glad."

"Have you finished yours?"

"Yes," he said.

"Let me look at your leaves."

She took his cup and held it at a slight angle to catch maximum light from the bedside lamp. She looked at it long, perhaps a full minute.

"What do you see?"

Both mother and son knew they were endowed with certain connections to thoughts and events that others did not have. These visions, feelings, were not controlled by intent. They just came. Akardy Zelach knew his mother was not reading the leaves but looking to them to give her a flash of insight. She and her son had no great intellect, but they did have the insight.

Akardy's mother felt the shudder of connection and put down the cup.

"What did you see?" he asked.

"Nothing," she said. "Sometimes there is nothing. Another poem please."

He obliged and she lay back with closed eyes, listening and wondering about the shadowy specter she had just seen. The vision was too dark to really see, but the dread, the certainty of death that clung to her son now, was evident not in images but in a certainty that pervaded without giving its name.

In the vision, the creature of dark dreams had been looking at her.

"You are still happy with the wedding plans?"

The studio apartment of Iosef Rostnikov was almost dark. The lights were out, but moonlight and street lamps managed to penetrate the drawn shade and thin drapes over the lone window. This was the way Iosef liked it when he slept, just a little light. He retained a dread of total darkness when he slept from an incident during his days in the army. The barracks held memories of a sleepwalker, Private Julian Gorodov, who appeared at Iosef's bedside babbling. Then there were thieves: Private Ivan Borflovitz had reached gently under Iosef's pillow looking for his wallet. Iosef had grabbed

Borflovitz's wrist and twisted until the arm of the transgressor strained with a pain that would endure for weeks. Sergeant Naretsev was not so gentle, and Iosef, a light sleeper, awakened to grab him by the neck and whisper a death threat.

"Yes," said Elena, who lay at his side.

Both Elena and Iosef, on their backs atop the blankets, were looking up at the shadows on the ceiling. Elena wore one of Iosef's gold T-shirts with the words "Lightning in the Woods" in crimson on the front. *Lightning in the Woods* was one of the plays Iosef had written, produced, directed, and acted in during the years after his military service.

Iosef, shirtless, wore a pair of gray sweatpants that he had cut off at the knees.

"We are too old for the nonsense," she added.

"I know," he said.

"Two days of eating and drinking and warding off drunken people I don't know."

"I agree. So do my mother and father."

"And then," Elena went on, "the ridiculous ritual of my being kidnapped and you having to get past guards to rescue me and find a way out of this apartment. Why can we not just go to our appointment at the marriage office, sign our papers, and have a small party at your parents' apartment?"

"I agree with you completely," he said. "That is what will happen. It will be as you wish. My mother and father and the guests know that."

"The point of the wedding is to make us happy, not to make us miserable. And the cost of food and drink . . ."

"Do you hear me doing anything but agree with you?" he asked, reaching over to touch her shoulder and move his hand down to her smooth stomach.

"No," she said, moving his hand and turning away.

"I propose we make love one more time and then get up to greet the sun. I will make breakfast."

"I accept that proposal," she said, turning back to face him as she considered whether it was the right time to tell him.

Iris Templeton entered the darkened tobacco shop not far from the Kremlin. Daniel Volkovich had opened the door with one of several jangling keys taken from his pocket. He had held it open so she could enter in front of him and have to touch him as she moved.

"You are not afraid," he said as he closed and locked the door.

"Should I be?" Iris asked, turning to him.

There was a single low-wattage lamp on the counter of the shop.

"Absolutely not," he said. "You do understand why I could not bring you here with your police escort?"

"Yes."

They had paused in the middle of the shop. Iris smelled an almost dizzying array of tobaccos. She had ceased smoking fourteen years ago while her father was dying from what he called "the last whacks of the Marlboro coffin nails."

"Good," Daniel said, and moved to a door at the rear of the small shop.

The door wasn't locked. She followed him through it and into another room not much larger than a closet. Still another door, but when this one opened there was a flow, not a rush, of light and the light was a golden haze. Inside the room, eight girls stood or sat talking and smoking. When the door opened, they looked at Daniel and Iris and stopped talking. It was not the first time Daniel had brought a female client. All the girls welcomed female clients. The risks of disease were diminished, and extra money could be earned from voyeurs at peepholes or watching on television monitors. One wealthy customer had a video hookup to all three rooms in the back. The girls knew that the price of such a selection in one's own home was enormous.

None of the girls were scantily clad. Most wore skirts and blouses or sweaters that accented their breasts. Others had the lean, slick, boyish look of models.

"You may talk to whichever one of the girls you wish," Daniel said. "But I suggest Svetlana. She is the best educated and probably the smartest."

He was looking at one of the svelte boyish girls. Svetlana paused in talking to another girl and looked at Iris openly with a smile.

Daniel motioned for Svetlana to come closer. When she did, her brown eyes were wide and fixed on Iris.

"Miss Templeton is not a client," he said. "She is a reporter from England. You will answer her questions and Miss Templeton will compensate you for your time."

Svetlana nodded.

"Room Two," he said.

As Svetlana led her through yet another door, Iris looked back at Daniel, who met her gaze and grinned, a dinosauric grin that Iris definitely did not like. She followed the prostitute to a dark hallway and into an unmarked room. The room had a bed, a comfortable chair, a hat rack, and a small painting of an early-nineteenth-century Russian village street on the wall. The yellowish light in the painting was the same as that in the room from which they had come.

"You're sure you don't . . . ?" the girl asked, touching her red lips.

"Certain," Iris said. "No offense."

The girl looked puzzled.

"It means 'please do not be offended.' "

"Your Russian is quite good. I wish I could speak English that well. I am learning."

She motioned to the chair. Iris sat. The girl moved to the bed and sat facing her.

Iris looked around the room.

"Yes," said the girl. "We are being watched and listened to. What do you want to know?"

Iris took out a small pad of paper and a click pen.

"How old are you?"

"Twenty."

"Are you ever seen by a doctor?"

"We are all seen every two weeks by a doctor to inspect us for AIDS and other diseases. We urge our clients to wear condoms, and they almost always do if we put it to them correctly. You know, we say, 'I'm much more stimulated by a man with a condom,' or some nonsense like that."

"Why are you a prostitute?"

"Money. I am from a very small town where there are few jobs and those that exist pay little and usually require that a girl please a boss or a foreman. I can make in one month here what it would take me a year to make in my town."

"Do you plan to stop being a prostitute someday?"

The girl shrugged.

"I do not know. I may save enough in three years to go to school here in Moscow and become a hotel manager or a pastry chef."

"Do you have any goals while you continue to work as a prostitute?"

"To move up."

The girl lifted her hand gracefully with palm down and wrist bent, reminding Iris of a swan. She made a note of the movement.

"Up?"

"We are above the lowest level, the girls who line up in tunnels, maybe twenty of them, in rain, cold, standing all night, hoping to catch the eye of a customer brought by one of the men whose job it is to bring them."

"And where . . . ?" Iris began.

"Do they take the customers? To reserved rooms in nearby hotels."

"So what is 'up' for you?"

"To be one of the women with their own hotel room or one who goes to hotel rooms of visiting businessmen from all over the world. We get double what the tunnel girls get, but the hotel room girls get more than double what we get."

"How would you get to be a hotel girl?"

"By being selected for looks and a certain sophistication and acting ability. Much of what we do is acting."

"I would guess that you have a very good chance at going up. Who do you work for?"

"Daniel."

"No, I mean who else? What is this operation called? Who runs it?"

"That I do not know," said the girl with an apologetic smile.

"You are acting now?"

"Perhaps. I do not know anyone involved but Daniel and the other girls. I do not wish to know. If you talk to any of the other girls, you will get less from them than you have gotten from me."

"Do you have regular customers?"

"A few."

"Do you know their names?"

"Only first names. Never last names. Just Sergei, Boris, Igor, never a Pavel Petrov or—"

"Pavel Petrov?" Iris jumped in.

"Random example of the anonymous names of my clients," Svetlana said, nervously glancing up at an air vent on the wall.

"I see," said Iris, displaying nothing and not writing the name in her notebook.

Pavel Petrov, unless this was a different Pavel Petrov, was a deputy director of Gasprom. Government-owned Gasprom was the largest provider of natural gas in the world, and possibly the largest corporation in the world. It was the economic razor that could be and had been held to the neck of Ukraine and Western Europe, and Pavel Petrov was one of Gasprom's principal spokesmen, a family man with a loving wife and three beautiful children. Iris knew this because she had interviewed Pavel Petrov the last time she had come to Russia for a story.

The dropping of Petrov's name was news on which Iris Templeton might be able to hang a scandal.

She wanted to place the name into the conversation, though she really had no more questions.

"Are you fed well?"

"We are not prisoners," Svetlana said. "We go out. We pay for our own food."

"You have friends among the other girls?"

"Not really. It does not pay. They move up or down or out quickly. It does not pay to have friends."

The door opened and Daniel Volkovich came in smiling.

"Time is up," he said. "You have one last question?"

"No," said Iris, rising but keeping her eyes on Svetlana, who was looking at Daniel with apprehension.

"Then we will thank our little Svetlana," he said. "And perhaps reward her for her valuable time."

"How much of a reward?" Iris asked.

"I would say two hundred euros would be sufficient. You agree, Svetlana?"

The girl said, "Yes," and tried to hide the quiver in her voice.

"If you don't have—" Daniel began.

"I have it," Iris said, opening her purse, putting the notebook inside, and removing her wallet.

When she finished handing the girl the money, Iris followed Daniel Volkovich toward the door. Daniel paused in the corridor just outside Svetlana's room.

"So," he said. "You have what you need?"

"I have what you want me to have," she said.

· "I do not understand."

"Svetlana's a fine actress," Iris said, facing him.

"Yes, but I do not understand."

"Pavel Petrov," she said.

His grin turned into a nervous laugh.

"How did you know?"

"She's too smart to make a mistake like dropping the name of a powerful client. You want me to have Pavel Petrov's name. Why?"

The man looked at the painting on the wall for about fifteen seconds and then made a decision and spoke after a sigh.

"You will write your story and expose Petrov. I will be left out of your story and emerge as the logical choice as his successor."

"We use each other," she said.

"Precisely, and if you want to seal the enterprise in Room Four just down the hall I will be happy to help you do so."

"A tempting offer," she said, "but I don't want to be on tape and get blackmailed as we are trying to do to Pavel Petrov."

"As you please," he said, opening the door to where the other prostitutes in the glow of a lamp were looking toward Iris. "I'll take you to your hotel."

"Thank you," she said as he went from the yellow room filled with the smell of women and perfume through a door into darkness and the pungent smell of tobacco.

On the drive to her hotel, Daniel did all of the talking. She absorbed little of it. There had been times in her career when she had been awake for three days and there had been others when she had grown tired and in need of sleep after a few hours. She had anticipated a three-day buzz. It had turned into an eight-hour day that rested heavy within her. But still, she had something she wanted to do.

"Do you still want to pretend to be a prostitute?" he asked as he pulled into the small driveway in front of the Zaray Hotel.

"No," she said, reaching for the door handle.

As pretty as her face was and well tended as her body was, she was no match for any of the girls in that yellow room. The only men who would select her instead of one of them would be either blind or in search of something Iris did not want to consider.

"Would you like company for a while?" he said.

"You are persistent," she said.

"And charming?"

"Not really."

His grin almost faded, but he held fast to his image.

"Good night," he said.

"Good night," Iris replied, standing at the open door.

"Tomorrow?"

"I'll see," she said.

"You would like Pavel Petrov's phone number?"

"I have it," she said. "Thanks."

"Be careful," he said.

She closed the car door and he drove away. In the lobby sat Sasha Tkach. Iris smiled. She had been about to call him on her cell phone.

"Do not come on the desk," Emil Karpo commanded gently.

As soon as he said it, he realized that he had just spoken to a cat and had some expectation that the animal would understand. Karpo had never addressed an animal before, not that he remembered, and his memory was nearly perfect. He had no pet as a child and none as an adult. He neither liked nor disliked dogs, cats, and domesticated birds. They were simply there.

The black cat had wandered in through the open window of his one-room apartment on a warm night four months earlier. She, for it was definitely female, had reappeared every week or so for a month and then once every nine or ten days and now almost nightly. In spite of a slightly lame right front leg, the black cat somehow made her way over roofs and down a treacherously steep slate roof to the open window.

She never made a sound. She simply wandered around the room and came to a halt next to the chair Karpo sat in at his desk. The cat remained there silently, curled up, sometimes looking up at him, sometimes appearing to be asleep. If he approached the cat, her large green eyes would open wide and she would then say something that sounded like *nyet*. She would also lift her lame leg and paw as if offering it to be shaken.

There were few places for a cat to go in the room. A bed stood in one corner near the open window. A dresser of unknown antiquity rested against the wall that held the door to the hallway. A wood and wicker wardrobe stood next to the dresser, and on the floor there stood a two-foot-high refrigerator. In the dresser were three pair of slacks, all black, two dress jackets, also black, two pair of black shoes, three white and two black long-sleeve pullover shirts, and a black zipper jacket.

His clothes, Karpo thought, were as black as the cat that had entered through the window.

The desk upon which Karpo did not want the cat to tread was one he had built himself. Its two-foot-wide polished wooden top extended from wall to wall, and behind the desk where he could reach over and remove a book was a four-tiered shelf filled with neatly arranged pages. Karpo had notes on every investigation he had been a part of, and each night after finishing whatever work he had for that day he took down his notes and revisited unresolved cases, some fifteen years old. The only things directly on the desk were a computer, a paperweight, a can filled with pens and pencils, and a pile of lined paper, some blank, some with the detective's current notes.

The pencils in black, red, and blue were always freshly sharpened; the paperweight was a half sphere in which there was imbedded a deep red beetle.

"Are you hungry?" Karpo asked the cat, telling himself he was not talking to the cat but to himself.

Karpo rose and moved to the refrigerator.

Karpo had stopped on his way home, telling himself he was purchasing the three cans of sardines in water for a lunch meal.

Emil Karpo took out a can, opened it, and tapped the sardines out onto a white saucer with a soft *tap-tap*. Then he moved back to his desk and pressed the button that brought the computer back to life. When the machine was purring, not unlike the cat, he punched in his access code and watched the screen fill with folders.

He worked till the clock in the upper-right-hand corner of the screen told him it was two in the morning. He was no more tired than he had been when he first sat down, but he put his notebooks back on the shelves and turned off the computer.

When he turned, the cat was curled atop his dresser asleep. Karpo took his toothbrush, tooth powder, and plastic container with his soap inside, plus a towel, opened his door, and closed it tightly behind him, after which he plucked a single hair from his head and placed it against a small invisible gummy dot on the door. If someone was to enter the room, the movement of the hair would betray them. It was a ritual Karpo followed whenever he left the room for whatever reason.

He walked with even paces to the washroom at the end of the corridor. There was no one inside. He washed, brushed his teeth, and shaved.

When he returned to his room, the cat was still sleeping on the dresser. Karpo stripped and put on a solid black T-shirt and boxer shorts. In the morning, when he rose, he would take a shower and shave again. He would do this in four hours, before anyone else on the floor was awake except for Adamski, who worked in the fish market. When Adamski had moved into the building almost eight years ago, he had run into the detective in the washroom well before the sun rose. Adamski had gone back to his room. He had never made the same mistake again.

A breeze kicked the shade. Karpo lifted the shade. He would be up while darkness still reigned. Karpo turned off the light next to his bed and lay atop the neatly tucked-in blanket.

Seconds after he lay down with his eyes open, the insight had come. The Maniac had made a mistake. Most humans would need to rise and make a note of their discovery or run the risk of losing it. Karpo had no such worry. The morning was soon enough to check his finding and to tell Rostnikov.

"*Spakoynay nochi*, good night," he said aloud, realizing less than a second later that he had actually spoken to the cat.

The cat did not reply. Seconds later Emil Karpo was asleep.

"It is almost midnight," Ivan Medivkin said when Vera Korstov entered her apartment.

"Yes," she said, placing her red mesh grocery bag on the table. "I have been talking to people, searching for whoever killed your wife and Fedot Babinski."

She took off her coat, hung it on the hook on the wall between the kitchen area and the front door. She had been gone for eleven hours, yet to Ivan she looked as if she had just arisen. He knew the look, the flow of adrenaline when he met people in the ring who thought they could get past the giant's paws. Surely the huge man must be slow, easy to hit. Surely they were wrong and paid for it, as they would with Vera.

"What have you found?"

"Four outstanding suspects about whom I would like to ask you some questions."

"These are . . . ?"

"Two women who were involved with Babinski and two men who were, apparently, involved with your wife."

"With Lena? She would never—"

He stopped himself, realizing not only that she would do it but also that she had done it with Babinski. Why not with others?

"I brought vegetables and eggs," Vera said. "Would you like an omelet?"

"No, yes, not now. In the morning maybe. You know how to find these people?"

"I do. I spoke to them, Ivan Ivanovich," said Vera, taking the few things she had purchased and putting them away in the kitchen. "Phone numbers, addresses."

"And you think one of them killed my Lena?"

"And your Fedot Babinski. Yes, I do."

"Why?"

"Ivan, I know people. I have learned to smell fear, anger, regret. I would wager much of what I own that one of them is a murderer. I am going to have bread and gooseberry jam. You sure you do not want any?"

"I will have some."

"Good, and coffee."

Vera moved to the small kitchen area where she could prepare the food and see him as they continued to speak.

"Were you all right here?" she asked.

"No," he said, getting up and looking around the room.

"I will pass what I know on to the police anonymously, and perhaps they will dig a bit more and pick out the murderer from among those on our list. Then you shall be free again."

"I want to get some sleep," he said.

"We shall eat our bread and jam and you may go into the bedroom and sleep."

"Yes," he said, rubbing his closed eyes with thumb and finger.

"May I ask you a question?" she asked from the kitchen.

"Anything," he said, folding his huge hands on the table.

"Would you like company in bed?" she asked.

"No, thank you," he said, accepting knife and platter.

She placed a plate of sliced brown bread and a large jar of jam on the table.

It was at this point that, without understanding why, he had decided to follow through on the enterprise that to this point had only been a vague thought.

If it worked, Ivan Medivkin might soon be either a free man or in prison. He wondered which it would be and then, when he had finished three slices of bread and jam, he thanked Vera and went into her bedroom, where, despite the undersized bed, he fell asleep less than two minutes later.

5

The Widow in White

"**What do** you see?" asked Paulinin.

The look on his face, Iosef Rostnikov decided, was that of either a madman or someone under the influence of a chemical substance. Paulinin needed a shave. Paulinin needed some sleep. Paulinin probably needed something to eat. Without his laboratory coat, Paulinin looked decidedly thin.

Zelach and Iosef looked down at the corpses of the man and the woman who were facing them with their eyes closed.

"Like two people who have been beaten to death," said Iosef.

"Yes, yes, certainly yes," said the scientist with a smile. "But what about the wounds?"

Zelach, never happy to be in this dungeon of alternatively sweet and acrid odors, said, "Their faces are purple and swollen."

"And?" Paulinin urged.

"The woman has been beaten more severely," said Iosef. "Broken cheek and nose. One punch to the face. Right here."

He reached over and touched the rubbery cheek of the corpse of the woman.

"All of the damage is to the right side of the damsel's face," said Paulinin. "Now look at him. Go on; go on."

Iosef and Zelach looked again.

"The woman was killed by someone left-handed. It took the killer only two quick punches. One to the face. One to the neck. Whereas the man was hit at least four times, with the heaviest blows from a right hand."

"So," said Iosef, "we have two murderers."

"Yes," said Paulinin. "Two people who are able to strike with great power, one left-handed and one right-handed."

"How tall?" asked Zelach.

Akardy Zelach seldom spoke in Paulinin's laboratory. Zelach's goal was to leave the large, cluttered room and its smells and visions as soon as possible. Speaking, asking questions, only prolonged the visit.

Paulinin and Iosef looked at Zelach as if he had suddenly appeared from nowhere. This was the second time he had spoken.

"That is a good question," said the scientist. "Judging from the angle of the blows, I would say the person who killed the woman was taller than she and the person who killed the man was about his height, unless of course . . ."

"What?" asked Iosef.

"Unless our victim here was on the floor when he was struck," said Paulinin. "Have I answered your question, Inspector Zelach?"

"Yes."

"And how is your mother?"

Zelach had spoken of his mother only once to Paulinin, and that had been several years ago. At that time Zelach had mentioned that his mother had great trouble breathing and that state doctors were doing little for her.

"The same," Zelach said, and then amended his comment to, "not so well."

"Wait," said Paulinin, holding up a hand and disappearing into dark shadows and narrow paths.

Iosef was looking down at the bodies now, examining them closely. In a few seconds, Paulinin emerged, carrying a small, brown bottle.

"Here, give one of these pills to your mother in the morning and one at night before she goes to bed," Paulinin said. "And, under your promise that she has no thoughts of suicide, tell no one where you got this. It is quite illegal."

Zelach took the pills, said nothing but nodded his thanks.

"There is something you have not shared with us," said Iosef, facing the scientist.

"There is," said Paulinin. "I wanted to finish a few more tests to be certain, but I am reasonably certain that I know who killed the woman."

"**Would you** give them to your mother if she were ill?" asked Zelach.

They were walking swiftly toward a crackling concrete-box apartment building. The something that fell from the sky was neither rain nor snow but a kind of penetrating gray slush that was peculiar to Moscow.

"My mother is ill. As you know, quite ill," said Iosef. "I would offer her something that Paulinin handed me, but he has not offered such a thing to me."

Zelach nodded. He could feel the brown bottle in his pocket, hear the pills tinkling against the brown glass.

They had entered dozens, perhaps hundreds, of Stalin-era buildings like this over the years. Dark stairwells that echoed sharply with each step and smelled of tobacco, food, and the sweat of a thousand bodies.

Zelach carried a small Chinese-made flashlight for situations like this. There was, however, enough light in this sagging building to see the numbers on the doors.

Iosef knocked. He knocked again. He knocked a third time. They heard a shuffling on the other side of the door, and Iosef, in his deepest and most commanding voice, said, "Police."

"I am not at home," came the voice of a woman.

"Open the door," said Iosef. "We are here to talk to you about your husband's death."

"I am expecting a visitor," the woman said. "Very soon."

"You have a visitor," said Iosef. "The police."

There was no sound from within for at least fifteen seconds.

"All right, but be quick. I am expecting a visitor."

The door opened and a large woman stood before them, her hair a wild, untamed dance of fading blond tips and stringy brown stalks, her face a mask of almost grotesque makeup. She wore a white nightdress that she held closed across her breasts.

She could have been any age from twenty to sixty, her face a round red-dappled apple with two quite beautiful blue eyes that seemed to have trouble focusing. She was clearly drunk at ten in the morning.

"I've had a few drinks," she acknowledged, correctly reading the look on their faces. "My husband just died. But you know that, don't you?"

"Yes," said Iosef.

"Come in," she said.

They entered and she closed the door.

They stood in a chaos of pillows, filled ashtrays, clothes piled on a brown sagging sofa, glasses, and two bottles on a small table.

She pushed a pillow out of the way on the sofa and sat heavily looking around when she was firmly in place.

"The cat, do you see the . . . no, never mind. The cat is dead. I plan to get a new cat and some new clothes with the money."

"Money?" asked Iosef.

Albina Babinski looked up, in an apparent moment of searching for sobriety to deal with her error.

"A friend owes me money," she said. "What do you want to know about Fedot? You want the names of his women too?"

"Too?" Iosef repeated as Zelach looked around the apartment without turning his head.

"I do not keep secrets well," she said, running a hand through her jungle of hair. "I am of too honest a nature."

Zelach moved to a low table against the wall on which were scattered cups, magazines, filled ashtrays, and a dozen or so small framed photographs. He picked up one of the photographs.

"Leave those alone, Cossack," the woman shouted at Zelach, who replaced the photograph.

"Someone has paid you to give him the names of women with whom your husband had affairs?" asked Iosef, ignoring the outburst.

"How did you know?" Albina Babinski asked, her hand coming down to partially reveal one full pink right breast.

Zelach could not keep himself from looking.

"You just told us. Who is he?" asked Iosef, apparently paying no attention to the naked breast.

"She, it is a woman. Do I keep the money?"

"When is she coming?"

"By ten o'clock," she said, reaching for one of the bottles on the nearby table and examining the glasses to determine which one was the least dirty.

Zelach looked at his watch. It was ten minutes to ten.

"What is the woman's name?"

"Vera something. She is a reporter for something, I think. I do not care about her name, just her money. Fedot Babinski has left me nothing but anguish and wasted years. I will need to go back to work again, but not at my old profession."

"Tell us the names of the women," said Iosef, who nodded at

Zelach, who, in turn, took out his notebook and began writing the names as Albina Babinski struggled to remember them.

"I think that is all," she said after finishing the recitation of names and a not-small glass of vodka.

She had leaned over in the course of giving her information. The tops of both of her breasts now showed, right to the nipples. She suddenly looked up and caught Zelach's eyes looking at her. He averted his eyes, but it was too late.

"You like what you see, shy policeman?" she asked.

"Cover yourself," said Iosef patiently.

"What did you see?" she asked, pulling the nightgown closed again.

"A small but distinct surgical scar on your right breast," said Zelach. "And another on your left. You have had small growths removed from both. There is a white spot just above the nipple of your left breast, indicating that you may have another growth there that needs attention."

Albina Babinski's mouth opened. She looked at Iosef, who had no intention of helping her. She had asked the question. Iosef was familiar with such bursts of observation from Akardy Zelach.

Before more could be said, there was a knock at the door. Zelach checked his watch. It was two minutes to ten.

They both woke up with the first light of dawn.

Iris Templeton reached out with her right hand and touched the chest of Sasha Tkach, who lay on his back atop the blanket. Then she moved her fingers down to his stomach, almost tickling, till she felt the curled hair between his legs and his ready member pointing straight toward the ceiling. She rolled over on top of him, looking down at his sad eyes, and eased him into her. She continued with small, steady strokes, which prompted him deeper and ever deeper. She breathed heavily, reaching down to press her thumb across his lips and into his mouth. Now she was frenzied and moving dizzily, her hair swirling, her voice uttering something in English Sasha did not understand, but he understood her need and met it. He sighed. She moaned as they suddenly stopped and met at the same moment.

They remained in that position till he slowly wilted. Then Iris rolled over and lay back on the bed in her room at the Zaray Hotel.

"Are you hungry?" she asked.

"Yes," he said.

"You are very good, you know," she said.

He did not answer, so Iris continued with, "Your body was hungry, but your thoughts were far away. Are you married?"

"Yes," he said.

"And your wife is . . . ?"

"In Kiev with our two children. She left me."

"Why?"

"Because of mornings like this," he said. "My clothes . . . ?"

"I laid them out for you," she said. "They are unwrinkled."

"I need to shave," he said.

"I have extra disposable razors."

"Elena Timofeyeva will be calling me soon," he said, sitting up.

"You would rather she not know that we spent the night together? You could get no closer in your responsibility to protect me."

"The Chief Inspector would not approve," said Sasha, rising. "He would not be surprised, but he would not approve. I need a shower."

"May I join you?" Iris said, standing and looking at him.

He shrugged and said, "Yes, of course."

The lack of enthusiasm for the offer was evident to Iris. She was good at seeing through lies and deceptions. He was bad at hiding them. He was afraid she would want more if she stepped in under the warm shower. He was sure he would want more.

"I think not this time. You have lots of scars. From dissatisfied women?"

"From criminals," he said. "The razor . . . ?"

"On the shelf above the sink in a plastic container."

"You have very smooth skin," Sasha said, looking at her.

"You mean for someone my age?"

"For someone any age."

"Thank you. I will order coffee and something to eat. You go shower."

He nodded, went into the bathroom, found the razors, and turned on the shower. While he waited for the water to turn warm, he picked up the thin bar of soap on the edge of the sink and looked into the mirror.

The Sasha Tkach he saw was quite different from the one with whom he had grown up. That Sasha Tkach had the face of a boy, a handsome boy who seemed to draw women of all ages. That boy had fallen in love with and married a beautiful Ukrainian girl named Maya. They had had two children. But he had been unable to control his animal desires. And she had left.

Now the Sasha Tkach in the mirror was a man, a handsome man with soulful eyes and no trace of boyishness. That man still held an animal within him. The evidence of that was the English-woman in the next room. He had not hesitated to come up here with her, to take off his clothes, to kiss and hold and make love to her and have her make love to him while all the time he thought of Maya and nearly wept believing he would never be able to control the animal within.

Steam covered the mirror and Sasha backed away, knowing that if Iris called he would return to the bed in spite of the hour, in spite of Elena, who would be calling him, in spite of his memories of Maya.

He stepped into the shower. It was too hot. His fair skin would be red for hours. He was tempted to make it even hotter, but instead he cleansed himself and then lathered his face with soap. His beard was light and came off with gentle, even strokes.

When he finished showering, he reached out for the towel on the nearby rack. Iris stood in front of him, still naked, towel in hand.

"Inspector Timofeyeva is on the phone."

"The room phone?"

"Cell."

Sasha eased past the smiling Iris, wrapping the towel carelessly around his waist. The phone lay on the bed. He picked it up.

"You did not answer your cell phone," Elena said.

He detected no hint of reprimand.

"No, I have not turned it on yet."

He was certain that she knew, and his certainty was confirmed by her question.

"Are you dressed?"

"No," he said.

"Get dressed and bring Miss Templeton down to the lobby with you. Daniel Volkovich is dead."

Iris was standing in the doorway of the bathroom meeting his sudden glance. Volkovich, the procurer who had allowed himself to be interviewed by Iris and who had let her into the brothel, was dead.

"What is it?" Iris asked.

"Get dressed quickly and come down. I have another surprise for you and Miss Templeton," said Elena. She hung up.

Sasha hung up, tossed the towel on the bed, and reached for his underpants, saying, "Daniel Volkovich is dead."

Iris dressed quickly. When she was finished, she spent a few moments in the bathroom preparing herself, doing her best to quickly brush her hair into a semblance of order.

They left the room together and used the stairs instead of waiting for the indifferent elevator. They found Elena Timofeyeva sitting in the lobby with a pretty young woman who had difficulty holding her cigarette steady between her fingers.

Elena looked at Sasha and Iris as they approached. There was no overt sign of reproach in Elena's look, but Sasha detected a distinct disapproval.

Elena stood and so did the nervous young woman.

"This is Olga Grinkova," said Elena. "She went to a police patrol car early this morning. She told her story and was taken to Petrovka, where she was directed to the Office of Special Investigations, where she sat waiting when I arrived. It was Olga who reported the murder of Daniel Volkovich. She is afraid that she too will be murdered."

The young woman's eyes were red and moist. Sasha detected an almost imperceptible quiver in her full lower lip. Olga Grinkova's eyes kept turning toward the lobby door.

"Why is she afraid that she might be killed too?" asked Iris.

"Because," said Elena, "she talked to you last night."

Iris looked at the young woman again and said, "Svetlana?"

Porfiry Petrovich Rostnikov was well prepared with reading material this morning. He had his usual Eighty-seventh Precinct novel and two newspapers. The skies had stopped dropping various kinds of moisture, leaving only a dark slush that seeped into the shoes of those who failed to take this weather into account.

Rostnikov had, thanks to his wife, been well prepared with ankle-high waterproof shoes. The left shoe had proved to be somewhat obstinate. In custom-manufacturing the foot, the craftsmen had made the left foot more than a half size too large. The artificial left foot of all three pairs of shoes that the Chief Inspector owned had been stretched. He kept a special German-made shoe stretcher in the left shoe he planned to wear each morning, but as soon as the device was removed the shoe began to seek its normal shape and size.

Porfiry Petrovich considered forming a self-help group for people with one leg to discuss all the things that the two-footed never thought about. He considered it, but he was certain he would not be forming such a group.

One thing he would have put on the agenda of the first meeting, had he actually proceeded with the idea, was the problem of walking. Now he was walking through Bitsevsky Park, pausing from time to time to search for a bird feeder. He found three among the trees at least fifteen feet from the path. As he walked, the policeman displayed only a slight limp, but he felt a distinct growing ache where his leg had once been. He would have to sit very soon.

People passed him coming and going. He noted but did not acknowledge them. These were people on the way to work as he was. They had no time for pleasantries and barely enough time for small unpleasantries.

There were few morning chess players. They had been greeted with wet benches and tables. The veterans had remembered to bring towels to dry enough space for them to begin their combat. If these veterans recognized those who had not come prepared, they might allow them to use their towels.

Rostnikov had planned to make it as far as the ski slope. There would be no skiing today. The hills would be sponges of cold water with puddles of melting ice.

It was too far and would be too much for his leg. He had not set the slope as a goal because he expected to find anything there. He had no clear objectives. He turned around and headed along the meandering path back to the entrance to the park from which he had come.

As he moved slowly, he encountered a small bridge over the creek and paused to listen to the rushing water. He went to a bench nearby, cleared a spot for himself with some wadded newspaper, and sat facing the water and the trees, most of which were weeks from bearing leaves again.

After listening and watching as people passed and birds began to chirp, cry, and caw, Rostnikov took out his novel and found his place. The book was in English. Porfiry Petrovich could understand written English far better than he could understand English when it was spoken to him or he spoke it. It also helped that this was the third time he had read this particular ragged-edged paperback.

"What are you reading?" asked the man who sat next to Rostnikov after picking up the wadded newspaper and using it to dry a space for himself.

"An American police mystery," said Rostnikov.

"What is it about?"

"A group of detectives in a mythical city who are trying to catch a serial killer."

Rostnikov looked at the man, who was neither young nor quite in the middle of life. He had good teeth, a knowing smile, and the face one sees on hundreds of Russian men every day.

"I saw you here yesterday," the man said. "Over by the chess players."

"Yes," said Rostnikov. "You were on the path walking toward Shavaska Street. You were carrying a grocery bag."

"Yes," said the man. "My name is Aleksandr Chenko." He extended his hand.

Rostnikov took it and said, "I am Chief Inspector Rostnikov of the Office of Special Investigations."

"May I ask why you spend time here?" asked Aleksandr Chenko.

"Pleasure and business."

"The Maniac," said the man knowingly.

"Yes," said Rostnikov.

"We are all worried about this madman," said Chenko. "You police have been trying for so long. I hope you catch him soon."

"We will catch him."

Aleksandr looked at his conservative black-band Swatch and stood, saying, "I cannot be late for work. Well, we will probably be crossing paths from time to time if you keep coming here. I come this way to get to my work, and when I have time I put some seeds into the bird feeders. You might want to try it. The birds, particularly the pigeons, come right down and perch on your arm if you hold up a palm with a few seeds on it."

"Your work?"

"My work? Oh, I fill shelves at the Volga Grocery Supermarket on the other side of the park. I am on my way there now. I had better hurry. I don't want to be late."

"No."

"I feel better knowing you are here, Chief Inspector," said the young man. "Do you play chess?"

"A little."

"Perhaps we could play a game sometime soon, or are you not allowed to play games while you are on duty?"

"I play games."

Rostnikov watched as Aleksandr Chenko moved quickly up the path. When Rostnikov was about to lose sight of him behind a bend of bushes, Chenko turned and waved. Rostnikov waved back. When he could no longer see the young man, Rostnikov took out his notebook and pencil and made the following note:

Aleksandr Chenko
Volga Grocery, does it carry Nitin wine? Is there any record of Chenko buying it? Where does he live? Does he drink guava juice?
?

Then Porfiry Petrovich went back to reading his book.

6

Tai Chi in the Rain

"I did not call them," said Albina Babinski.

She sat, as disheveled as she had been the previous day when Vera Korstov had come to her apartment. The widow of Fedot Babinski seemed to be wearing the same housedress and holding the same fingerprint-besmirched glass of vodka.

Vera was certain that the two men who now stood before her were the police.

She considered stepping back quickly, pulling the still-open door closed, and dashing for the stairway. Vera was, after all, a former athlete who still competed from time to time in park district competitions. She could certainly outdistance the slouching, sad-eyed man who stood facing her on her left. She might even be able to make it down the stairs ahead of the broad-shouldered dark man who stood to her right.

What Vera did not know was whether there might be more police waiting at the bottom of the stairs.

"You have my two hundred euros?" asked Albina. "You promised. I trusted you."

"Who are you?" asked Iosef Rostnikov.

"Who are you?" Vera responded.

"I am Inspector Rostnikov. This is Inspector Zelach."

Zelach moved behind Vera and closed the door. All thought of flight was now gone, so she decided to lie.

"I am a journalist with *Sputnik Secrets Magazine*," Vera said.

"You owe me . . . ," Albina muttered but was ignored.

"You have credentials?" asked Iosef.

"I can get them," said Vera.

"You do not carry them?"

"I have broken no laws," said Vera.

"I am keeping the money you have already given me," said Albina. "And that is that."

"Your identification cards, please," said Iosef.

Vera reached into the black cloth bag slung over her shoulder. Zelach stood close by, ready in case a weapon was drawn. Vera came up with a wallet and extracted several cards.

Iosef examined the cards and handed them to Zelach, who punched a number into his cell phone. Vera glanced at Zelach and then with a sigh faced the more formidable-looking of the policemen.

Zelach was far more comfortable with a standard phone, one with buttons, one that looked like a phone and not like a box such as the one in which his mother held her daily pills. In truth, Zelach was not comfortable with any phone. He disliked the silences that he was expected to fill.

Vera could hear Zelach talking softly on the phone. Albina, the widow, sat mumbling softly to herself. The policeman named Rostnikov spoke. Vera tried to focus on his words, to buy time for Ivan Medivkin, but the policeman was not selling time.

"You think the weather is really about to change?" Iosef asked.

"Why do you ask me that?" said Vera.

"Because I am trying to bring you back to the conversation

from the world in which you appear to be searching for a way to deal with me."

"I have nothing to say," she said.

Iosef looked at the window where a lone cluster of gray ice about the size of a hand was slithering down the glass. He nodded and turned to watch Zelach press the "end" button on his phone.

"I have it," said Zelach.

"Good. Let us go."

"Where are we going?" asked Vera.

"To your apartment," said Iosef.

Albina began to rise. Iosef raised a hand to signal to her to resume her seat. She sat reluctantly.

"I am a widow," said Albina, examining her now-empty glass. "I have rights."

"And which of those rights do you wish to invoke?" asked Iosef.

The question puzzled the widow, who ran her fingers through her wild hair, allowing her breasts to spread the nightgown.

"Akardy," said Iosef. "Call for uniformed backup. Have them pick us up here as soon as possible. We may be walking in on Ivan Medivkin."

Iosef looked at Vera Korstov again.

"Have I guessed correctly?"

"Let me talk to him," said Vera. "He will not give you trouble."

"We shall see when we get there," said Iosef.

"He did not kill them," she said.

Iosef said nothing.

"Ivan will not give you trouble," Vera repeated.

Iosef certainly hoped this would be true. He had never arrested a giant before, particularly one who might well become the heavyweight champion of the world if he was not in prison for murder.

Olga Grinkova bore little resemblance to the woman who had called herself Svetlana the night before. Iris found the transformation incredible, the material of which prizewinning stories are made.

Olga was no more than twenty, cheeks slightly pink, eyes wide and frightened, hands at her sides, more girl than woman. Her dark skirt hemmed below the knee and her white up-to-the-neck sweater fit loosely. Olga kept pushing her sleeves up and the sleeves kept refusing to cooperate. When she spoke it was with the voice of a shopgirl who had lost her confidence.

Svetlana had been sultry, dark, confident, almost bored, and carefully made up for the evening. Her dress had been formfitting, with the revelation of promising cleavage. Svetlana's voice had held a promising huskiness not unlike that of a young Lauren Bacall.

They were seated now at a table in the hotel's small breakfast room. There was a buffet of yogurt, cold cuts, hard-boiled eggs, and cheese. A pitcher of water was surrounded by glasses.

"Room number?" asked the plump blond girl who stood over the table.

Iris tried to imagine Olga transformed into a sultry prostitute named Svetlana.

"Room Four-eighteen," said Iris. "Does anyone want breakfast?"

"Coffee," said Sasha, looking at Elena, who met his eyes.

Coffee was agreed upon and the blond girl moved off slowly. There was only one other person in the breakfast room, a well-dressed man of at least seventy who read a newspaper and ate very slowly.

Olga Grinkova kept her hands in her lap to hide their trembling.

"They killed Daniel," Olga said, forcing herself to speak slowly and distinctly.

"Why?" asked Iris.

"Because he spoke to you," said Olga. "That is why they want to kill me. You have already been told that. It is not right that they should want to kill me. I did not ask to speak to you. It was Daniel who told me to do it. Now . . . I am alive only because I mentioned Pavel Petrov and saw the car, the black American car with the little flag on the . . ."

She made a motion that looked as if she were miming the act of pulling a thin piece of string into the air.

"Antenna," said Sasha.

"Yes," said Olga. "Antenna. I recognized the car parked across the street from the entrance to my apartment building. It belongs to them, the two men who even Daniel was afraid of."

And with good reason, it seems, thought Iris, who wanted to pull out her notebook but thought this a time for consoling and not writing.

"I knew when I saw them," Olga said. "I knew."

"How did you know Daniel was dead?" asked Elena.

Olga looked at Elena, who touched her arm and said gently, "Go on."

"I did not go to my apartment," said Olga. "I found a cab and went to Daniel's to ask him why the men in the American car were waiting for me. Daniel lives . . . lived not far from where we . . . where we work. His apartment is on the first floor. If you work the outside door just right, it will open. I also know where Daniel hid his spare key, under the carpeting on the sixth step at the end of the hall."

"You have been there many times?" asked Iris.

"Sometimes Daniel wanted one of us to visit him," Olga said. "He liked me as I am now, not as Svetlana. He treated me gently. He treated us all gently."

"You found him," Elena said.

"Yes," said Olga. "He was . . . He had been . . . I do not know. Violated."

"Daniel Volkovich had been stabbed at least twelve times and his throat cut," said Elena.

Olga closed her eyes tightly and bit her lower lip. She made a small, clipped whimper and shook her head. The blond waitress returned with four coffees and a full hot pot, which she placed gently on an ornately decorated stone trivet. The waitress looked at Olga and then retreated through the door to the kitchen.

"Tell them who owns the black car with the little flag," said Elena gently.

"Pavel Petrov," said Olga. "He sat in the back each of the four times I saw the car. He sat in the back behind closed and tinted windows while the two men terrorized us. I saw him when the light hit the car windows just right. I saw him. I saw him today. He was reading a newspaper. The two men were murdering Daniel and he sat reading a newspaper. And if they had gotten to me, I would be cut to pieces like Daniel and he would sit there reading the newspaper. Arrest him. I will tell you everything I know. Arrest him and get me out of Moscow."

"It will not work," Sasha said. "She saw no murder taking place, and even if she did, she is a prostitute. Her testimony is worth little. He will not be convicted in any court."

"Not in court perhaps," said Iris, "but I can certainly convict him in print. Remember, I have an interview with Pavel in less than two hours. I will put the needle to him and record his confessions."

"He will kill you," said Olga.

"No," said Iris. "I have the police to protect me."

She patted the hand of Sasha, which rested on the table.

Olga Grinkova tried to pick up her coffee with both hands, but they refused to cooperate. She put the cup back down and said again, "He will kill you."

Nine police officers, including Iosef Rostnikov and Akardy Zelach, entered the small apartment of Vera Korstov ready for whatever might come from Ivan Medivkin. The blue-uniformed officers, one of them a woman, carried stun guns, electric riot batons, and

heavy rubber truncheons. Iosef Rostnikov and Akardy Zelach were
unarmed.

Iosef had knocked at the door and announced loudly that the
door should be opened immediately. The door had not been opened
immediately. Two of the uniformed police threw their shoulders
against the door, which opened abruptly with a shattering of wood.

There was no one in the tiny living room/kitchen area and
no one in the bedroom. There was, however, a note in small pen-
ciled words:

> *Vera, I cannot stay. It is torture to pace these floors waiting. I am
> calling someone who will help. It is better you not know who. I
> will come back to you when this nightmare ends.*

"How far can a giant run without being seen?" asked Iosef.
None of the police had an answer.

"Shall we check every apartment in the building?" the highest-
ranking of the uniformed police asked.

"Yes," said Iosef, looking at the note one more time before
folding it and tucking it into his jacket pocket.

Armed and very dangerous, the uniformed police hurried out
of the apartment.

Iosef and Zelach could hear the high-ranking officer calling out
orders for two people to check all exits and entrances from the
building and to secure them. The other four began their apartment-
by-apartment search while Iosef and Zelach went down the stairwell and out the front door just as one of the policemen was about
to secure it.

On the way into the building, they had seen people on the
lone patch of green and under the only tree within sight. This was
not a day to be enjoying nature. A fast-rushing rivulet of melting
slush ran along the curb on both sides of the street.

Iosef and Zelach approached the people, who were all in yellow sweatpants and sweatshirts except for one old Chinese man who appeared to be leading them in some kind of slow-moving dance.

"Have you seen a giant come out of that building this morning?" asked Iosef.

The old man in blue looked ancient now. His head was bald and dotted with meandering blue veins. He was clean-shaven and smiling. He was in the middle of a movement of legs and hands as he gently urged his extended right hand upward, palm forward. The others were mirroring the old man's moves.

The old man closed his eyes, dropped his hands at his sides, and bowed his head smoothly forward and back.

"A giant?" the man in blue said.

His look was one of incredulity. He turned toward the people in front of him and said, "Have any of you seen a giant?"

They all shook their heads no except for a woman in the group, who said, "Yes," so softly that it almost escaped without notice.

"You saw the giant?" Iosef asked the woman.

"Yes. He came out of that building."

She pointed to the building in which Vera Korstov lived.

"Where did he go?" asked Iosef.

"He got into the car that was waiting for him," the woman said. "Then the car drove off."

"What kind of car was it?" asked Iosef.

"Blue," said the old man.

"Green, definitely green," said another man. "I saw it clearly. One of those little tiny cars."

"It was a large dark red car with a significant dent in the left rear fender," said the old man with calm finality.

"Thank you," Iosef said with only slightly disguised insincerity. "You have been very helpful."

As he turned to go back to the apartment building to tell the others that a search was unnecessary, he saw Zelach pause, put his feet together, roll his shoulders forward, and place his open palms against each other pointing skyward. Then Zelach bowed his head slowly. All of the sweat-suited people returned the gesture. It was brief. Zelach and the people exchanged a small smile.

As they walked back toward the apartment building, Iosef said, "What was that?"

"The bow is a sign of respect," said Zelach. "A sign that you are giving up self-importance."

Iosef shook his head and grinned.

"Akardy Zelach, you are probably the least self-important human I have ever known."

"It is good to remind oneself."

"How do you know this?" Iosef asked as they walked.

"My mother and I used to do tai chi exercises three times a week. We did it since I was eight years old. She is not well enough to do it anymore. She insists that I do it without her, but I do it with an empty heart."

Now they were standing at the curb, more or less where the car had picked up Ivan Medivkin. There was nothing there to see. Iosef looked back at the Chinese man and the others, who had returned to their graceful slow movements. Iosef could not imagine Zelach doing this, but Zelach was not lying. In fact, Akardy Zelach was the worst liar Iosef had ever known.

"Akardy, you are a fountain of confounding information and new revelations. Now if you could only tell me what color that car was . . ."

"It was a large dark red car," Zelach said as they stepped onto the sidewalk.

"The Chinese man is the only one who got it right?"

"Yes. He is the only one both focused and seeing everything around him."

Iosef looked back at the Chinese man. His eyes were closed as he moved his arms and hands gently and brought his left leg slowly forward with his foot not touching the ground.

"He is looking at us now?"

"Yes," said Zelach.

"With his eyes closed?"

"He senses and sees," said Zelach, looking across the street at the man about whom they were speaking.

"A red car?" said Iosef.

"Yes," said Zelach.

"With a dent in the left rear fender?"

"A significant dent," said Zelach.

"Let us find it."

"Out all night. I thought you were dead."

So Lydia Tkach, mother of Sasha, widow of Borislav, shouted at her son when he came through the door of his apartment, which she had moved into with him almost a year ago. She stood, a small stick of a woman with arms folded, looking at him with a reprimand Sasha had known since he was a small child.

"I was working," he said.

"What?"

Oh God, thought Sasha, she is not wearing her hearing aids.

"I was working. Working," he shouted.

"At what?" she said, matching the volume of his words.

There was no point in trying to pass on to her the complexity of what had happened. And even if he did, he would certainly not mention that he had gone to bed with the Englishwoman. Lydia Tkach was a bigot. She distrusted anyone who was not Russian and every nation that was not Russia.

"Protecting someone. I have just come home to shower and change clothes."

"You smell of perfume," she answered as he moved toward the bedroom. "You should shower and change your clothes."

Lydia followed him, arms still folded, into the bedroom where he took clean clothing from the closet and bureau drawers.

"Who is this woman of perfume?" she demanded.

"I must shower and perhaps shave," he answered as he began to undress.

"She is a flower and a slave?"

"Yes," said Sasha. "I took her from the harem of a Turkish pasha."

"She was in a bare room and you took her Turkish kasha? You are going mad or you are trying to make jokes at the expense of your mother."

Sasha was now wearing only his underpants. He looked at her as he put his thumbs under the elastic. If nothing else would give him respite from his mother, perhaps the sight of his nakedness would force a retreat. He took off his underpants, looking at her as he did so.

"Did she bite you on the thigh? I see a red welt. Did she bite you?"

"No."

The truth was that he seemed to remember Iris Templeton indeed biting him.

Sasha moved into the tiny bathroom and reached over to turn on the water as he muttered a prayer that he would not have to shave and shower with cold water. He looked over his shoulder at Lydia, who was in the doorway examining his body in search of other violations of his flesh by this woman.

"Mother, leave me in peace for a few minutes."

"Leave you a piece of what?"

A peace of mind, he said to himself, thanking whatever gods might exist for the hot water he felt with his hand.

"You look like your father," Lydia shouted without going into a retreat. "He was too skinny like you. You should be in Kiev on your knees begging Maya to come back to Moscow with my grandchildren."

I have been there and I have done that to no avail, he said to himself as he washed.

"You should not be a policeman," Lydia cried.

There were few conversations with his mother during the nine years he had been a policeman that she did not show her disapproval of his profession.

"Policemen got shot," she shouted. "There are crazy people out there. Remember when someone shot Karpo?"

Seven years ago, he thought. That had happened seven years ago and the wound had long since healed.

Sasha shaved.

"I have decided," she shouted. "I am going to Kiev to convince Maya to come back to Moscow."

"Good luck," he shouted.

A visit from their grandmother, who frightened them, would add their voices to a *nyet* for Moscow and their father.

"Do not use language like that in front of your mother," she cried out.

Sasha had no idea what distortion of language she had created, and he thought the less he considered it, the better off he would be.

"Soup," she shouted when he stepped out of the shower and began to dry himself with the blue beach towel he and Maya had bought shortly after they were married. The towel was still soft against his skin.

"Yes," he said, moving past Lydia and beginning to dress.

"Soup is on the table," she said.

He nodded, unwilling to engage in conversation that would certainly and creatively be distorted. When he had fully dressed, he moved back into the living room and to the round wooden dinner table near the wall by the kitchen area. On the table was a large bright green cup of soup filled with vegetables and beef and a piece of dark bread next to it on a small plate. The cup was one of five Maya had bought for almost nothing at a stall on the Arbat shortly after Pulcharia was born. Everything, everything in the apartment, was a reminder of his wife and children. She had taken nothing but her clothes and those of the children when she had left.

He sat and drank the warm soup with his mother sitting across from him.

"Good," he said.

"You are my burden, Sasha," she said with a shake of her head. "You are my only son, my only child. You should be a comfort and a joy as I grow older. Instead you are out all night with sweet-smelling Polish women and you are killing people with a gun."

Sasha considered correcting her, but the effort would certainly be doomed to failure. *Who*, he thought, *is the burden at this table?*

"I should have named you Konstantin," she said. "That means 'constant,' 'reliable.' I could have called you Kolya. Instead I named you Sasha. Do you know what your name means?"

" 'Defender of men,' " he said. "You have told me this hundreds of times. 'Defender of men.' "

" 'Defender of hens'?" she said.

"Where are your hearing aids?" he asked, pointing to both of his ears.

"Too loud," she said. "I hear well enough. You are changing the subject. Like your father. You are changing the subject. Is it any wonder poor Maya left you?"

"None," he said. "None at all. Have a good trip to Kiev."

"You are missing two bodies, maybe more," Paulinin said to Emil Karpo, who sat across from him under the bright lights of the laboratory.

They sat at the scientist's desk, space on which had been cleared to hold the two mugs of almost black, almost boiling tea in front of

them. The laboratory smelled of fetid decay from the two bodies
on the table about a dozen feet behind Emil Karpo.

"I have looked at all you have brought me so far," Paulinin said,
taking a sip of tea.

His glasses steamed. He removed them and placed them carefully on the desk.

"And you have discovered?" Karpo prodded.

"Bodies in a state of unseemly deterioration. The homeless
are treated with as little respect when they die as when they lived.
However, I did learn some things."

Paulinin drank some more tea. This time Karpo waited patiently.

"Two of the dead were not the victims of your Maniac. Copycat. Buried hastily in the park, heads crushed from behind, but not
by a hammer, by a metal pipe or rod. The killer of those two, killed
within a few days of each other, was taller, heavier, than your Maniac. When those murders were taking place, your Maniac was hit-
ting harder and with greater efficiency, but the leap in murderous
quality is too abrupt. It should be more gradual, which leads me to
believe—"

"That there are some bodies we have not yet discovered,"
said Karpo, looking over the mug in his hand.

"The dolts who were in charge of the case before you took
over missed this and, I am certain, missed much more."

"Can you tell what time of day each victim was killed?"

"Ah, good question. Stomach contents. Most of these victims lived on vodka or cheap wine, but the contents of the stomachs with food suggest they were killed at night. But you knew
that. Our Maniac would be unlikely to strike in the gray light of
day."

That was Karpo's theory. More than fifty people, all killed at
night. What if the Maniac could only kill at night because he

worked during the day? Karpo had already told this to Porfiry Petrovich, who had not been the least bit surprised.

Paulinin had supplied Rostnikov and Karpo with information about how tall the Maniac was and that he was right-handed and urged his victims to drink Nitin wine while he indulged in guava juice. More would come.

"Where is Porfiry Petrovich?" asked Paulinin, putting his glasses back on.

"In Bitsevsky Park."

"Searching for more bodies?"

"I believe he is walking the pathways, sitting on the benches, and watching the chess players."

"In other words, he is working," said Paulinin.

"Yes," said Karpo.

"You are going to look for the copycats?"

"Of course."

"Becker at Moscow University has run their DNA. They do not appear in the files and I doubt if they themselves were homeless."

Karpo knew the dead men as Numbers 30 and 31. There had been several differences from the other victims of the Maniac and these two. Numbers 30 and 31 had been buried more deeply than the others. While a number of the victims had little or no identification, none appeared to have been robbed and all had something in their pockets, slip of paper, an appointment card, something. These two had been stripped of everything. This had been attributed to nothing more than a slight deviation in pattern for the Maniac. After all, he was mad.

"And?" asked Karpo, sensing that Paulinin had something more to tell.

"Fingerprint," he said. "In spite of decomposition. In spite of pitiful irreverence for the dead, I managed to retrieve a fingerprint from the jacket of one of the two victims."

Paulinin reached over on his desk to pick up a thin, square white envelope. He handed it to Karpo, who put it in his jacket pocket.

Before the end of the day, Emil Karpo would identify both of the copycat victims, discover that they had disappeared leaving everything behind, which included not very much, for their niece, the daughter of their long dead sister. The niece, who believed herself very clever, broke down after being interrogated by Karpo in a room at Petrovka.

Thus, two of the murders attributed to the Maniac were solved, leaving only approximately fifty more that were the work of the still-unidentified Maniac.

7

A Prince of Industry Plays with Fire

Pavel Petrov met Iris Templeton in the lobby of the office build-ing not far from Red Square. He was a bit heavier than when last she had seen him, but he was still handsome and smiling. His suit, Iris could tell, was Italian and almost certainly custom-made.

"I am very glad you could come," he said in English, taking her extended right hand and holding it in both of his. "You look as lovely as when last we met at the Trade Congress in Belgrade in 1994."

"You have been well briefed," she said.

Petrov shrugged and said, "I confess. Come."

He led her across the lobby, which included a desk for two uniformed guards and a smattering of well-placed pots with plants sprouting large succulent green leaves. Somewhere a voice, probably in conversation on a telephone, echoed through the lobby and remained with them until the elevator doors closed behind Iris and Petrov.

"Are you enjoying Moscow this visit?"

"I have only been here one day and one night," she said as the elevator slowly rose.

"And I trust you have been well treated night and day by the members of our incorruptible Office of Special Investigations?"

"Yes," she said.

He knew. She was certain he knew she had been with Daniel Volkovich before Volkovich was murdered, certain that he knew where Olga Grinkova, otherwise known as Svetlana, was, certain that he knew that Sasha Tkach had spent the night in her room.

"Good," he said.

The elevator doors slid open and Petrov stepped to one side to allow her to pass onto the highly polished wooden floor.

"This way," he said, moving to her side and gesturing with his right hand toward an unmarked and unnumbered door. Through the floor-to-ceiling glass window of a reception area they saw where a young man, in a suit not quite as expensive as that worn by Petrov, looked up from behind his desk as Petrov opened the unmarked door.

She followed him into a large but not ostentatious wood-paneled office that carried the scent of forests. The desk was ancient and highly polished mahogany and the chairs a matching wood and hue.

He pointed with a palm to the left of the office, where a dark leather love seat and matching chairs faced a low glass table on which sat a pair of cups and a plate of assorted chocolates.

"I took the liberty," he said, sitting at the sofa. "I am, I confess, addicted to chocolate. Coffee? I believe you drink coffee and not English tea?"

You not only believe it, you are certain of it, and you want me to know that you know everything about me.

"Coffee is fine," she said, sitting.

"Black."

"Black."

He pressed one of the buttons of the console on his desk and said, "Are the chocolates all of the latest choices?"

He smiled at Iris, pressed another button, and folded his hands on the smooth, shiny brown surface of the desk.

"Now," he said, smile broad and voice apologetic, "if you will turn off the tape recorder in your briefcase. I will make a statement and try to answer your questions."

"How will I be able to provide evidence of what you say?" she asked.

"I intend to deal with you honestly, but there is always the chance that I will say something I regret," he said. "It has happened to me before. Now, the tape recorder please."

He held out his hand.

"You object to my taking notes?" she asked.

"Not at all."

His hand remained out, palm up, waiting. Iris took a tape recorder from her purse, pushed the button to turn it off, and sat back.

"Next," he said after checking to be sure the tape recorder was off and placing it within her reach. "If you will please disengage the listening device hidden somewhere on your person."

"I don't have one," she said, meeting his eyes.

"Then you are a fool, and I do not believe you are a fool. No, I've read your work. I do not believe you are a fool. Disengage or you will leave without coffee, chocolates, and conversation, and I assure you the cookies are the best to be found in all of Moscow."

He watched with a smile as Iris reached down her dress between her breasts and removed a small microphone taped to her skin. She held it out for him to look at, which he did. Then he took it and crushed it easily in the palm of his hand.

The door opened without a knock and Pavel Petrov dropped the microphone fragments into a polished mahogany trash basket.

A tall woman in a green knit dress came to the desk and set down a tray with a fresh plate of chocolates, although Iris, on the one hand, had not touched the first plate. Pavel Petrov, on the other hand, had devoured the small confections.

"I did not have time for breakfast," Petrov said with a nod to the woman in the green dress, who retreated out the door. "I know it is not healthy to have a breakfast of chocolate and coffee, but it is very satisfying. I shall have a generous portion of chicken for lunch to atone for this."

Petrov held out the plate.

Iris reached for a chocolate with a glazed cherry resting precisely in the middle of its raised circular surface. The chocolate did not melt between her fingers. She placed it in her mouth and bit down, half-expecting to taste a hint of poison.

"Good, eh?" he asked.

"Yes."

"Hmm, you want to begin. All right. We will begin. Whatever answers I give to your questions will not leave this room. If they appear in print, two things will happen. First, I will bring suit against the magazine or newspaper. I will win. I have almost endless resources."

"Then why am I—?" she began, holding her growing anger in check.

"So that your curiosity will be satisfied and you will understand."

"You said two things would happen if I published this interview," she said, taking a bite of chocolate, happy that her hand was steady.

"Why, I will have you killed of course," he said.

She was certain that he meant it, but she was not at all certain that she would not try to find a publisher who would be willing to print the story.

"Did you kill Daniel Volkovich?"

"Yes," he said.

"You yourself?"

"Yes," he said with a smile.

"And you want to kill Olga Grinkova?"

"Certainly," he said.

"I see," Iris said. "You are the head of a prostitution ring?"

"Business, a prostitution business. I provide a public service. The girls and women are well paid, given excellent medical care, and treated with respect."

"All of them all the time?" asked Iris.

Petrov shrugged and reached for a chocolate.

"No, not all of them all the time," he said. "Loyalty is sometimes betrayed."

"And the price is death?"

"On occasion."

"How big is your organization?"

"At the moment, six hundred and twenty-eight prostitutes in eight cities, with a staff of one hundred and eighty-two."

"Income?"

"Approximately three hundred and forty million euros a year," he said, eyes wide, examining her for signs of surprise.

"Why? You are already a rich man."

"I could not resist the opportunity to employ business techniques of the highest quality to the rental of women's bodies. Women are the product. Beautiful women mostly. We advertise exclusively through cabdrivers, bartenders, hotel clerks, waiters, and alert office workers."

Pavel Petrov held up the coffeepot. This time Iris accepted his offer.

They sat drinking coffee and nibbling at chocolates without saying a word until Petrov said, "Did I tell you that if you reveal anything said in this room, you will be raped before I murder you?"

"No, you did not say that."

"Well, consider it said."

"And you will personally . . . ?"

"With great pleasure," he said. "Will that be all?"

"Yes," she said.

Petrov handed her the tiny tape recorder. Iris dropped it into her purse and rose.

"All too brief a visit," he said, also rising and extending his hand. She did not take it. "I like you. And for that reason I will give you a present. Olga Grinkova can live. She can go back to Lvov and continue to work for the company. As long as she remains silent about what she knows, she will live unharmed. To ensure this, I will be sure that she remains frightened. I will promise the deaths of her mother, brother, sister, and at least one cousin. You can trust me. My word is good."

Iris believed that he would do what he said he would do. She also believed that his word was good.

"Now I would like the real reason you do this?"

He made a soft clicking sound with his tongue, looked toward the window, and said, "The reason is not as satisfying as the excitement of heading an illegal prostitution business. I have always courted danger. I need it. It is built into me. That is why I am talking to you. Do you understand?"

"Not completely," she answered, meeting his suddenly wild-looking eyes.

She chose at that moment not to raise the issue of his also being a murderer. She could see by the man's face that such a mention would not be a good idea.

"Yes," she said.

Petrov's fingers were restless in his fists. He did not look away from her face, and then, quite calmly, he said, "Would you like to take a box of chocolates with you for the police officers waiting for you in the car?"

"Yes," she said.

"Good. I will get a small box for you. It will be ready for you by the time you reach the lobby. You can tell them that whichever one of them bites into the one filled with glass wins the prize. No, I am only joking."

"You can always turn to a life of comedy. Good-bye for now."

Iris left him standing behind the desk. She moved slowly, deliberately, through the doors and to the elevator. She pressed the lobby button and felt nothing as the elevator descended. In the lobby, a woman behind the reception desk held up a small, neatly wrapped box. Iris took it and walked out the doors to the street, where she got into the back of the waiting car.

"Did you get it?" asked Elena, who sat behind the steering wheel.

"Yes," said Iris.

Elena pulled away from the curb and Sasha in the front passenger seat reached back to take Iris's purse. As they drove, he reached deep into her bag and, pushing toiletries, notebook, pills, and makeup aside, lifted the flat bottom of the bag and carefully extracted an ultra-thin recorder. He pressed a button. There was a pause and then a voice, a man's voice singing in French.

"He recorded over your recording," said Elena.

The man on the recorder continued to sing.

"Yves Montand," said Sasha. " 'Le Temps des Cerises.' "

"Then Petrov wins," said Iris. "That gloating, sadistic—"

"I know a young man," said Elena, almost to herself.

"A man?" asked Iris.

"A boy really," said Elena. "He does magic with electronics. Maybe he can . . ."

"Worth trying," said Sasha.

"Can it be done? Can the original recording be gotten to?"

Pavel Petrov stood by his window. He looked out at the many new central Moscow office towers as he spoke, his back to the tall woman who gathered the coffee cups and the last few chocolates on the plate and placed them on a tray.

"Christiana?" he asked, turning to look at her as she picked up the tray. "Can it be done."

"I do not know," she said. "I doubt it."

"We need certainty," he said.

Christiana Davidonya was forty-two years old and had lived through many men and many dark days. She had never experienced certainty. She did not believe in it. She believed in having options and escapes. Pavel Petrov, she knew, believed in taking risks. He lived dangerously. He loved backing himself into corners and then using his charm, cunning, and position to get out of trouble. Christiana Davidonya believed that his neurotic behavior would eventually lead to his downfall.

Daniel Volkovich had almost succeeded in making this happen. Volkovich was dead now, a victim of his own ambition.

Christiana had no desire to rise either in the ranks of the massive infrastructure of the company or within the growing reach of the prostitution ring. Her relative comfort, safety, and longevity were perfectly suited to her needs. She had spent time in jail. She did not wish to return. Ambition would lead to a cell. She was invested in Petrov's success but feared what she believed would be his inevitable crash.

"There is no certainty the conversation was overridden," she said, standing with the tray in her hands.

Petrov scratched his head. He trusted her far more than anyone knew, and he relied on her advice and companionship far more than he did on that of his wife, who now resided most of the year in their dacha forty kilometers outside the city.

Christiana, tall, dark hair tied back severely, was still a lovely woman. She had been one of the highest-paid prostitutes in the organization. She had her own apartment for clients who paid not only in rubles but also in dollars and euros. Pavel Petrov had slept with her many times over the years. Then he had hired her as his personal assistant. As a prostitute, Christiana had brought in a great deal of money and a mass of information about clients. Still, she was invaluable as an assistant. On the day that he had given her the job, he took her to bed to celebrate. She did not mind. In fact, she acknowledged something like love for Pavel Petrov, but love would not save him from his precarious behavior.

Christiana had dutifully and skillfully placed the button-sized receiver in Iris Templeton's case. She had inserted it in the lining at the bottom of the case. Christiana's skills, learned on the streets of Vilnius as a child, included picking pockets. This task had been no problem at all.

Now Petrov sat listening to Iris and the two police officers in the car. Moments ago he had leaned over and turned a dial on the small monitor that had been in his desk drawer. The conversation continued to record, but the voices no longer crackled from the tiny speaker.

"I think we shall have to kill her," he said.

"And the two police officers?" Christiana added.

"An accident," he said.

"Of course," she agreed, already planning an exit from this madness and a flight, which she had long planned for, to Brazil.

She still held the full small tray.

"This is a request, not an order," he said. "Would you like to spend the night with me?"

"Yes," she said, and she knew that she meant it.

She would do whatever he wished her to do until the moment she could escape.

He felt the stirring between his legs and grinned.

"Yes," he repeated.

Porfiry Petrovich stood looking down at the body of a disheveled man who was probably about sixty years old. The corpse had been covered by a tangle of branches, dirt, and long dead leaves, one of which had rested in his open mouth. Rostnikov knelt awkwardly and removed the leaf.

On Rostnikov's left when he stood was Emil Karpo. On his right stood Paulinin, wearing a heavy coat and shifting his weight from one leg to the other. Neither Rostnikov nor Karpo was the least bit cold. Paulinin did not like leaving his subbasement laboratory even to go home.

Rostnikov had discovered the body not more than a dozen feet from one of the park's makeshift bird feeders, which had been moved from a limb next to a nearby path.

Paulinin made a puffing sound through his pursed lips. "He has been here for a few weeks," said Paulinin. "Like the others, his skull has been crushed from behind. I will tell you more after we get him to my laboratory, where eager hands of the medical examiner's office are going through my notes and records."

"What can you tell us?" asked Rostnikov.

Birds were chirping away loudly, possibly in battle. The afternoon was clear. The sun was shining.

"I can tell you his name is Julian Semeyanov. He came to Moscow from Neya. He had been a soldier, a sniper. He has a wife and two grown daughters and one grandson. He abandoned them all and came to Moscow to become a zoo worker. He became alcoholic, lost his job, and has wandered the streets for about seven years. His liver was in the last throes of existence when he was struck down. He had no more than a year to live. His favorite foods were sardines and shrimp."

"And you got this from simply looking down at him?" asked Karpo.

"No," Paulinin said with irritation. "I made it all up. How am I supposed to know anything till I look at him on the table? Search the area around here for evidence. Bring me whatever you find. Bone fragments. Bloody leaves. Whatever you find."

"Yes," said Karpo.

"He was dragged here," said Rostnikov.

"Yes," said Paulinin.

The dead man's arms were at his sides, shoulders up.

"From over there near the bird feeder," said Karpo.

"You will see to it that the body is transported to Dr. Paulinin's laboratory," said Rostnikov.

"Yes," said Karpo.

Rostnikov looked down at the dead man, walked slowly to the bird feeder, and looked inside it. The feeder was full of a variety of seeds. Rostnikov reached in, picked up one round yellow seed, and placed it in his mouth. It was dry and fresh tasting. Someone was keeping the feeder full. Could that be done without noticing the dead man? Possibly. Rostnikov turned to Karpo, who was talking to Paulinin, who was now down on one knee, white rubber gloves on his hands, two fingers inserted into the open wound at the back of the dead man's head.

"Emil Karpo," he said. "Leave the body where it is for now. See that Dr. Paulinin gets back to his laboratory; then take a position where you cannot be seen and observe who approaches the feeder. Take photographs of anyone who approaches and follow them. Get names and addresses if you can."

"I need this man now," said Paulinin. "It may rain. It may snow. Every hour, every minute, he is left in the open means more information lost. How can he talk to me if you take away part of his essence?"

"It will not be long," Rostnikov said, evenly taking a handful of seeds from the feeder and heading for the path.

"Where are you going?" asked Paulinin.

"Shopping."

With that Rostnikov continued to walk to and down the path, eating birdseed as he limped forward.

"Inspector Karpo," Paulinin said, probing more deeply into

the wound with his fingers. "Sometimes I think your Chief Inspector is a little bit mad himself."

Since Emil Karpo thought that the scientist he was talking to was more than a little bit mad, he said nothing.

The man stood at the side of a brackish pool of green water. He was a short, bald man of no more than fifty with a substantial belly. His face was the map of a man who had seen violence. Nose broken. Right ear curled. A faded four-inch-long white scar across his forehead. He had a large white beach towel wrapped around his nonexistent waist. Both of his hands were occupied, one with what looked like a small cucumber, the other with a cell phone.

The ride that had taken Klaus Agrinkov and Ivan Medivkin forty miles outside of Moscow had been particularly uncomfortable for Ivan. The front seat of the small red BMW forced him to ride with his knees up almost to his chest.

They had stopped before a large wooden door in the wall that surrounded the Saslov Community. The young man at the door, pink faced, hair short, wearing a cap with a Molson beer logo on it, leaned down to the window and recognized Agrinkov. Then he turned and slowly pulled back the metal bar across the doors and then pushed open the doors. Agrinkov pulled in.

"You will be safe here," said Klaus.

"I should be in Moscow finding out who killed Lena," said Ivan. "I should be finding him and beating him to death."

"No, you should be here waiting to hear from me," said Klaus as they walked up a muddy road. "I will keep the police away and try to find what I can about who killed Lena and Fedot."

"I do not care about Fedot. He and Lena were . . . I do not care who killed Fedot."

"But," said Klaus, stepping off the path with Ivan towering over him at his side, "it is the same person."

"Maybe," said Ivan.

It was then that they saw the near naked man with the large
belly at the side of the green-water pool. The man kept talking on
the phone and eating his cucumber as he looked up and acknowledged the arrival of the two visitors with a nod.

When they were close enough, Ivan could hear the man say
into the phone, "Yes, the Archbishop will be joining us. The church
will be ready."

The man looked beyond the pool and down a small, low val-
ley where workmen were removing lumber from a large pickup
truck. A few feet from the truck a small building, clearly a church,
was somewhere near completion.

"It will be perfectly safe to bring our friends in the Duma. I
have to go now. Visitors."

The near naked man put the phone down, placed the cucumber in his mouth, and held out his hand to greet Klaus and Ivan.

"Good to meet you," the man mumbled around his cucumber.

His grip was firm, not as firm as Ivan's but definitely among
the stronger and more confident that Ivan had encountered.

"Artyom will take care of you. We are old friends," said Klaus,
reaching up to place a hand on Ivan's shoulder.

"You will be safe here," Artyom Gorodeyov said, hitching his
towel up a little higher. "Our people have already been informed
that they are not to notice you. Do you know anything about us?"

Gorodeyov motioned for the two visitors to follow him up
four wooden stairs to a deck of the one-story house they approached.

Ivan knew a little about the Union of the Return and a little
about Artyom Gorodeyov, and what he knew from the newspapers
and television was not flattering.

"No," said Ivan.

"We were founded twenty years ago by seven former military
officers, some of whom are now in important positions in the gov-

ernment. We are dedicated to returning to the time when Russia was respected throughout the world, a return to the order brought by Stalin, a return to the religion of our past. An expulsion of the Jews, who have been responsible for our failures since 1917. We are a peaceful fellowship of diverse but like-minded people determined to exert our political power and raise a new generation of the young who will have direction and principles."

There had been nothing in the diatribe that Ivan had not heard before. He barely listened to the man, who spoke without expression or enthusiasm.

"We have eight girls and eleven boys here," he went on. The visitors were led into an office so small that there was barely room for a simple wooden desk and three chairs.

Gorodeyov took his time settling himself in behind his desk.

"No one is forced to remain here," he said. "If they want to go, even the boys and girls, they simply say so. We call parents or relatives to pick them up. Adults can just pack up and leave after telling someone else that they no longer wish to stay. Very few, I tell you, leave us."

"I must get back to Moscow," Klaus said, rising. "How much   ?"

"There is no charge for staying here. If you wish to make a donation because you believe in our cause, you may do so. Please take some of our literature from the table in the front hall. You are sure you do not wish to stay for dinner? We live off of food we grow and produce ourselves. Nothing in all of Russia is fresher."

"I must go," said Klaus, holding out his hand.

Artyom Gorodeyov took it and Ivan said, "I am going back with you."

"Why? So that you can be arrested for murder?" asked Klaus. "You will be recognized the moment you step out in public."

"Everyone here is happy," said Artyom, whose face conveyed

no sense of happiness. "You are free to talk to anyone here about what they think and what they are doing. There is only one rule: obey. If you stay, obey."

"All right," said Ivan. "For a few days."

Then Klaus was gone and Ivan was alone with Gorodeyov.

"Hungry?"

"Yes," said Ivan.

"Good. We will have some soup made from our own vegetables and you will talk to me about the murder of your wife and . . ."

"Fedot Babinski," said Ivan. "His name was Fedot Babinski."

The Volga Supermarket II was busy. It was early evening and people on their way home from work added to the people who did not go to work but prepared the evening meal for their families.

The aisles of the supermarket were wide, the shelves no more than shoulder high, so that all items could be reasonably in reach, the lights high above were brightly fluorescent, and constant chatter was indistinguishable.

Aleksandr Chenko, in a clean apron in spite of the lateness of the day and the frequent contact with meats, fruits, and vegetables, was rearranging a freestanding display of canned soups. The number of cans had slowly dwindled and the display had to be restocked and restacked.

He was lost in his work, a can in his hand, when he had a feeling that he was being watched. He turned his head and saw the policeman from the park standing in the canned fruit and vegetable aisle. There was a small package under the policeman's arm and a look of sadness on his face.

Aleksandr went back to doing his work, stacking, building, perfecting. When he had taken all of the cans of chicken soup from the cart and was satisfied with the display he had created, he turned to Rostnikov with a smile.

"What do you think?" asked Chenko as a short, fat woman

with a scarf tied tightly around her red face reached up and took down a soup can to take a critical look.

"About what?" asked Rostnikov.

"The display."

"Very neat," said Rostnikov. "Are you always so neat?"

"I try to be," Chenko said as the short, fat woman reached up to place the can she examined back on the stack.

Chenko took the can down and carefully replaced it.

"You cannot do that every time someone looks at a can or buys one."

"No, but I can try to stay one step ahead of them."

"Them?" asked Rostnikov.

"The customers. You do not usually shop here."

"I do not."

Rostnikov shifted his packet to underneath his other arm.

"Is there something with which I can assist you?" asked Chenko.

"Yes, you can tell me why you do it."

"It?" asked Chenko.

"Why you take the path through the park when it is neither on the way to or from this store from your apartment. It would be far more direct and much faster to walk along the outside walk."

Emil Karpo had supplied Rostnikov with the address of Aleksandr Chenko.

A man with thick glasses squinted painfully at a shopping list as he pushed his cart between Chenko and the policeman. The man wore a heavy blue denim jacket with an insulated lining.

"I like to walk different ways. You have taken an interest in me," Chenko said.

"You are a person of interest."

Aleksandr Chenko began pushing his now-empty cart toward the back of the store.

"Why?"

"You are an interesting person," said Rostnikov, keeping up with him.

"Me, interesting? No one ever thought I was before."

"Do you like guava juice?"

"What? You ask some very odd questions for a policeman."

"I have been told I am a very odd policeman."

"I drink all kinds of juice."

"Including guava?"

"Including guava. Has it become a crime to drink guava juice?" Chenko asked.

Rostnikov shrugged his shoulders and stopped trying to keep up with him. The policeman stopped and watched Chenko hurry away.

He told himself to resist, not to turn and look at the policeman. There would be nothing guilty in his doing so, but nonetheless . . . This policeman was playing a role. He probably dealt with the guilty and the innocent in the same way, trying to make them think that he knew something when, in fact, he knew nothing. He had probably harassed several other "persons of interest" today before coming to the Volga.

Chenko turned his head and almost ran the cart into a stylishly dressed young woman pushing a small cart. The policeman was no longer behind him.

"Watch where you are going," shouted the woman he had almost hit.

"I am sorry," he said.

"You could have killed me," she said loudly.

"I am sorry," he repeated, moving on.

This policeman, this Chief Inspector Rostnikov, would be back. He probably had a checklist of people he went to trying to intimidate. The list must constantly expand. What did he expect? A mistake? A confession? That would not happen. It would not.

Guava juice? he thought. *What was this business about guava juice?*

It then struck Aleksandr Chenko that the policeman might be a little bit crazy.

Rostnikov sat on a bench at the edge of Bitsevsky Park looking across the street at a trio of six-story concrete apartment buildings of no distinction.

A wind was whispering through the trees behind him, and the clouds were gray and listless, moving quickly to the east.

The boy put down his school book bag and sat next to him without speaking. "What are you looking at?" asked Yuri Platkov.

Rostnikov pointed with a gloved hand to the center building.

"What is in there?" asked the boy.

"Someone I know lives there."

"The Maniac?"

"Perhaps."

"What will sitting here accomplish?" asked Yuri.

He was beginning to doubt whether the crate-shaped man at his side was indeed a policeman and not just another of the crazy people who had nothing to do but hang around the park and create worlds and realities where none existed. Yuri's father had warned him of such people, but Yuri, who planned to be a writer of fiction when he grew up, was fascinated.

"So far, my sitting on park benches has resulted in my meeting you and the person who lives over there. You told me about the bird feeders that had been moved."

"And that was helpful?"

"Yes."

"Good. I think I will write a story about you," said the boy, pulling his hat down lower over his ears.

"I should like to read it when it is finished."

Rostnikov rose slowly, making sure his ersatz left leg was firmly under him.

"You are leaving?"

"Yes," said Rostnikov.

"Then I shall also," the boy said, rising and slipping the bag of books over his shoulder. "You will be here tomorrow?"

"I will be somewhere tomorrow," said Rostnikov.

"That is not an answer. Everyone is always somewhere."

"I have known many people when they were nowhere."

Yuri nodded, not certain whether the somber-looking man who said he was a policeman was saying something very deep or something rather stupid.

"You should go home, Yuri Platkov."

Yuri shook his head in a slight acknowledgment of affirmation.

"And you?"

"I should cross the street."

He called himself Tyrone. His real name was Sergei Bresnechov. He hated his real name. He hated almost everyone in addition to himself. He tolerated a few people, including his own mother, and he felt more than mild affection for the policewoman Elena Timofeyeva because she had let him go after six hours alone in a cell. She had not charged him. Besides that, she was pretty and just ample enough to meet his fantasies.

Tyrone was at best a gawky seventeen-year-old. He was somewhat pigeon chested, extremely skinny, with a frenzy of wild dark hair and a large nose on top of which was poised a pair of glasses. He wore an extremely rumpled T-shirt on the front of which was a faded photographic imprint of Gene Simmons with his tongue sticking out. Tyrone had promised the pretty policewoman with the large breasts that he would no longer hack into the files of the National Socialist Party. They had complained. They had threatened. Tyrone was a Jew. The National Socialist Party was a Hitler-loving hodgepodge of skinheads, would-be Nazis, and zombies. Tyrone's mission had been pure sabotage. Quite illegal. He was fortunate that his case had made its way to the desk of Elena Timofeyeva, whose distaste for the National Socialist Party was admittedly stronger than her commitment to the law. The law, she had learned in her five years as a police officer, was often quite clearly wrong. She felt little guilt in circumventing a bad law. Porfiry Petrovich Rostnikov served as a model for her behavior. He had once told her, "If you break the law, do so with the understanding that you believe you have done what is right and are willing to accept the consequences should you be caught."

Tyrone did not stop hacking into the National Socialist Party's computers. He just did so with far greater caution and discretion.

Now he sat hunched over some piece of electronic gear on the table in the small living room. The table housed two computers, all manner of electronic equipment, and a plate bearing a large sausage and lettuce sandwich. The few pieces of family furniture in the room had been exiled to a nook in the corner of the room, a nook in which all furniture faced a large television set.

"Yes, I can," Tyrone said, picking up his sandwich and taking a great bite. "I will need time."

"How much time?" asked Iris over his shoulder.

"Yes, how much time?" asked Sasha

"A day, maybe two. I have to barter with an acquaintance for an oscilloscope."

"We need it soon," said Elena, standing at the end of the table with the filtered light through a window behind her.

Tyrone chewed and looked up at her, squinting.

Elena did not seem to notice that the boy was clearly infatuated with her. Sasha noticed.

"Tonight," Tyrone said, still chewing. "Call or come back at nine."

"Tell no one about this," Elena said.

"I will not," he said, watching her. "My mother is spending the next two days at the dacha of the man who likes to be thought

of as my uncle and not my mother's boyfriend. It is not really a
dacha. It is a shack surrounded by a forest of weeds."

"Nine, Tyrone," Elena said. "We are counting on you. This is
very important."

She touched his shoulder and smiled, at which point Tyrone
would gladly have hacked into the files of the CIA and the Kremlin offices.

"He does not know you are getting married," Sasha said when
they were back outside.

"Why would he care?" asked Elena.

"You underestimate your power to charm," said Iris. "He did
not even look at me."

Sasha, who had been looking at Iris, averted his eyes.

"We will take you somewhere safe with Svetlana," Elena said,
quickly changing the subject.

"Is there somewhere safe in Moscow?" said Iris.

"Petrovka," said Elena.

"The central office of the police? You think that is safe from
Pavel Petrov?" asked Iris.

"Yes," Elena lied.

"I will stay with you," said Sasha.

"Is there a bed?" asked Iris, looking at Sasha.

"A cot," said Elena.

It was clear to Elena that the British woman was trying to
make Sasha uncomfortable. And she was succeeding. Elena had no
objection to this. Sasha had spent the night in this woman's bed. He
deserved to be uncomfortable. It was a small enough consequence
for having been caught.

A cell phone rang. All three of them started to reach into
pocket or briefcase.

"Mine," said Elena, taking her phone from her pocket.

The misty gray rain had begun again. While Elena talked, all
three moved to the car and got in. When they were inside, Sasha

behind the wheel, Elena in the rear with Iris, Elena continued her conversation, asking, "Where? . . . When? . . . How bad?" She paused after each query to listen to the answer. Then she said, "Thank you," and hung up.

"Olga Grinkova has been attacked. She is in the hospital. If we hurry, she may still be alive when we get there."

8

The Ghost of Tarasov's Wife

Ivan Mediukin decided to leave the compound of the Union of
the Return less than five hours after he had arrived.

He had eaten with Artyom Gorodeyov, whom the men,
women, and children in the compound obeyed without question,
happy to get a nod of approval or a new task from Gorodeyov.

This baffled Ivan, who saw not a benevolent father figure but
a dour, ill-dressed, and sloppy man of neither wit, wisdom, nor
charisma. Ivan wondered why Klaus Agrinkov had brought him
here.

"I have decided to go," he announced to Gorodeyov as they
took a walk down a muddy road outside the compound walls.

"There is no place safe for you but with us."

"I should be in Moscow looking for a murderer."

"It is not a good idea."

"Do you plan to try to stop me?"

Gorodeyov, a sprig of radishes in hand on which he had been
munching, stopped and looked up at the giant beside him.

"It would be very difficult to stop you. But it would be a great risk for us to help you go back."

"All I need is a vehicle to borrow."

"In the barn, there is a backup truck. It is not in the best of condition. You may take it. You disappoint me, Ivan Medivkin. You have failed to allow yourself to remain and thus learn that you can be a great tool in getting all of Russia to know that there is a force rising throughout the land, a force to return our nation to glory and respect."

"I am going," said Ivan.

Gorodeyov shrugged and said, "Suit yourself. Think about what I have said. Consider. The Union of the Return is here to welcome you as a brother."

"Yes, I have a red car," said Klaus Agrinkov.

The fight manager and the two policemen were sitting in a corner of the gym, where Agrinkov held in place a heavy dangling canvas bag. A big heavily perspiring young man in sweat-soaked gray shorts and a green T-shirt pounded away at the bag, pushing Agrinkov back half a step with each blow.

There was no one else in the gym, which smelled even more stale and rancid to Iosef than it had earlier.

"Popovich here is big, strong, willing," said Agrinkov, "but he lacks something."

"Heart?" said Iosef.

"Power in his left jab," said Zelach.

Both the fighter and the manager looked at Zelach, and Agrinkov said, "You've seen him fight?"

"No," said Zelach. "But he does not put his weight from his left leg into the blow."

"See?" said the manager to the boxer. "If the policeman knows, everyone will know. Go take a shower."

"No hot water," said the fighter, chest rising and falling.

"Then shower cold or towel down and go home and shower."

Popovich walked off, using his teeth to take off the lightweight gloves he wore.

"Only one Medivkin," said Agrinkov, watching his fighter walk away. "He is not just a giant of a man. He has the determination, the will to win. I had it, but not the size to make it to the big money as a heavyweight or the ability to get my weight down to where I could be a middleweight."

"Red car," said Iosef.

The fight manager considered, folded his arms over his chest, and pursed his lips in thought. He wore a gray cotton shirt with long sleeves and the word "Medivkin" across the front.

"Ivan did not kill her," he said. "I would stake my life on it. I would stake my mother's soul and that of my father on it. He could not. I am certain."

"Not because in losing him you would also lose your most precious asset?"

"Of course I want to keep him fighting, winning, making us both rich, but he is my friend first. He did not kill Lena. He loved her beyond reason. She did not deserve his love, but he loved her."

"You picked him up at the apartment of Vera Korstov," said Iosef. "He called you. Where did you take him?"

"I took him to the new Russia Hotel."

"You did not," said Iosef. "We would know by now if you had. A famous giant boxing champion wanted as a suspect for murder does not just check into a large hotel unnoticed."

"That is where I left him," Agrinkov insisted.

Zelach was staring at the battered nose of the manager, the badge of pugilistic honor. The image of the old Chinese man moving in slow motion near the single barren tree came to Zelach. He wondered if this man had ever tried tai chi.

"We can arrest you for assisting in the hiding of a fugitive," said Iosef.

"What good would that do?" asked Agrinkov.

"None, other than to let the world know that not only is your meal ticket wanted in association with a particularly unpleasant murder but that you too are wanted in connection with the crime. It might make it very difficult for you to continue to function as a manager."

"The public will thank me."

Iosef knew Agrinkov was right, but the policeman pressed on.

"He is just postponing the inevitable," said Iosef.

"Aren't we all?" said Agrinkov.

Agrinkov shook his head, unfolded his arms, and slapped his calloused hands against his thighs.

"I tell you I do not know where he is. He did not ask to be taken to a hotel. He asked to be taken to a Metro station and . . ."

"Compound of the Union of the Return," said Zelach.

Both of the other men looked at him.

"In your office where we were this morning," said Zelach, "there are photographs on the wall. One was of a training camp in Saslov. You were smiling and so were Artyom Gorodeyov, the head of the Union of the Return, and Deputy Russian Minister Borodin. His arm was around your shoulder. The Union of the Return compound is no more than two hours from Moscow."

Iosef smiled.

"I could be wrong," said Zelach. "I probably am."

"But maybe you are not," said Iosef, who turned his head to Agrinkov, who was rubbing his thumbs against his fingers nervously. "I think you are not."

"I have told you nothing," said the manager.

"You have told us everything," said Iosef. "We are going to this compound to get Medivkin and you are going with us."

Iosef motioned for Agrinkov to move ahead of him. Were the

former boxer to put up a fight, Iosef, though certainly strong, and Zelach, a zealous combatant, would probably be no match for him. For an instant Iosef wondered if his partner might possess some strange martial-arts moves in slow motion that would subdue even the strongest of men. Little that Zelach could do would surprise Iosef.

"Artyom Gorodeyov will not easily give up someone under his protection," warned Agrinkov as he moved ahead of them.

"Then it will be his mistake. Move."

Iosef did not want to draw his gun, but he would have if the man in front of them showed any signs of resistance. Iosef Rostnikov, unlike his father, had a very short temper, which he strove, usually with adequate success, to keep under control, but he would not actually fire his weapon on an unarmed suspect.

Zelach shuffled at the rear. The image of the slow-moving Chinese man under the light rain returned and Zelach had an almost uncontrollable urge to call his mother to see if she was all right.

Emil Karpo had been slowly taking notes as he went through the building in which Aleksandr Chenko lived. Karpo had spoken to twenty-two tenants, all of whom, with the exception of an older blind couple, answered his questions with some degree of nervousness. They were anxious to rid their apartments of this pale specter of a policeman who stood erect, asked questions slowly, listened carefully, and watched them without blinking.

From most of those to whom he spoke he learned little or nothing. Few people, even those who lived on the same floor, remembered Chenko at all. Those who had encountered him said he was a pleasant young man who smiled when he passed and seemed pleased to see them when they encountered him at work at the nearby Volga Supermarket II. Most important, Karpo found that the blind woman, Kesenia Ivanovna, who was sixty-two years old and on a pension from the Moscow sewage authority, knew the histories of almost all her neighbors.

Aleksandr Chenko, she told Karpo as her husband sat nodding in agreement and confirmation, had suffered a rejection about six years ago. A young woman had told him that she planned to marry another man, an acquaintance of Chenko's. In fact, Chenko had moved into this building just to be near the young woman.

"Tragedy," said the blind woman, looking at a blank blue-white wall. "The man she was to marry had a tragic fall from his apartment window and the young woman disappeared."

"Her name?"

"I do not remember," the woman said.

"Hannah," said the old man.

"Yes, Hannah," the woman agreed.

"Hannah . . . ?"

Both of his hosts shook their heads to indicate that they did not know.

"His name, the dead man who fell from his window—," the blind man began.

"Or jumped in grief," said the woman.

"But he died before she was missing," said the man

"That is right," the woman agreed.

Rostnikov caught up with Karpo on the third floor of the apartment building as he came out of the apartment being shared by three friends in their forties from Novosibersk who all worked as custom brick shapers for the dozens of new construction projects around the city. The trio had appeared quite guilty, but of what Karpo did not know or care. They knew nothing of Aleksandr Chenko.

"Luck?" asked Rostnikov.

"Some," said Karpo, who spoke softly of the missing girl and the dead young fiancé.

"I have a job for us both," said Rostnikov.

As they went down the stairs slowly, the Chief Inspector told Karpo what he planned to do. Karpo knew better than to express his lack of enthusiasm for the plan. Too often plans of Porfiry Petrovich Rostnikov made little sense to Karpo, but just as often they met with success.

"Aleksandr Chenko," said Rostnikov shortly after shaking the hand of Aloyosha Tarasov in the latter's office.

"Coffee?" asked Tarasov with a smile that gladly revealed even, white teeth.

The MVD Major was in a civilian suit with a striking purple-and-black tie. His steel blue short-shorn hair was brushed back. Rostnikov was reminded of the American actor Viggo Mortensen.

"No, thank you," said Rostnikov, taking a seat across the desk.

"I was about to leave," said Tarasov. "Since you have taken over the Maniac case, I now have time for leisure activities."

Those "activities," as Rostnikov knew, were centered on eligible and ineligible women of ages ranging from twenty-two to forty-five. Tarasov believed that his pursuit of beauty was implicitly condoned by Prime Minister Putin himself, who was reputed to keep company with women half his age. At least Aloyosha Tarasov was not married, as the Prime Minister was. Major Tarasov had removed his wife from the scene years ago. He felt no guilt over having thrown her out of their apartment window. *Everyone dies*, he told himself. *It is just a matter of when.*

"Now, Porfiry Petrovich, what can I do for you?"

"Aleksandr Chenko," Rostnikov repeated, resisting the urge to scratch madly at the line where the stump of his real leg met the nesting cup of his false extension.

"Who is that?"

Rostnikov paused. There were several ways to go about this, each reeking of potential danger.

"A possible suspect in the Bitsevsky Park murders."

"So soon?" said Tarasov. "Congratulations."

"He was questioned by you and held for sixteen hours before being released," said Rostnikov.

"We arrested so many that—"

"This one is different."

"So?"

"I would like whatever files you have on Chenko. There was nothing about him in the material you gave us."

"I will look tomorrow and get back—"

"Tonight would be much better," said Rostnikov.

"Porfiry Petrovich," Tarasov said with a smile. "You should spend more time at things you enjoy. What do you enjoy, my friend?"

"My wife, son, two little neighbor girls, plumbing, working with weights, and American detective novels. I also derive satisfaction from my job."

Tarasov's smile disappeared. The Chief Inspector who sat across from him was not joking.

"Plumbing?"

"Yes. Did you enjoy spending time with your wife before she died?"

"Of course," said Tarasov, now wary.

"I understand she fell or jumped from a window."

"Yes."

"The window was closed. She went through the glass and out onto the street. She could easily have opened the window before she jumped, but she chose to leap through a glass window that she could not with certainty penetrate."

Tarasov's smile broadened with mock cooperation as he said, "It is puzzling, isn't it? I will see if I can find any file on this Chenko."

When Tarasov left the room, Rostnikov immediately began to massage the end of his leg. If he scratched any harder, he knew, the itching would be even worse. He checked his watch. Almost four. He would go to Petrovka, see the Yak, and probably have time to get home for dinner and to talk to his wife. He would have just enough time to work out with the weights stored under the cabinet in the living room and work on the mystery of the backed-up drain in the apartment of Mr. and Mrs. Bortkin.

Tarasov returned with a folder that he gave to Rostnikov, who placed it on his lap.

"Those are copies of everything about our interrogation and findings concerning Aleksandr Chenko."

"You interrogated Chenko personally," Rostnikov said, opening the file and lifting a printed sheet so that he could better see it.

"Yes, now I remember."

"He is difficult to forget."

"I really must be going," said Tarasov. "Why don't you take the file and—"

"It is thick for the file of a man who was never truly suspected."

"No thicker than several of the others," said Tarasov. "If you will just—"

"I will be quick as a fox pouncing on a skittish rabbit," said Rostnikov, running his eyes across the pages.

Tarasov leaned back against the wall and took a cigarette from his pocket. He watched Rostnikov and smoked and waited.

After about five minutes, Rostnikov closed the file and rose.

"Chenko approached you when you came to look at the park," said Rostnikov.

"I do not remember. There were so many suspects."

"He approached you and wanted to talk to you, to tell you about his theories concerned with the murders. You told him to leave."

"He is an annoying, bitter man," said Tarasov.

"Like me?"

"You are very annoying, but you do not appear to be bitter."

"In your investigation, did you come across the last name of a missing young woman named Hannah?" asked Rostnikov. "I see nothing about it in the file, but I have not looked closely enough perhaps. And if she is not in here, I will find her."

The Major was not smiling.

"Chenko was questioned about six years ago about the disappearance of the girl," said Tarasov. "He was released."

"And the young man, the girl's fiancé?"

"An accidental death."

"Fell from a window accidentally," said Rostnikov. "Like your wife."

No more need be said. The ghost of Tarasov's wife stood in the corner.

"Perhaps we will talk again soon," said Rostnikov, leaving the office.

Pankov was mopping his forehead with an already moist handkerchief when Rostnikov entered the outer office of the Yak. The little man behind the desk stuffed the handkerchief into his pocket. He was certain Rostnikov had seen him, had added a mental note of evidence to his already substantial collection about the existence of Pankov's fear.

"You have arrived early," said Pankov.

"I ran all the way," said Rostnikov, stepping forward in his awkward gait, a file folder in his hand.

Pankov's smile came out as a nervous tic. He picked up the phone from his desk and punched in the Yak's number, hoping that he was not disturbing the Colonel. The Yak had never really chastised or punished Pankov for errors small or great, but he lived in perpetual dread of the moment when the Yak entered a state of fury.

"Chief Inspector Rostnikov is here," Pankov announced.

He moved the phone several inches away from his ear lest the

Yak send a threatening sound. The Yak smoothly told his frightened assistant to send in the Chief Inspector.

"You may go in."

Rostnikov shifted the file folder to his left hand and moved to the inner office door as Pankov set the phone back gently in the cradle on his desk.

Rostnikov's mind held momentarily to the question of handkerchiefs as he opened the Yak's door. No one used handkerchiefs anymore, at least no one Rostnikov knew, except for Pankov. Had the man an aversion to paper tissues? How did he clean the handkerchiefs? In a washing machine? In the kitchen sink? Did he strip to his underwear to iron them as he stood before the television watching and listening to the late news?

The Yak, head shaven, imperially slim in a dark blue suit with a pale blue tie, sat not behind his desk but at the conference table to Rostnikov's right. There was nothing on the shining table except a pad of white paper and a fine-point pen at a place opposite the Yak. For an instant, Rostnikov imagined Pankov furiously using his handkerchief to coax out the nearly perfect finish on the table.

Rostnikov placed the folder he had brought on the table and sat with the white pad and pen in front of him. Porfiry Petrovich was certain that the conversation would be recorded and, given the nature of what he was about to impart, was reasonably certain that most, if not all, would be edited and deleted.

"I have approved five days' leave for both your son and Elena Timofeyeva for their wedding and honeymoon."

"Thank you," said Rostnikov.

"That is provided their departure will not stop the progress of ongoing investigations."

The Yak fixed his eyes on those of Rostnikov, who picked up the pen and began taking notes.

"If need be, Inspector Karpo can assist Inspector Zelach in the pursuit of the boxer and Inspector Tkach can continue his mission of protecting the British journalist with the assistance of two assigned people from the uniformed division."

Rostnikov wrote a single word in small block letters, "Yalta," and put a dark box about it to remind himself to confirm the honeymoon arrangements.

"Zelach and Tkach," Yaklovev said. "The former does not and never has impressed me, and the latter continues to appear to be unstable."

"I trust them both," said Rostnikov, starting to draw a square with a circle inside touching the top, bottom, and both sides of the square.

That was what the Yak wanted on record and what Porfiry Petrovich was quite willing to give.

"You will be coming to the wedding?" asked Rostnikov.

The Yak shifted his weight in the chair. The invitation had been a surprise to him, as it had been to Rostnikov. Porfiry Petrovich could not remember ever having seen the Colonel uneasy. Now Rostnikov expected an excuse or a lie or a simple "no."

"Yes."

Rostnikov expected the wedding gathering would consist of, as other such weddings did, hours of eating, noise, and drinking. Rostnikov could not imagine this officious man at any informal function.

"It will be an honor," said Rostnikov. "And, of course, I will when I leave remind Pankov that he has agreed to come."

The box with the word "Yalta" inside was now upon the head of stick figure of a man with a crude hammer in one hand and a can marked "Soup" in the other. The man was standing on a compact disc. Yes. Rostnikov owned a compact disc player given to him by his son. Gradually, slowly, Rostnikov's collection of cassette tapes was being replaced with CDs of his favorites—Dinah Washington, Ella Fitzgerald, Billy Eckstine, Sarah Vaughan, the Basie band, and Italian opera.

The Yak sat silently waiting for the reason his Chief Inspector had asked them to meet. In response to the unasked question, Rostnikov stood, but not completely, and pushed the file folder in front of the Colonel, who opened it.

"One year ago Major Aloyosha Tarasov, who was then in charge of the investigation of the Bitsevsky Park murders, allowed a very suspicious suspect to walk free after being held for sixteen hours and interrogated."

"A very suspicious suspect?" asked the Yak, reaching into his inner jacket pocket to extract a pair of glasses and perch them on his nose.

"The suspect was and continues to be almost certainly the murderer," said Rostnikov.

The Yak read quickly, turning pages in the file, pausing once to say, "Aleksandr Chenko?"

Rostnikov nodded "yes" and added, "Notes on the interrogation of Chenko are reasonably conclusive, but the interrogator stopped just short of extracting a confession."

"The interrogator was . . . ?"

"Major Tarasov."

"And General Misovenski knew this?"

"His initials are on the last page."

"Why did they let Chenko go and why did they not destroy this file?"

"Aleksandr Chenko claims to be the nephew of the Prime Minister," said Rostnikov.

"How do you know this?"

"Internet family tree. Emil Karpo found it. There is a Chenko on the Putin family tree."

The Yak was shaking his head in understanding.

"And you are sure this Aleksandr Chenko is one of the family on that tree?"

"No," said Rostnikov. "I think he may be taking advantage of a coincidental name."

"Misovenski and Tarasov were taking no chances. They did not want to embarrass the Prime Minister by exposing his nephew as one of the worst serial killers in the history of Russia."

"Almost certainly the worst," said Rostnikov.

"This cover-up goes all the way up to Putin?"

"I do not think so," said Rostnikov.

"And so they dropped the case on us."

"Yes."

"So we would be almost certain to find the murderer and we, not they, would be responsible for embarrassing the Prime Minister," said the Yak softly, contemplating aloud. "If our suspect is indeed his nephew."

The Yak no longer needed an answer to the question of why the evidence had not been destroyed. Tarasov and probably Misovenski were holding it as insurance should the Prime Minister need to be informed about his nephew. The situation was now one that required some caution. Colonel Yaklovev had long courted the rumor that he and Putin were judo workout partners. In fact, the Yak had, twice a week, left the office giving no information on where he was going, not even to Pankov. The truth was that the Yak indeed worked out at a judo club with a personal instructor, but Vladimir Putin was neither a member nor a friend. All that might change one day when Colonel Yaklovev was ready to ascend to a higher level of influence.

"I will see what I can discover about this Chenko's claim of being a nephew to Prime Minister Putin. Why did Tarasov give this evidence about Chenko to you?" the Yak said.

"Because he does not wish me to open a closed case of suicide," said Rostnikov, "which I believe was not a suicide but a murder."

"Who was murdered?" asked the Yak, hands now folded atop the file.

"The wife of Major Aloyosha Tarasov."

The Yak was silent for a long minute looking at Rostnikov, who continued to allow his fingers to draw without giving thought to the images. He had drawn the compact disc flat beneath the feet of the man with the hammer and soup can. Now he began writing on the disc itself.

"With your approval, I would like to move a very old couple from their apartment and into a hotel for a few days," said Rostnikov.

"They are in danger? They are witnesses to Chenko's crimes?"

"No."

"Then . . . ?"

"I have need of their apartment."

"Their specific apartment?"

"Yes."

"You have my approval. I will order Pankov to draw whatever funds you may need. Keep me informed. Thank you, Chief Inspector."

A sincere "thank you" from the Yak was almost unheard of.

The Yak rose. So did Rostnikov, looking down at what he had written, actually printed, in very small block letters: "Georges Simenon and Fyodor Dostoevsky."

The plan for Porfiry Petrovich Rostnikov was definitely inspired by the two authors. He was sure that if he could open the CD cover he had drawn and play what was on the disc, he would hear the two novels that his plan brought to mind.

When Rostnikov had closed the door behind him, the Yak moved to his desk and picked up his phone without sitting.

"Pankov, approve anything Chief Inspector Rostnikov requires and get General Misovenski on the telephone when the Chief Inspector leaves. Do not indicate to the Chief Inspector whom you are going to call. You understand?"

"Yes," said Pankov in the outer office, where he was perspiring again. He looked up at Rostnikov, who stood patiently and told Pankov what he needed.

Rostnikov was reasonably certain that the Yak had just told the little man behind the desk that he wanted to talk to General Misovenski

"You will be attending the wedding party of my son and Elena Timofeyeva?" Rostnikov said.

"Oh yes," said Pankov.

Forty six years old and Pankov had never been to a wedding, not even that of his only sister. Trina, who had married only two years earlier, had made it clear that he would not be welcome. He made Trina uneasy and nervous. He made his mother uneasy and nervous. He made everyone he knew uneasy and nervous. And now the son of a man on whom Pankov spied on a daily basis had invited him to his son's wedding.

Pankov reached inside his pocket for his handkerchief and realized that he was not sweating.

9

In Which High-Ranking Policemen Have Coffee

Ivan Mediukin parked the small pickup truck in a dead-end alley-way alongside the old gymnasium. The trip had been somewhat painful. It had required him to drive with his knees up high, al-most against his chest. His foot wanted to fall heavily on the gas pedal. It was a strain to keep it from dropping and sending the little truck into a mad dash that was certain to cause attention and possible destruction.

He had worried the last fifteen kilometers. The gas gauge had insisted that the tank was nearing empty. He could not stop for gas without being seen and remembered. He was the Giant, Ivan the Terrible, the Man Who Would Be King of the Ring, the Man Wanted by the Police for Murder.

Ivan managed to get the door open and drop his feet to the ground. Then he bent over and came out of the truck crouching. Night was coming soon. There was still a pale wash of dying sun and long gray shadows.

There was a huge green Dumpster against a wall. The top of

the Dumpster was open. Things scuttled among paper and garbage, and the smell was sweetly decaying. Ivan walked behind the truck and moved to a wooden door behind a trash can. Something scuttled in that too. Ivan pushed the trash can out of the way and tried the door handle. It was not only locked; it was also held in place by decades of not being used.

The door was wood, once a thick wood, now a wood decaying from the outside in. Ivan threw his shoulder against the door. The door shot open. The ease with which he had opened the door surprised him. He fell over into the equipment storage room, breaking the fall with the palms of both hands. Then he rolled on his side and looked around the room panting from the effort and surprise. Dim twilight through the doorway covered him.

Two heavy punching bags, both with holes that would leak sawdust if they were moved, leaned against each other in a corner, suggesting, at least to Ivan, a pair of dead bodies. A cardboard box stood against a wall, a thick rope dangling from it like a snake that had died trying to escape. A stationary bicycle faced the door, its chain broken. A few feet from Ivan Medivkin lay a deflated brown leather punching bag. The punching bag seemed particularly sad, a defeated head on its side with no eyes with which to see and no body to carry it.

Ivan had spent little time training in this gym in the early days of his career. He and Klaus Agrinkov had moved to the more upscale boxing facility on a one-block street off of Kalanchevkskaya. Ivan rose and moved to the door to the gym. This door had felt frequent openings and closings. He opened the door and stepped through, closing the door behind him. He could hear voices ahead of him down the dark, narrow corridor. He followed them and came to yet another door. This one he opened slowly, cautiously.

The gym was large, a great dank-smelling place. The ring was opposite where he stood in the doorway. Two men were sparring, young men. Both were small, fast. Ivan knew that without being told. Sitting in a wooden chair outside the ring, his back to Ivan, was his manager and friend, Klaus Agrinkov.

Ivan took a step forward and stopped. From the shadows on his right and left the familiar, and not unpleasant, smell of dank sweat engulfed him. He felt a sad murmur of mourning for his damaged career.

Something emerged from the nearby shadows. Two men. One man was large, well built, though not nearly as large or well built as Ivan. The other man looked less formidable. He slouched forward and wore a look of great sadness on his face. He wore round simple glasses with reflecting glass. He turned his head toward Ivan.

That was the point at which the well-built man lifted his hand to reveal a gun pointing at Ivan.

Ivan considered turning and running back through the open door. The man with the gun might shoot, but he probably would not. Ivan began to raise his hands.

"That will not be necessary," said the man with the gun.

"Thank you," said Ivan.

"We have been waiting for you," the man with the gun said.

"You knew I would come here?"

"Where else would you go?"

They met on neutral ground, the British chain Costa Coffee shop on Pushkinskaya Square. Colonel Yaklovev could not bring himself to suggest one of the new Starbucks or the Moka Loka and did not want to go to a Shokoladnitsa coffeehouse, where there was a slight chance he might be recognized. Yaklovev was secretly addicted to frothy flavored lattes, particularly those made at Shokoladnitsa. With Moscow's ratio of one coffeehouse for every 3,187 people, however, it was not difficult to come up with a suggestion that General Misovenski did not veto.

Coffeehouses were especially good places to meet in public.

They were crowded and noisy and the two men were unlikely to be recognized. Indeed, without their uniforms, they simply looked like businessmen out for a coffee break.

A few people might comment that Yaklovev looked somewhat like Lenin or that the dark Misovenski with deep-set eyes looked a little like the British actor Ian McShane.

Given the subject that they were going to discuss after having a satisfying sip of their drinks, both men felt confident that the other would not be recording the conversation. What they were about to discuss could lead to the fall of both men.

"It is good," said the General in the gravelly voice that was familiar and forbidding to his department of 220 men and women.

The Yak put his cup down and nodded his agreement.

He did not like drinking coffee from paper or Styrofoam cups. He thought the coffee before him only minimally satisfying. To avoid the possibility of future profiling for the General's files, the Yak had ordered a straight medium-sized black coffee.

"If Aleksandr Chenko is arrested and brought to trial," said the Yak, "he will very likely tell the prosecutors and the court that he is related to Prime Minister Putin and that you had him in your grasp a year ago, as many as twelve murders ago, and that you let him go to protect the reputation of Prime Minister Putin."

The Yak, with evidence provided by Emil Karpo, knew that Chenko bore no relationship to Putin. The familial tie was an invention of Chenko.

"I am listening," said the General, offended by the lack of political subtlety being shown by this man he outranked.

"I have that evidence, or at least a copy of it, in my possession," said the Yak as a young and pretty girl with long black hair bumped into their table. The girl said, "Oops," and moved her coffee cup away before it spilled on either man.

"And what do you propose?" asked Misovenski.

"If Chenko does not make it to trial, perhaps does not even

make it to arrest, my office will be given credit for catching the worst serial killer in the history of Russia, and neither your office nor mine will have to embarrass Prime Minister Putin. You can simply issue brief congratulations to the Office of Special Investigations. My name need not be mentioned. The case will be closed. We can both control the flow of information about Chenko, perhaps even manufacture a suitable biography."

Since Karpo did not have the imagination for such a task, the Yak had given the assignment to Pankov, who would certainly stain any hard copy with sweat. He would sweat, but he would do a good job.

The General nodded to show his approval.

"It will have to be accomplished soon," said the Yak.

"You have a person in mind for the task?" asked the General.

"Yes," said the Yak, deciding he could drink no more of this coffee in a cardboard cup, listen to no more of the babble of boys, the chatter of women, the laughter of girls.

"You approve then?" asked the Yak.

"Yes," said the General, rising.

Protocol and his superior rank meant that the General should choose his moment of departure and that the Colonel should remain in place till the higher-ranking officer had left.

"You have not finished your coffee," the General added.

"Perhaps in a moment or two."

Another nod from the General and he made his way through the evening crowd and out the door.

Yaklovev left as soon as he could, dropping his half-full cup in a trash container whose lid opened greedily.

Igor Yaklovev had written nothing, but he had come well prepared. Before the meeting he had carefully gone over the Bitsevsky Maniac files pulling out names, searching. An hour before the meeting with Misovenski, the Yak had narrowed the list down to five.

Half an hour before the meeting his list was down to two, and now, after this meeting, the list was down to one.

The only problem might come from Porfiry Petrovich Rostnikov or one of his people who might get hurt or even killed. It would be tragic but acceptable, though the Yak would far prefer not to lose Rostnikov. The Chief Inspector was vital to the Yak's plans, but even that could be dealt with.

He had decided who would kill Aleksandr Chenko.

Two dented cans of Norwegian salmon.

In twelve years, Aleksandr Chenko had not been responsible for a single dented can, not one can. Nor had he broken a jar or caused a hole in a box of cereal or noodles or anything else.

He had watched the blue-and-white cans roll across the aisle. He had heard them clunk to the floor and wobble in three directions. Customers had been present. He wanted to tell them that nothing like this had ever happened to him before, never, but he said nothing, just chased down the cans and gently dropped them in the carton on the flatbed before starting to return them to the shelf with great care.

That was when he had found the two dented cans.

He would have to tell Juliana Horvath, the storeroom supervisor. He hoped she would not make the dented cans a subject of extended conversation, but he knew she would acknowledge this event in some way. And she did.

Juliana Horvath was just over fifty, stocky, homely, with short, straight dyed yellow hair. She was neither too smart nor too stupid for her position, and she took it seriously.

Aleksandr had carefully restacked the cans in the same display form as before, replacing the dented cans with new ones. Everything was even, symmetrical. A customer would sooner or later remove a can, but that did not matter. Aleksandr would have done his job.

As it turned out, Juliana Horvath had simply accepted the two dented cans and made a small x on the bottom of each so that they could be placed in the reduced-price bin at the front of the store. The saving would be small. The store would still make a profit.

"You look pale," said Juliana Horvath in her slightly hoarse cigarette-destroyed voice.

"I am fine," Aleksandr had said.

"You do look a bit—" Ilya Grosschekov had started to observe, but Aleksandr had cut him off with an uncharacteristic firm, "I am fine."

"It is just two dented cans," said Juliana Horvath.

They had no real pride in their work. They came, did the job, collected their pay. Aleksandr took pride. What was the point of working eight or ten hours a day if one did not derive satisfaction from what one did? As it was for cans of Norwegian salmon, so it was for the lost souls in the park.

When he checked out later, Aleksandr had walked slowly, full cloth grocery bag in hand, containing the two cans of Norwegian salmon that he had purchased, to Bitsevsky Park. He had come there earlier, on his lunch break, on this cool, clear, crisp day, in search of the policeman with the artificial leg, but the policeman had been at none of the benches. Aleksandr had eaten his cheese and lettuce sandwich on a fresh roll while he searched. No policeman.

Maybe he was ill. Maybe he had been taken from the case, as had been the previous police detective Aleksandr had approached. That policeman had taken Aleksandr into custody, put him in a room for many hours, asked him hundreds of questions, and then released him, causing Aleksandr to lose half a day of work. His mentioning a family connection to Putin may have helped. Aleksandr lied extremely well and was proud of his ability to do so.

The policeman with the artificial leg could not be gone. He was to complete the task. He was, if possible, to be the sixty-fourth sacrifice. Aleksandr planned to approach the washtub of a detective, lure him into the bushes with the excited promise of evidence accidentally uncovered, and then crush the man's skull from behind with a skilled blow with the hidden hammer. He would do all this in broad daylight, probably on his lunch hour, this time leaving the bloody hammer next to the body, and return to work.

As he now walked through the park looking for the policeman, he considered that the man might not be Number 64. Aleksandr had been counting the first two he had killed, the young man he had pushed from the window and the girl he had strangled and buried far from the park. Maybe he should do more than fill the board just to be sure.

It was the girl who had started him on this path, given him the idea after she had kissed him twelve times in eighteen days and told him that she liked him. Then she had said her boyfriend had come back. Come back from where? No boyfriend had been mentioned. They were in the park. She was being kind and sincere. Aleksandr had strangled her with hands grown strong from honest, hard work. He had buried her and then sought out the boyfriend and pushed him from the window.

Those two were the impetus Aleksandr needed to start the task, and now he had almost achieved the goal. Maybe he would be caught when he finished. It would not matter greatly. If they did not catch him, he might stop, but then again he might not. He might start a fresh 64. He wanted to win this game and then be recognized as the champion, the record holder, the one who stood in a steel cage at his trial imagining a gold medal around his neck.

Aleksandr took the path he almost always took and went winding toward the street and a block of Stalin-era high-rise apartment buildings. Twilight was upon him. There were adult couples and trios and joggers. Few were alone in Bitsevsky Park as the hooded sun sank under gray clouds. Later there would be the drunks, the mad elderly, the occasional fool who had not heard of the Bitsevsky

Park killer. He did not like being called "Maniac," but he had little choice and, besides, it had a satisfying frightening echo to it.

Stepping out onto the sidewalk, Aleksandr looked both ways at the light traffic and crossed in the middle of the street directly in front of his apartment building. He took out his key as he moved and opened the outer door to the cigarette smell that would never go away. He opened the inner door with the next key to what most considered the sickening-sweet odor of strong cleaning liquid. He did not find it distasteful.

He did not wait for the unreliable elevator. He never did. He climbed the stairs to the fourth floor, strode to his apartment, opened the door, went in, and locked the door behind him. Then, eagerly, he moved to the small kitchen area, where he removed two slices of fresh lake trout from the newspaper in which they were wrapped. He put a pan on the larger of the two burners atop his stove and prepared the pan with a generous dollop of real butter. He kept the fire very low and, after washing the small potatoes he had brought home thoroughly, cut them into slices and carefully placed them around the rim of the large pan. Finally, he placed the two slices of fish in the pan and seasoned them with salt and pepper.

He had almost forgotten the two dented cans of Norwegian salmon.

Later, after he had eaten, Aleksandr allowed himself a small glass of Nitin wine, on sale last week at the Volga at a bargain. He was not particularly fond of the wine, but it held memories.

After cleaning up the kitchen, Aleksandr took off his clothes and put on a pair of loose-fitting gray jogging shorts and an over-sized red T-shirt. He moved to the sole window and sat down in his comfortable chair. A headache, which he had up to now refused to admit, made one last effort to burrow into him.

It was then that he looked out the window and across the space between his building and the next. Sometimes he would see the old couple in the window, sometimes only one. They sometimes nodded to him and he nodded back. They sometimes had their heavy curtains completely draped closed. But not tonight. To-night the curtains were open. Tonight seated in the window directly across from him was, not two nodding old pensioners, but the policeman with the artificial leg.

The policeman with one leg had not been on the bench.

On his way home from school, and a decidedly unpleasant experience resulting from a confrontation with two other stu-dents over the Russian invasion in Georgia, Yuri had looked for the policeman for about ten minutes before heading home.

Now, Yuri opened the door of the apartment to the smell of *shchi*, cabbage soup, and *tefteli*, meatballs, and the sight of his grandfather sitting across the room in his personal chair. Yuri Michaelovich spent most of his time watching news and interview shows on television. He cursed and shook his head in disagree-ment with almost everything he witnessed on the screen. He even grew red in the face second-guessing soccer coaches and players when he occasionally watched a game.

Young Yuri's grandfather, lean, with shoulders sloped forward and wild mop of white hair bobbing, glanced up at Yuri, waved a hand, and turned his eyes back to the television.

Yuri's mother stepped out of the cupboard-size kitchen when she heard the door open and said, "You are on time today."

His grandfather rubbed his stubbled chin, contemplating the folly of all but himself and those of the past who ran the world as he had known it. The Communists had run a much bigger world with much greater efficiency.

Young Yuri's mother ladled food into two blue ceramic bowls in the kitchen and then stepped around her father and nodded to-ward the table.

"Sit," she said.

Olga Platkov was thirty-five and very pretty. She had passed on her large brown eyes and curly dark hair to her son. *Now*, Yuri thought, putting down his backpack, *she looks tired.*

Six mornings a week she got up before dawn, dressed, ate what was left over, and began her almost-two-hour train and bus trek to the Coca-Cola bottling plant. She had recently become a shift manager, which meant she got up even earlier and came home later.

Yuri went around the blaring television to the bathroom, where he washed his hands, after which he went briefly into the bedroom he shared with his grandfather. There young Yuri removed the book he was reading and took it back into the living / dining room. He sat at the table in his usual seat. There were only three plates on the table, which meant his father had already left for the Volga Restaurant, where he worked behind the bar.

"Father," young Yuri's mother said.

Yuri's grandfather held up a hand to silence her.

"One minute," he said.

Yuri and his mother sat and each reached for a thick slice of dark bread.

"I met a policeman in the park," Yuri said. "He is looking for the Maniac."

"There is no Maniac," Yuri's grandfather shouted, rising from his chair and joining them at the table. "It is a rumor created by this new government working with capitalists."

Yuri's grandfather had been a commissar before the fall of the Soviet Union. Yuri did not remember it, but he was often told by his grandfather that they had lived in a large apartment on Kalinin Street, a high-rise with an elevator. Young Yuri's grandfather had been the Communist Party commissar for the entire street, a big job with a small office on the first floor of the building in which they lived. It had been his job to respond to political complaints and nonpolitical complaints ranging from the price of fish at the market to requests for annuities.

"You know what we need?" he asked, reaching for the bread and butter and looking down at his soup.

"Stalin," said Yuri automatically.

"Stalin" was the answer to almost every question Yuri's grandfather posed.

"Yes," he said. "Stalin. Stalin was a Georgian, like us. Did you know that?"

Yuri knew it well.

"Stalin would have taken care of the problem," said Yuri's grandfather, starting to eat the thick soup before him.

Yuri did not know what the problem was, but he nodded his understanding and agreement. His mother smiled at him and slowly began to eat.

"There is no Maniac in the park," his grandfather repeated more to himself than to his daughter and grandson.

"The policeman has one leg," Yuri said.

"He is not a policeman. He is a molester of children. No one with one leg is allowed to be a policeman. Stay away from him."

Yuri knew better than to argue. They ate in silence to the ranting of voices from the television set. When the meal was over, Yuri's grandfather rose once more, saying, "Policemen with one leg. Maniacs in the park. You read too many wild stories."

With that Yuri's grandfather left the apartment to go downstairs and outside, where he could smoke two cigarettes. He had been told by doctors that he had to stop completely, but he had no intention of doing so. He was only sixty years old. Others he knew who smoked were older than he. Doctors since the fall of the Soviet Union told everyone they had to stop smoking.

"There is a Maniac and there is a policeman," Yuri said, helping to clear the table and put the leftovers in plastic containers. "And he is not a molester of children."

"I have heard these tales of a Maniac," Yuri's mother said,

turning the volume of the television set down to a whisper. "I think there was even something on the news. Was that in our park?"

"Yes," said Yuri.

"And your policeman with one leg is there to catch him?"

"Yes."

Yuri had not mentioned the candy that the policeman had shared with him. He knew it would not be a good idea.

"Solachkin is a jackass," his grandfather said, bursting through the door. "A fool, a jackass, a . . . jackass."

Yuri welcomed his grandfather's return. It interrupted the conversation with his mother, a conversation about the policeman that was beginning to make Yuri uncomfortable.

"You know what that *ti sleepoy, asleyp mudak*, that impotent bastard, said?" Yuri's grandfather said between his nearly closed teeth. "He believes in your Maniac? I told him that it was just a trick to divert the minds of the public from the invasion of Ossetia by Putin and his puppet Medvedev. When the police have wrung the last sweat of rumor from the streets they will find some fool to accuse of their make-believe murders and lock him away or even shoot him."

Yuri had an open book before him. As he was picking it up to retreat to the bedroom, his grandfather strode across the room, beating Yuri to the bedroom. Wherever his grandfather roosted, Yuri would go in the other room.

Through the open door of the bedroom, Yuri heard something rattling and the voice of his grandfather saying, "Betrayed, betrayed by Putin. I am not afraid to say it. Betrayed. I thought KGB Putin would resurrect the Communist Party, but what has he done?"

Yuri's grandfather emerged with a small wooden box and a board tucked under his arm.

Without a word, Yuri's mother got up and touched her son's cheek. She looked so tired. Yuri touched her hand and smiled.

"You set up," his grandfather said, placing the chessboard on the table.

Olga Platkov moved across the room and through the door to her bedroom, closing the door behind her. Yuri opened the wooden box and placed the chess pieces in the center of each box.

"You have white. You open," his grandfather said. "You want tea?"

"Yes."

"Good. I will heat the water. You get the tea."

The two prepared the tea side by side.

"You have white," Yuri's grandfather said. "I have black."

It was the same thing he said before every one of their games of chess. He had said it since Yuri was five years old. The truth was that Yuri looked forward to these games, to chess with his grandfather, who ceased ranting as soon as the game began.

"School is good?"

"Yes," said Yuri, reaching for the pawn directly in front of the King's knight.

In the six years they had been playing, Yuri had not won once. This did not seem to bother either him or his grandfather. Yuri knew he would soon start winning.

He changed his mind and moved the knight over the line of pawns.

"A new gambit," his grandfather said, reaching into his shirt pocket to pull out a cigarette and put it between his teeth. He would not light it. He never did when he was inside the apartment. "Well, let us test your mettle."

Maybe this would be the game Yuri finally won.

"**Now for** the reports," said Paulinin to the couple at his table, the woman next to him, the man just beyond.

The problem and the particular value of Paulinin's reports

was that they were meticulous and detailed, written with a dark, ultra-thin-point pen. There were thirty-two identical fine-point black gel pens in the drawer of his desk right next to the two small jars of pain pills. Paulinin always wrote in clear, small letters. He wanted no mistakes or distortions. When he finished each report, he carefully transferred his notes to the computer.

Before beginning his report, he had turned off the CD of Beethoven's *Fidelio*. It was Beethoven's only opera and the only opera that the scientist really liked. There was an inevitable melancholy to the overture, an echo from the pit in the cell. Most of Paulinin's guests appreciated the opera.

He had already examined and written reports on five of the victims of the Bitsevsky Maniac and on the latest corpse, that of one Daniel Volkovich, which Inspector Iosef had sent him. Paulinin was not at all sure that the simple case required his special forensic skills. Oh, he was pleased that the son of the Chief Inspector thought highly enough of Paulinin's skill to bring him this guest. However, the visitors were piling up. Six were in the refrigerator one flight up, and two were before him in the laboratory.

He looked down at the quite pretty woman with her eyes closed and began, "Lena—"

A lightbulb crackled. He began again.

Before writing the reports on his own form and not that of the government, he spoke to both the tape recorder and the two corpses.

"Lena Medivkin and Fedot Babinski were murdered by . . ."

". . . **two different** people," said Iosef, who had received the report from Paulinin confirming what he had thought.

Iosef and Akardy had remained in the musky gymnasium, neither sitting. Handcuffed, Ivan the Giant stood between the two policemen. Across from them stood Klaus Agrinkov, the manager, and at his side stood a bewildered middleweight with a completely

smashed nose. A towel was draped over the shoulders of the middleweight, whose name was Osip. He had no idea what was going
on. The only thought in his mind was of getting home and
telling Maria that he had met Ivan Medivkin, who was as big as
his myth.

"Different people?" said Agrinkov.

Ivan did not appear to have heard. His mind was focused on
escape.

"So our expert tells us," said Iosef. "Both of the victims were
beaten to death. However, the blows to Lena Medivkin were short,
hard, much more powerful with a right hand than the left. And Fedot Babinski was killed by crushing straight punches to the face,
neck, and stomach with a left hand, which suggests . . . ?"

"Two assailants in the room," said Agrinkov, nodding his head.

"But not necessarily at the same time," said Iosef. "Our laboratory has not yet fully established how far apart they were killed,
but it appears the woman was killed first."

"Ivan," said Iosef. "Both your wife and Babinski were dead
when you entered the hotel room?"

"Yes. Who killed Lena?"

"We know Fedot Babinski killed your wife," said Iosef. "What
we do not know is who killed Fedot Babinski."

Knock at the door.

Tyrone was close to calling Elena Timofeyeva. There were only
a few more passages, bits of dialogue that needed work to restore
them to the point at which they could be heard clearly. It was late,
closing in on midnight. He had her office phone number and he
had hacked into her unlisted home phone. She had not answered,
but at eight o'clock he left messages on the machines telling her
that he was running late, very late, but he had good news. He would
bring the tape and perhaps somehow she would show her gratitude.

Knock at the door.

He smiled. Elena the voluptuous policewoman had heard his message and could not wait for him to bring the good news.

Tyrone had been moving slowly to the door, chewing on a caramel, which he could not resist and would certainly contribute to the destruction of his teeth.

Knock at the door.

Only when he was standing before the door did he wonder who besides the policewoman might be knocking at this hour. Had his mother come home a day early and forgotten her keys? Was PoPo Ivanovich here to report on some newly discovered treasure trove of information he had hacked into? No, it had to be the policewoman. Tyrone swallowed his caramel and ran his tongue over his teeth.

Knock at the door. He opened it.

Two men stepped forward. One was thin, not as thin as Tyrone, and wore a suit that fit him reasonably well. He was about fifty, with white hair and blue eyes. His teeth, Tyrone noted, were perfect and seemed to be his own as he spoke.

"You know why we have come," the man said.

At his side was a considerably larger man wearing brown denim pants, a black T-shirt, and a smile Tyrone definitely did not like.

Tyrone knew, but he said, "Tell me so that I make no mistake."

"The tape," said the white-haired man.

The man's hands were folded in front of him. The larger man in the black T-shirt had his considerable hands at his sides.

Tyrone considered asking, *Which tape?* but he appreciated the possible consequences of such a question.

"I have given it to the police," he said.

"You restored it?" asked the white-haired man.

"I did, at least most of it, but I paid no attention to what was being said."

The two men who had entered his life suddenly now looked at each other and considered.

"Even if I did hear something," Tyrone added quickly, "I could not testify to what I heard. No court would believe me, not with my background."

The larger of the two men stepped forward and pushed Tyrone. Tyrone staggered back and almost fell.

"To which policeman did you give the restored tape?" asked the man with white hair.

"His name is Sasha Tkach," said Tyrone.

The white-haired man nodded. Tyrone felt just a bit safer.

"And you made copies," said the white-haired man.

It was not a question.

"No," said Tyrone. "I was asked by the police to make no copies, and I did not have the time."

"Oleg?" said the white-haired man.

The other man shook his head "no."

"Oleg does not believe you," said the white-haired man.

The slaps came in quick, stinging seconds, two with the open palm of Oleg's right hand and then two with the back of the man's right hand. Oleg was wearing a large ring. It cut into Tyrone's cheek. Tyrone reached out to steady himself on a chair that was not there. He sat backward on the floor with a brittle thump.

Oleg stood over him. Tyrone tried to think.

"No copies," he said. "I swear on the graves and bones of all the saints who have ever lived, on every holy icon that has ever been discovered. I swear."

"Empty your pockets," the white-haired man said.

Tyrone, cheek bleeding and certainly in need of surgical closure, came to his knees and emptied the contents of his pockets onto the floor. Then Oleg lifted him to his feet and patted him down.

Agreement passed between the two invaders.

"Come here. I have something important for you to do," said the white-haired man.

Tyrone put a hand to his cheek and shuffled his way to the man, who said, "Do not drip blood on me."

The white-haired man took a small spray can from his pocket. He unscrewed the lid of the can and handed it to Oleg, who began spraying its contents generously around the room.

"Now," said the white-haired man. "Be thankful you are alive and, as you consider your luck, run through the corridors shouting, 'The building is on fire.' "

Oleg produced a lighter, turned it on, held it to a piece of paper he tore from a discarded newspaper on the sofa, and set the apartment ablaze.

The white-haired man and Oleg pulled Tyrone into the hallway and closed the apartment door.

"You will have a scar," said the white-haired man. "It will remind you to be careful about working with the police. Now run."

Tyrone, hand to his burning cheek, stumbled, then ran awkwardly, calling out, "Fire, fire, fire."

When he looked back over his shoulder, the two intruders were gone. He paused for an instant to be certain and then shambled back to his apartment door. The heat from inside threatened the door. Almost everything of his and his mother's was now gone. His equipment would be useless. Almost everything was gone. Almost.

He knelt and dug his fingernails into the cover of the electrical outlet near the door. The heat stung his fingers, but the outlet cover popped off, revealing an empty space just large enough for the copy of the tape he had placed there less than half an hour earlier.

It was a time to panic, but Tyrone did not panic. Instead, he walked slowly out the door past the people who had come out of their apartments to find out whether there was a fire or they were the victims of a drunken joke.

In bare feet, Tyrone moved to the stairwell, his right hand to his bloody cheek, his left hand clutching the tape.

10

The Evidence of Bloody Knuckles

Sara and Porfiry Petrovich sat in the apartment on Krasnikov Street.

"It will happen and we will have grandchildren," said Rostnikov. "And they will grow and ask impossible questions, which we will delight in answering."

"And they will be strong and beautiful," she said.

"Of course."

She had fixed him a bag of food, including a bottle of orange juice and a thermos of coffee, when he told her he would have to work through the night. She wanted to ask if what he was going to do might be dangerous, but she did not. What was the point? Everything he did each day might result in anticipated or unanticipated danger.

The wedding. How could there be a wedding when the bride, groom, and father of the groom were all involved in solving different violent crimes? How could there be a wedding in which bride and groom feared the loss of their independence?

Was it too late for them to change their minds? Yes. Things

she had already ordered could be kept reasonably fresh at the markets, at least for a few days, but not beyond that. People had been invited and had accepted.

When Porfiry Petrovich had kissed her and gone through the door, Galina and her two granddaughters came up from their apartment to keep Sara company.

"Where is Porfiry Petrovich?" asked the younger granddaughter. "Is he fixing someone's toilet?"

"Perhaps," said Sara.

Galina had brought *vatrushka*, sweet cottage cheese–filled pastries, from her work, and the four of them had eaten the pastries with tea and told of their day. Sara had the least to say. She had gone to her treatment earlier in the day, treatment to keep the malignancy from returning. She was reassured once again by her cousin Leon, who was also her doctor, that she was cancer free. The cost of remaining cancer free, however, was an ever-present fatigue, which she fought to keep under control.

Sara kept from slouching like Zelach or shuffling like her husband or looking blank like Karpo. She had wonderful examples in her life of how not to look. Leon had suggested that she merely remember to walk heel down first and chest up to maintain erect posture and a firm step.

Sara had reached out and touched the cheek of Galina's older granddaughter, who smiled through her disappointment. On the one hand, nothing delighted the girl more than serving as Rostnikov's assistant when he went on an apartment mission, tools in the box in one hand, to repair a fissure or diagnose a change in pressure. Only a complete rupture of ancient piping pleased her more. The younger girl, on the other hand, was particularly taken by Porfiry Petrovich's nightly ritual of taking his weights out of the cupboard, pushing his bench away from the wall, and lifting. She was convinced that he was the strongest man in the world.

They had departed more than two hours ago and now Sara lay on the bed with a night-light on, glasses on her nose. She was trying to read one of her husband's detective novels in English, but her English simply was not good enough to make the effort even slightly enjoyable. She began to think of the wedding once more.

The apartment was really too small for the wedding reception, which was to take place after the official sanction of the government wedding bureau. It would have to spill out into the hallway outside their door and probably down the stairs.

She had wanted to rent the former neighborhood Communist Party Headquarters offices, now a meeting hall for groups of almost all persuasions and perversions. Iosef had said no. He and Elena needed no meeting hall. Sara and Porfiry Petrovich, who had not had a wedding party of their own when they got married, both understood. So all would be crowded into the apartment in which she now lay.

She would have help. Some of it, like Galina's, was welcome. Some, like that of Lydia Tkach, was most unwelcome but impossible to reject. The effort of communicating with Sasha's mother was not worth the small woman's willing and ever-moving hands, which jumped into service. Anna Timofeyeva had volunteered to help and Sara had said it would be most welcome, though, in fact, Anna Timofeyeva had already survived three heart attacks and seldom left the small apartment in which she lived with her niece Elena.

There would be no pretense of impressing Igor Yaklovev, who had, to Sara's surprise, said he would attend. He had never been to the Rostnikov apartment and she had never met him. He would find it small, with old but serviceable furniture and marvelous plumbing.

Sara had tried to go back to work at the Metro Music Shop near the Kremlin. She and Porfiry Petrovich needed the income.

She had been unable to handle the eight or nine hours a day on her feet and being almost constantly engaged in conversation, not to mention the need to be always well-groomed, always presentable.

It was no use. She could not read the English words. She put the book aside and turned off the light. As she did, a wonderful idea came to her, which she vowed to implement in the morning. She was asleep within three minutes.

In the morning, the wonderful idea was gone.

"Your wife was killed by Fedot Babinski," said Iosef. "It is her blood on his hands and knuckles."

Ivan Medivkin and Klaus Agrinkov stood silently, absorbing the information. Osip the middleweight was simply bewildered.

"Fedot killed Lena?" said Agrinkov in disbelief.

"Of that there is no doubt, according to our laboratory," said Iosef.

"Then who killed Babinski?" asked Klaus Agrinkov.

Eyes turned to Ivan.

"Your nose is bruised," said Iosef. "Let us see your knuckles."

"His knuckles are always bruised," said Klaus quickly. "His nose bleeds. Ivan is a boxer. He works out on the bags. His hands bleed and scar and grow harder. Bruised knuckles prove nothing."

"You do not understand," said Ivan. "When I got the call saying Lena and Fedot were at the hotel, I was here. My hands were taped."

"Fedot Babinski killed your wife," said Iosef.

They still stood in the same semicircle in the gym, Iosef, Zelach, Ivan the Giant, his manager, Klaus Agrinkov, and Osip, the young boxer with a towel draped around his neck.

"Fedot Babinski?" asked Ivan, looking at each face for an answer he did not receive.

"Her blood was on his hands," said Iosef. "He hit her so hard that he broke a knuckle on his right hand."

"Weak knuckles," said Agrinkov. "That is why his career was over. He had to wear pillow-sized gloves just to spar with Ivan."

"Why did he kill her?" asked Ivan.

"We do not know with any certainty," said Iosef. "Not yet. A quarrel over something. Tryst gone wrong."

"She had a fierce tongue," said Agrinkov. "And a temper that could sting."

Ivan was shaking his head, trying to figure out what he had heard.

"Our theory," said Iosef, "is that you came to the hotel room, heard your wife being beaten, entered, and then, seeing her bloody and probably dead, became enraged and beat him to death."

"I would have," said Ivan. "But he was dead when I went into the room."

"How did you get into the room?" asked Zelach.

"The door was unlocked and not completely closed," said Ivan. "I went in and saw them both there dead. Then I ran and someone tried to stop me."

"And you went to the room because someone called and told you to go there?" asked Zelach.

"Yes."

"Did you recognize the caller's voice?"

"No. I think it was a man, but I am not certain."

If Ivan was telling the truth, it was very likely the caller had killed Babinski. The caller may even have used the telephone in the hotel room. Iosef whispered something to Zelach, who nodded and moved to the gym door.

"I dressed quickly and did not remove the tape till after. . . . I did not kill him. I would have, but they were both already dead when I got to the hotel room."

"To which you were directed by an anonymous phone call?"

"Yes."

"Man or woman?" asked Iosef.

"I am not certain," said Ivan.

"And your bruised and bloody nose?"

"I tripped and fell when I ran from the hotel room."

He was certain what he should do.

Iosef also believed the Giant, which was why he did not bring forth his gun when Ivan bolted back through the door of the room from which he had entered. Instead of firing, Iosef darted after him. Catching up with Ivan was not a great problem. Stopping him was an insurmountable difficulty.

Iosef tried. And failed.

If he had hopes that Agrinkov and the young boxer would help him, such hopes were quickly dashed. In the darkened room, Iosef leaped upon Ivan's back. Ivan shook his shoulders and threw the policeman against a wooden crate.

Ivan hurried through the room to the back door that led to the alleyway. Iosef, now in pain, forced himself up and tried to run after the Giant. The consequences and embarrassment of allowing the suspect to escape were too great to contemplate.

Ivan threw open the door and dashed into the alley with Iosef a few wracking steps behind him. It was a useless pursuit. *Perhaps*, Iosef thought, *I can shoot him in the leg.* No, if Ivan Medivkin was innocent, Iosef might well be ending his career and find himself responsible for having done so.

Once in the alley, Ivan turned to his left. Something hurtled toward him. He was unprepared for the sudden battering ram to his stomach. He went down, sitting awkwardly, and tried to catch his breath. Before he could rise, Iosef was through the door and twisting Ivan's arms behind him.

Iosef had witnessed the scene but could not fully appreciate what had happened.

"Is he injured?" asked Zelach.

"You knocked the wind out of him," said Iosef, looking down at the still-seated but now-cuffed Giant.

Iosef had seen Zelach launch himself headfirst into Ivan an instant after the boxer cleared the door.

"You were supposed to go to the hotel," said Iosef, looking through the doorway at Agrinkov and Osip, who were now standing there.

"I was going to, but then I thought that Medivkin might bolt and that you were alone with him," said Zelach. "I did not think you would shoot him. I thought the hotel room could wait till we brought Medivkin in."

"You were right," Iosef said.

The policemen helped the huge boxer to his feet.

"Ivan did not kill Babinski," said Agrinkov as the boxer was ushered back into the gymnasium.

"How do you know this? Did you kill him?" asked Iosef.

"Me? No, of course not," said Agrinkov. "No more than Osip killed him."

The young boxer was quite confused now.

"I did not kill Babinski or anyone else," said Osip.

"No one thinks you did," said Agrinkov, touching the young boxer's shoulder reassuringly.

"I must try to find the killer of Babinski myself," said Ivan, starting to breathe almost normally again.

"Why must it be you who catches the killer?" asked Agrinkov. "The police can handle it."

"I do not know," said Ivan, dropping his shoulders in defeat. "Sometimes . . . I do not know. I want to know why Fedot killed Lena. I want to know who killed Fedot. I want something, someone I can pound until they talk."

"We will find him," said Iosef.

Zelach was going to alter Iosef's words but thought better of it. He needed a bit more evidence before he named the killer of Fedot Babinski.

"Ivan, no one would blame you for killing him if you walked in on Babinski right after he killed Lena," said Agrinkov.

"I did not kill him," said Ivan Medivkin.

"I believe you, Ivan Medivkin," said Agrinkov.

"Thank you," said Ivan.

Ivan repeated his innocence a few minutes later when he was squeezed into the backseat of the marked police car. He repeated it when he was fingerprinted. He repeated it when he was examined by a doctor. He repeated it again when he was placed alone in a cell. He repeated it again when he was allowed a telephone call and spoke to Vera Korstov.

"I did not kill him. They are not even looking for the real killer."

"I know," Vera said. "I will find out who did this."

Iosef whispered something to Zelach, who nodded and shuffled out the door of the gymnasium.

Iosef had held back one essential piece of information that Paulinin had given him. Babinski had been struck from behind by a heavy object. The blow had cracked his skull, the crack not visible until Paulinin had shaved the dead man's head, chiseled and sawed his way into the skull, where blood had seeped into the brain of the fallen boxer, killing him almost instantly. Babinski was dead before the first punch crashed into his face.

Iosef had sent Zelach to bring in the object that had felled Babinski. It had recent fingerprints on it, clear prints that matched nothing they had on file or could access through the computer. The fingerprints were definitely not those of Ivan Medivkin.

"**What was** he doing there?"

Aleksandr had two possible answers to the question he asked himself.

One was that the man with the false leg, Chief Inspector Rostnikov, was now certain that Aleksandr was the Bitsevsky Maniac, and was there to make him panic and confess. He wanted to be caught. He had trod dangerously close to the policeman, fascinated by the flame of discovery.

The other was that the man with the false leg was not there at all. Aleksandr was hallucinating, imagining. It was possible. As vivid as the image of the policeman was in the apartment across from him, it was possible that Aleksandr was creating him.

When Aleksandr was a child and told his mother stories he made up of killing nightmare creatures with a club, she had attributed his tales to a vivid imagination. She had told him that he might one day write books, possibly books for children. He had battled and slain imaginary enemies from the age of two until . . . When did it stop? Had it ever stopped?

If the policeman in the apartment across from him was not real, then how could Aleksandr ever know when something was real and when something was not? No, Aleksandr Chenko would have to assume that he was not going mad. The policeman was there. Did he sit there waiting for a sign of guilt? Well, there would be no sign. Aleksandr felt no guilt. He had murdered many and felt exhilaration, excitement, a sense of accomplishment. All people were but animals. What difference did it make if one or ten or twenty or fifty were slaughtered? They were all doomed anyway, as was he. It felt so good, so sweet, so right, when he struck with a godlike hammer. Few had the courage to play God on earth, to decide who would die and who would live. The role of God suited him. He was certain there was no real God to challenge him.

On television just the night before, he had witnessed a weeping woman who had survived a car crash on the Outer Ring. Five had died, including an infant. The weeping woman had sobbed, "Thank God I am still alive."

And, Aleksandr had thought, *thank God I killed those others. Maybe I should kill a baby or a young boy who is on the way home from school. Maybe it would be the boy I saw seated on a park bench talking to the one-legged policeman. Talking about what? About me?*

Stop, he told himself. *Control your thoughts. Cope. Do I ignore him? Do I acknowledge him with a smile and go about my business?*

It was a test of wills. It was a game Aleksandr could play and win. The policeman thought he could drive Aleksandr to confession. He would not confess. It would be the policeman who would give up and go home.

Aleksandr cleaned the last of his dinner dishes and finished preparing for bed. He took a long time, far longer than he usually would. He put on a fresh T-shirt and blue briefs and when he was finished turned out all the lights.

In the protection of darkness, he put his back against the wall and slowly made his way to the window. At the wall, he went down on hands and knees. At the corner of the window, he parted the curtain slightly and looked out.

Chief Inspector Porfiry Petrovich Rostnikov was looking directly at him. There was a look of what appeared to be great sadness on the face of the policeman.

In the apartment from which Rostnikov had gently removed the old couple who lived in it, Rostnikov considered what Aleksandr Chenko might do.

A major difficulty and also a blessing was that Chenko would probably not commit another murder with a policeman peering into his apartment and, in all likelihood, following him when he left. He would probably not kill, but Rostnikov could not be entirely certain. Maybe Chenko would decide to kill Porfiry Petrovich Rostnikov. It was a distinct possibility.

Chenko would find it difficult to avoid acknowledging Rostnikov's presence, not if he wanted to maintain the charade that he was innocent. He had awaited a smile, a wave, a look of amusement or curiosity on Rostnikov's face. There was none, nothing but that face of sadness.

Rostnikov could see nothing in the near total darkness in the rooms. He kept looking, waiting for a fuss of curtain or the full face of bravado. It took a few minutes, but the vigil proved worthwhile. Rostnikov saw the curtain on the right move slightly. He turned his attention to the curtain and fixed his eyes at the spot from which Chenko would probably look.

Rostnikov was right. The curtain rustled.

Tyrone was feeling decidedly unwell.

He had trod bare of foot and bleeding to the apartment of Dr. Simotva, two blocks away. Dr. Simotva worked on a strictly cash basis and asked no questions, which, oddly enough, made people want to talk to him.

Tyrone's cheek had been cleaned, treated, and stitched. Dr. Simotva had offered to give the young man a more than ample injection of morphine, but Tyrone had rejected it. Tyrone wanted to be awake for what he had to do. And so he had withstood the pain. Normally he would have welcomed any drug that would dull or eliminate the pain, but not on this night.

"You are now a work of art," Dr. Simotva said, standing back to admire his work.

The doctor was forty-nine years old, a short, ash-bearded man with a rapidly receding hairline. He thought he looked quite dapper. The world did not agree.

The basin next to the chair in which Tyrone sat was heaped with bloody hand towels.

"I have an old pair of shoes that I think might fit you," said Dr. Simotva. "Socks too and maybe a shirt. I have several I do not wear. I do not even know why I keep them."

"Thank you," said Tyrone.

Dr. Simotva smiled benevolently. Socks, shoes, and shirt would be added to the bill his patient was about to receive.

"Take these," the doctor said handing Tyrone a small plastic bottle of pills, "every four to six hours for the pain. It is not morphine, but it may suit you."

Tyrone pocketed the bottle and touched the small tape in his pocket with his fingers. He stood on weak legs and asked, "What do I owe you?"

"Fifty euros."

"I will be back with it before the night is through."

"Now would be a better time."

"I have only twelve euros and I need them. I will give you a hundred euros when I return."

Dr. Simotva considered the offer. After all, what could he do about it now, remove the stitches and throw the boy into the street?

"I know where you live," the doctor said.

Tyrone nodded, not mentioning that the apartment in which he had lived no longer existed.

"I have business associates who can come for you should you not pay what you owe. They would not be gentle."

No less gentle than the two men who had beaten him and destroyed his equipment and the apartment, thought Tyrone, who tried not to imagine what his mother might think when she returned to nothing. He and his mother had little to do with each other. Their paths seldom passed. There was no joy in their encounters. She would smile sadly and go her way, and he would smile back and go his. He had not been a wanted baby. His mother had planned a career as an office manager, but the unexpected birth had led her to a life of being nothing more than a waitress.

"I understand," said Tyrone. "They would not be gentle."

"Good. I will get you shoes and clothes."

"And a cap to cover the bandage," said Tyrone.

"I have just the thing, an orange Netherlands cap from the 2004 Olympics," said Dr. Simotva.

When Dr. Simotva left the room, Tyrone pulled out his cell phone, pulled up his list of recent calls, and punched in the number of the Zaray Hotel. When the night clerk answered, Tyrone asked to be connected to the room of Iris Templeton.

Sasha rationalized. He was usually very good at this, though his confidence had been eroding for the better part of a year.

There was really nothing wrong with being in the bed of the Englishwoman he was guarding. This way he could be at her side twenty-four hours a day, his gun, a Makarov/Shigapov pistol with a twelve-round magazine, within easy reach.

When they had returned to the hotel earlier that night, they had changed rooms and informed the desk that no one was to acknowledge that Iris Templeton was even in the hotel. The consequences of not complying with the police were enough to get full cooperation.

Sasha had volunteered to remain with Iris. Elena fully understood what this meant, but she was too tired and had far too much on her mind to object.

When the phone rang through the darkness, Iris moved out of his arms and reached for it before Sasha could stop her.

"Yes," she said to the night clerk, "put him through."

She reached over, phone in hand, to push the button that turned on the light above the bed. Sasha was awake now, listening to her side of the conversation.

"Tyrone . . . When? . . . We had an agreement. . . . I am sorry you have been put through— Two thousand euros is far too much. I can get my editor to approve one thousand. . . . All right. One thousand, five hundred. . . . Bring it to me now and I will give you a check. . . . Yes, I can give you a thousand in cash. . . . One hour."

She hung up and looked at Sasha.

"You have a very sad face, policeman."

"I am a sad policeman," he said.

"You had better put on your pants," she said, climbing out of the bed. She looked incredibly slim and healthy as she moved nude across the room. Sasha tried to compare her to his wife. He found that he was no longer certain what his wife looked like without her clothes on.

"A sad policeman," he said to himself as he swung out of the bed.

11

The Policeman in the Window

Aleksandr Chenko had awakened after a fitful night.

Over the last five years since he had pushed his rival out of a window—he could no longer remember the name of the lean, weak young man—Aleksandr had not had a troubled night of sleep. Indeed, he had seemed to sleep more soundly with each drunken, homeless, or surly lout he lured into the park and struck from behind with his hammer. The feel of steel against skull, the shatter of cracking bone, the last sounds without words from each victim had given Aleksandr days and even weeks of near perfect peace. After marking off each attack, he had always returned to his daily ritual, breakfast of hot or cold kasha with a little milk.

But last night, last night had been different. He had dreamt; the dream had the feel of a nightmare. He had sat on a stone bench in the park across from a man to whom he could assign no face. The chessboard between them had only a few pieces left. Each empty space was trickled by a drop of blood that shimmered with each hand placed on the table.

"Your move," the man had said.

It was quite vivid, even now, in the light of a sunny day.

"Your move," the man had said patiently.

Aleksandr had raised a hand toward his remaining knight when the man said, quite calmly, quite certainly, "With that move you will lose."

Aleksandr had withdrawn his hand. He had looked at the board, the remaining pieces, the spots of blood, and none of it had made any sense. He did not know whether he was ahead or behind.

It was then he had awakened with no doubt that the man across the way, the policeman with one leg, was the man of his dream.

Aleksandr Chenko needed a plan. It was his move.

But first he forced himself to shave, shower, and dress before deciding to boldly throw open the curtains to be sure that he had not also dreamt of the policeman he had seen last night.

As soon as he had opened the curtains, he saw the policeman, cup of steaming coffee or tea in his hand, sitting in the opposite window. The policeman did not look Aleksandr's way but continued to read, or pretend to read, a paperback in his hand. The policeman was dressed and looked quite awake.

Should Aleksandr try to get his attention or should he too act as if this were all very normal? He decided to wait out the block of a man across from him. Aleksandr would not crack. The man who had calmly killed more than sixty people was not going to crack. He would not allow the lawyers, judges, newspaper reporters, television news crews to see a broken man. Of course this all depended on whether or not he was going to be arrested. He was determined to hold out. He was determined not to give them what they wanted. Now, if only the policeman with the false leg would understand. Aleksandr did not want forgiveness because he did not feel that he had done anything that needed to be forgiven. But understanding would be acceptable, and it was possible this bulk of a policeman could understand that Aleksandr was not the Bitsevsky Maniac, that calling him a maniac was to dismiss him as simply having acted insanely. Aleksandr knew that he was not insane.

When he exited his apartment building, the first thing he saw was a bus moving toward the corner. If he hurried, he could catch it and it would bring him to within a few hundred yards of the Volga Supermarket II. Even during heavy rains when he carried an umbrella or deep snow and frigid cold when he had to wear his down jacket and hood, he had not chosen the bus. The park was his.

But this morning he was tempted by that bus, for the second thing he saw was the policeman sitting across the street in front of the park on the bench that faced the apartment building.

Aleksandr, pretending he had not seen the policeman, did not hurry toward the bus. He hitched his backpack, in which was packed his lunch of beef soup in a thermos, and crossed the street. He entered the familiar park path certain that he hardly had to hurry to outdistance the policeman.

When Aleksandr emerged from the park, he saw the one-legged policeman again sitting on a bench, a book in hand. As Aleks moved, he was within ten feet of Rostnikov. No one was in sight but a woman a half block down, her back to the park. The element of surprise was with Aleks. He could kill the policeman here and now during this break in late-morning traffic. The only question was how did the man get here so quickly? Was there a police car lurking, watching? No. This was neither the place nor the time. Aleks decided to acknowledge the policeman.

"Good morning."

Rostnikov finished the sentence he was reading and looked up, shielding his eyes from the sun with his right hand.

"Good morning."

"Do you plan to haunt me night and day?"

Rostnikov did not answer and so Aleks continued with, "Are

you trying to get me to say something I will regret? *Nyet*, no, never mind the question. You will either give up in time or arrest me for something. Meanwhile, I must get to work."

"Tell me," said Rostnikov as Chenko started to step away. "Do you like birds?"

"Birds?"

"Yes. When I go to the coast of the sea on vacation, I sit and watch the long-beaked, long-legged white creatures that step with the grace of Bolshoi ballet dancers. And when they soar, it is a thing of great beauty. Do you find anything beautiful?"

"Beautiful? Perhaps a neatly lined-up and stacked display of some fresh fruit. Oranges, apples, melons. The ones that give out a sweet smell. But vegetables also—"

He stopped abruptly.

"What?" asked Rostnikov.

"What did you do with the old couple whose apartment you sit in?"

"Moved them out for a while," answered the policeman.

The next reasonable question was, "Why?" but since Aleks knew why, the slayer of dozens did not ask.

Aleks hurried away wondering if the one-legged policeman would emerge during the day, at the end of a display in the produce department, down the aisle of canned soups and canned vegetables, seated on a bench at the end of a checkout aisle.

Aleks paused a moment to look back at the policeman, who was now in the distance. The man had gone back to reading his book.

Lydia Tkach did not expect her grandchildren to run to her arms. Lydia knew that her voice was high and shrill and her manner that of a Gulag prison camp commander. Still, they were well behaved and suffered themselves to be hugged. The hug was long and the children were patient.

"Other room," said Maya.

Lydia's daughter-in-law had changed, and definitely for the better. Her dark beauty had returned. There was confidence in her manner. The small apartment in the heart of Kiev was clean, comfortable looking, and bright.

Both children headed back across the living room and entered a room at the rear of the apartment.

"Please sit. I'll make some coffee."

"Maybe in a little while," said Lydia, who was, reluctantly, wearing the hearing aids her son had purchased for her.

Maya sat on a modern-looking chair with arms and rested her folded hands in her lap.

"No," Maya said.

"No? You don't know what I was going to ask," said Lydia.

"I do," said Maya. "The answer is 'no.' You will always be welcome in my home because of your grandchildren, but I do not want to hear the reasons why the children and I should go back to Sasha."

"I have come far and spent much to talk to you of such things. At least listen. Time me. Ten minutes. No more."

"Ten minutes."

"Yes, ten minutes, well, maybe fifteen."

"Begin," said Maya.

And Lydia did.

"I am a pest, I know," said Vera Korstov.

She had knocked at the door seven times before it opened. In front of her now stood Albina Babinski dressed in tan pants and a buttoned long-sleeve red shirt. For an instant, Vera thought she had knocked at the wrong door, but when the woman spoke, Vera knew she had not. Fully made up, the widow of Fedot Babinski looked almost pretty.

"I do not intend to contradict you. You are a pest. What do you want?"

"To find something, someone, to prove Ivan did not murder his wife and your husband."

"I told you what I know." She hesitated, sighed, and held the door open. "Oh, come in."

She stepped out of the way and Vera stepped in. Albina closed the door and motioned toward the couch, where Vera sat down. The room had been cleaned.

"A drink?" Albina asked.

"Maybe. Yes. I have been running everywhere," said Vera. "Now I am going back, looking for a small sign."

"Fedot was a womanizing devil of no character," said Albina as she sat in the armchair facing Vera.

"You used to be a boxer," said Vera.

"I used to be a boxer," Albina confirmed.

"A good one?"

"Yes, but there was little market for women boxers in Russia at the time. Is there a point to this question?"

"Your hands, particularly the left one, are covered in makeup."

"Are they?"

"Yes. You showed them as little as possible the last time I was here."

"Very observant. Do you have some point to make?"

"Your knuckles are red and raw."

"Yes. I have a skin condition. I use a lotion from the Dead Sea. Would you like some tea?"

"I think you killed your husband," said Vera.

Albina Babinski coughed. The cough was followed by a sigh.

"That he deserved destruction I do not deny," she said. "That I did the deed I do deny. I'm having tea. You may join me. Or you can simply get the hell out."

The latter was said gently and with a smile.

"I have a word that will prove your crime," said Vera.

"Speak it," said Albina, moving across the room and into a small kitchen from which she continued to address her visitor.

"DNA," said Vera, still seated.

Albina was back in the living room, a blue ceramic teapot in her left hand.

"I plan to tell the police to check the DNA at the crime scene. I am sure they already have it, but they have had no reason to check it against yours."

Albina weighed the ceramic pot and considered what to do.

"You watch too many American television police shows."

"I watch none of them," said Vera.

Albina moved across the room, teapot now at her side. Vera considered moving quickly to the door. The woman with the teapot was much bigger than Vera and, besides, she had been a boxer. Vera had entered the apartment looking for further information. She had talked herself into finding a murderer.

"Do you plan to kill me?" asked Vera.

"Plan? I have no plan. I do not want to go to prison. Not for killing that bag of lying, cheating filth. I do not wish to hurt you. I do not wish to hurt Ivan. I followed them to that room, called Ivan, and told him to hurry to the hotel room. Then I heard the sounds inside. They were not screams of ecstasy. The door was open and they were in the middle of the room. He was beating her with his fists. He did not even notice my presence. I picked up the vase or whatever it was, hit him. He let her go. She crumpled to the ground as if her bones had turned to water. I hit him three or four times and then I punched him in the face. I do not know how many times."

"Maybe you can convince the police and a judge that you lost your mind for a . . ."

Albina was shaking her head "no."

"I knew what I was doing."

"Soon the police will check the DNA even without my asking them to. Then you will have to answer for two murders. And what will you do with my body?"

"Get something to wrap you in and carry you out of here tonight."

Albina towered over her guest with a look of great sadness.

"I will scream."

"Few will hear and those few will not respond. You are not in a luxury high-rise building, not even a fully respectable Stalin concrete tower."

Vera looked around for something with which to fight back. Nothing was close enough to get to before the larger woman could beat her to death with teapot or fist.

It was at this point that Albina raised the pot high. Vera held her arms over her face and tried to rise with no plan but to get to the door. But the blow did not come. Slowly, cautiously, Vera lowered her arms.

"I cannot do it," said Albina, looking at the pot in her hand. "Can I get you some tea? A glass of wine?"

"Tea will be fine," said Vera.

Albina nodded and moved back to the kitchen, her voice now coming to her visitor as if she were in a cave.

"Where was I? Oh yes. He did not even notice I was there." I picked up something, I do not remember what, and hit him in the side of the head. I hit him hard. I watched the blood come as he turned his head to look at me. There was so much blood. I had seen a great deal of blood when I was a boxer, but this was different. This was Fedot. I would say he was astonished. It came to me that he had sinned and now knelt before me in prayer. Do you take sugar?"

"Yes," said Vera.

"I waited for someone to come and count him out. A fight without a winner."

Albina Babinski returned and continued.

"The pot is on. It does not take long."

Once again she sat across from her guest. This time Albina folded her hands in her lap. Was her makeup giving way? Vera thought so. The two women were quiet for a while.

"I met Fedot Babinski in Gomel; that is in—"

"Belarus," Vera added.

"Yes. I was working in a hair salon. I went to see the fights one night. Fedot was in the main event. He won. After the fight I went for a drink with my friend. Fedot came in. I was not as you see me now. I was considered to be a beauty of sorts. Maybe I can go back to hairstyling if I am not hanged."

A high-pitched whistle came from the kitchen. There was time enough to get up and run to the door when Albina rose, but Vera simply continued to sit.

Minutes later, the tea was on a trivet on the table and the two women were silently drinking.

"Fedot taught me to fight. I did well, far better than he. He enjoyed the additional money but complained about my ability. Gradually, he wore me down and I stopped boxing while he continued to both box and be the Giant's sparring mate. He also continued to bing-bang every willing woman of even passing good looks. I complained, but it did no good. Oh, I am sorry. I do have some cookies to offer you."

"No, thank you."

Albina's head turned as if on command and she looked at the television sitting on top of a table across the room.

"I watch a lot of television," she said. "I spend most of my days looking at that little screen and waiting, waiting for him. I cheated on him just once, three years ago. A young boxer with a fine body and a nose already flattened. I cheated once and felt guilty. Fedot Babinski cheated often and felt no regret."

"Perhaps you could argue that you were trying to save the woman. After all, she was beaten to death by him."

"I hit him two or three times with whatever I had in my hand and then I pummeled him with my fists."

"You could have followed him to the hotel intending to confront him, but you came upon him killing the woman."

Albina poured the tea and considered her options.

"That is exactly what did happen," she said. "But I was not there to save her."

"I suggest you call a lawyer and then turn yourself in to the police. I assume you are full of regret for what you have done."

"No," said Albina with a very small smile. "Are you sure you will not have some cookies?"

Ivan Medivkin, a man of considerable height, strength, and weight, was subdued, cuffed, and seated in the interrogation room with the two detectives.

"When I get up, I will get free and kill whoever beat Fedot Babinski after I get him to confess."

Iosef sat in a wooden chair. He tugged his shirt from under his arms. He knew he was sweating in the room that reeked of the smell of human bodies.

"I do not think much of your plan, Ivan Medivkin," said Iosef. "You proclaim your innocence and plan a murder."

"Not a murder. An execution," Ivan amended.

Iris Templeton put on a clean white blouse and a comfortable blue cotton skirt. She straightened her skirt and stood up. Then there was a knock at the door. She almost asked who it was when Sasha, gun in hand, emerged from the bathroom and motioned for her to be quiet and move to the bathroom as he walked slowly to the door and slowly opened it as the knocking continued. During the night, Sasha had changed rooms, moved into the room directly across from that of Iris Templeton, but he had awakened at her side.

Sasha threw the door open. In front of him now at the threshold stood a very muscular man with a shaved head and another man, a thin man with very white hair.

"Breakfast?" said the man with white hair.

He sounded cheerful, cheerful enough that Sasha hesitated, but only for an instant, only long enough to see the guns suddenly appear in the intruders' hands.

"Come in," said Sasha, dropping to the floor. The two men came in firing at the bed and looking toward the bathroom. Then Elena came out of the room across the hall behind them firing her weapon. Sasha did the same. The noise was familiar but not welcome to the two men in the doorway. Then both intruders fired, the white-haired one at Elena, the bald one at Sasha.

At this point, Elena stepped back and three SWAT-uniformed policemen armed with automatic weapons came out from behind her. The bald man dropped his gun and went to his knees.

The white-haired man dashed toward the open doors of the elevator at the end of the corridor. He had propped the doors open with a small wedge of wood so that he and the bald man could get away quickly after they killed Iris Templeton.

The man hobbled, grunting, leaving a trail of blood on the gray carpet. Sasha went after him. The man had a foot in the door of the elevator when Sasha landed on his back. The man twisted his hand behind him and fired his weapon. Sasha tore the gun from his hand, battered his face against the floor, and rolled onto his back.

"Are you all right?" asked Elena, who stood over Sasha as he moved over onto his back, from which vantage point he could see a small, old chandelier.

"I am," he said. "Iris Templeton?"

"Unhurt. She crawled to the bathroom when the shooting began. The two men with guns were remarkably poor shots."

"Just like in an American movie."

Sasha was fascinated by the dozens of lights in the small chandelier in the ceiling directly above him.

A pair of policemen in protective wear hurried down the corridor dragging the bald prisoner, who looked back over his shoulder at Sasha.

"I think they will both live," said Elena. "I will have them put into separate small cells."

"The older one, make him comfortable. The bald one, give him some food and water and something to drink. . . ."

"I know," said Elena.

They would play the two men against each other. Maybe Chief Inspector Rostnikov would take care of that part of this. If they were lucky, one of them might turn Pavel Petrov in and with the tape from Sergei Bresnechov, Tyrone, they might be able to arrest Petrov.

Over Elena's shoulder appeared the face of Iris Templeton.

"Are you shot?" she asked the fallen detective.

"No," Sasha said. "I just want to lie here for a while. I like the view."

12

In Which a Serial Killer Copes with a Surprise

Had his father ever come home sober from the furniture factory where he worked? He must have, but Aleks could not remember such a time. He was certain that his background must be known to the police. He was certain a dolt of an officer had or would come to the conclusion, with the help of a no-nothing psychologist, that in killing the alcoholic old men in the park Aleks was killing his father. Aleks did not want to kill his father. He was alive, still working, and quite available if Aleks wanted to kill him.

Perhaps Aleks could take this opportunity to lull the policeman into a nighttime stroll in the park from which only Aleks would return.

Aleksandr Chenko decided to take a walk. His apartment had begun to feel like a tight suit his parents had made him wear for a parade at the Kremlin. He had been eight years old and he was too short to see much of anything, though he could hear the grinding of tanks and the claps of marching boots. Aleks remembered the tight and itching suit and the fact that he had wet his pants. He had not told his parents, and when he got home he had hurried to the bathroom, stripped himself naked, and stepped into the shower. The shower had been cold. It was always cold. He ran it on his penis and between his legs where the redness itched.

Aleks's father had shouted at him when he came out, called him a fool while his mother just shook her head and looked at the pile of clothes her son brought out.

Perhaps it would be a good idea to kill his father.

13

What Does a Monster Dream?

"**Once more** I tell you, I do not know who killed your boxer, but I do know it was not your giant," said Paulinin. "He was there, but DNA insists on another wielder of the weapon."

"You are sure?"

There was a long pause and then Paulinin said, "When have you known me to speak without certainty?" He hung up before Iosef could say more.

Then Iosef said, "Who do you know who did not like Fedot Babinski?"

"His wife," said Zelach. "Her knuckles."

"Knuckles?" asked Ivan.

At the entrance gate of Petrovka stood a young man who held on to the fence's iron bars and shifted from one leg to the other. He had told the guards whom he wanted to see, though he did not know the man's name. The young man did know from Elena that she worked in the Office of Special Investigations. Therefore, he had asked for the boss of that department.

"What do you want?" asked the guard, who looked remarkably like one of the men who read the news on *Russia Today* television.

The guard stayed well back when he asked the question and waited for an answer.

"To give him something of great value. It is my civic duty. Tell him it involves the man from Gasprom in whom he is interested."

"Wait."

The guard moved away, replaced by another guard who looked like a little boy with a big gun.

Tyrone had done his best to dress respectably, which meant he had to buy new clothes with some of the money he got from the British journalist. He had been given the money in the hallway after he turned over the tape. He did not say it was the only copy, and it was not. In his pocket was another copy.

Tyrone's request was brought to the Yak's assistant, Pankov, who weighed it carefully and moved to the window where he had a partial view of the gate. The young man looked harmless, but who knew these days? Two Chechen suicide bombers had attempted to enter Petrovka in the last three years. Neither had succeeded, but there might always be a first. The young man seemed to be in some pain, but that might be Pankov's imagination.

"Wait."

Pankov rubbed his palms against the sides of his pants to keep from revealing his perspiring hands. He had worked for Colonel Yaklovev for five years, yet the prospect of entering the office with news that the Yak might not like still terrified Pankov.

He knocked and was immediately told to enter. Behind the desk directly in front of him sat Igor Yaklovev under a portrait of Lenin that one might be forgiven for thinking was a portrait of the Yak himself.

"What?"

"A young man wants to see you," said Pankov. "He claims to

have something you would like to have, related to the man from Gasprom."

The Yak pondered the situation for a moment. In his three years as Director of the Office of Special Investigations, no one had ever simply come to the gate seeking him.

"Have him thoroughly searched, every thread of his clothing and every tooth in his mouth and all the recesses of every orifice of his body."

"Yes, sir," said Pankov. "Then should I bring him here?"

"No," said the Yak. "Turn him loose naked and tell him never to return."

"I—" Pankov began.

"It is a joke, Pankov," said the Yak with some exasperation.

"Oh. . . ."

Pankov had never before heard the Yak utter anything that even sounded like a joke.

"Bring him," said the Yak, and Pankov hurried out the door.

Ten minutes later the young man was ushered into the office of Igor Yaklovev.

"You have been beaten," the Yak said to the boy who stood before his desk, "beaten by professionals."

"By people who wanted to destroy what I have for you," the young man said.

The boy was skinny, pigeon breasted. He had made some attempt to pat down his wild hair, but that had only made it worse.

Tyrone would have liked to sit. Sleep would be even better, but the man who looked like Lenin did not offer him a chair.

"Your name?"

"Tyrone."

"Your real name."

Tyrone hesitated.

"It would not be difficult to find out what it is without your cooperation."

"Sergei Bresnechov."

"Sergei Bresnechov, what do you have for me?"

"A recording of Pavel Petrov gladly confessing to murder."

"Let me see it."

"It is not on my person," said Tyrone. "I am not a fool."

"What do you want?" asked the Yak.

"Three thousand euros or one hundred and eighty-five thousand rubles."

"I think you want something else in addition to money," said the Yak.

"I want to work for you, handle all your electronic needs, you know, listening to your enemies, uncovering secrets they think are hidden on their computers, things like that."

"And what would you want to be paid for this service?"

"We would negotiate it job by job."

"Sit."

Tyrone sat as if he felt no pain.

"If this recording is authentic," said the Yak, "we can negotiate your terms. Does anyone else have a copy of this confession?"

"An English journalist named Iris Templeton thinks she has, but she will discover that she has a blank tape."

"She will be very angry when she discovers the truth," said the Yak.

"I hope so. Elena Timofeyeva works in your department."

"Yes."

"I have done a few things for her in the past. I do not think she will like what I have done to the English journalist."

The Yak could see the hint of adoration behind the young man's languid look. Such adoration might well be of value in the future.

"I will take care of that," said the Yak. "The recording?"

"You have the frightened little man outside your office be at bottom of the escalator of the Olegskaya Metro station at exactly ten tomorrow morning."

"I have no intention of betraying you," said the Yak. "It is far easier to simply buy you, but if you wish to play games, I will oblige."

Tyrone rose from the chair with some difficulty. His head still ached and dizziness prevailed when he stood.

"Are you all right?" asked the Yak.

"Perfectly," said Tyrone, though he ached from deep bruises on his face, back, and stomach.

Something came to his mouth and Tyrone was certain that if he spat, it would be bloody.

"No more games after tomorrow morning," said the Yak in warning as Tyrone crossed the room and opened the door.

"None," he said. "I know how easy it would be for you to find me. I have left a gift to prove my loyalty."

"A gift?"

"Maybe we should call it a good-faith offering. You will know about it soon."

"I look forward to it with great anticipation," the Yak said quite flatly. "And now, work."

Tyrone left and Igor Yaklovev folded his hands and said, "Very easy.".

In the apartment in which Vera Korstov sat talking to Albina Babinski, Vera was trying to get the much larger woman to agree to confess to the murder of her husband. It was proving to be a most difficult task.

"It was not murder," said Vera, cup of tea in her lap.

They were having a very civilized discussion of the consequences of Albina having cracked her husband's skull with a blunt instrument.

"It was murder," Albina said, looking at the knuckles of her hands. "He was not a bad man. He was not a good man. He was not a good husband."

". . . and he killed Lena Medivkin," added Vera.

"And he killed Lena Medivkin," Albina repeated.

"If you do not tell the police what happened, Ivan Medivkin will suffer, go to prison, possibly be executed."

"True, but if I tell, I will suffer. Would you like more tea?"

"No, thank you."

"I have killed once. I think I can kill again. Let me show you something."

She stood and crossed the room to the chest of drawers and opened the top drawer. Then she brought something out. It was a gun.

"I know almost nothing about guns," Albina said. "Fedot said it was always loaded, that all one had to do was point it and pull the trigger. It was not unusual for him to take it out and aim it at my face."

"Why did you stay with him?" Vera asked, trying not to look at the gun.

"I do not know," said Albina, returning to the chair directly in front of her visitor. "I never considered leaving, probably never would have, had I not followed Fedot to that hotel."

"I think we should finish our tea and call the police, or perhaps we should simply go to them."

"I know a bit about prisons," said Albina, looking first at the gun in her hand and then nowhere. "I know what will happen to me. I will be destroyed, violated, my body and mind insulted by the hands and tongues of foul-smelling strangers."

"It is the right thing to do."

"The right thing?" asked Albina "What do I care about doing the right thing? I care only at this point for staying alive."

Vera put down her teacup and said, "I have changed my mind. A little more tea would be nice."

"No," said Albina, standing, weapon now aimed at her visitor.

"Neighbors will hear gunshots," said Vera.

"In this outpost of the indifferent, no one will care. I can kill you and wrap you in something, maybe this carpet, and carry you out tonight. I can carry your body to the Metro station very late tonight, and when no one is looking I will sit you up on the bench at the entrance and leave with the carpet. The problem is that I like you. You have stuck by your man to the point at which your loyalty is about to lead to your death."

"It would be very nice if we could think of a solution other than your shooting me and carrying my body through the streets of Moscow."

"I am too tired to consider options."

"Since my life depends on such considerations, let me present a few problems with your plan."

"A few problems?"

Vera should have noticed long ago, but the woman had kept it covered by a shroud of pseudo- or perhaps real grief: Albina Babinski was drunk.

"Yes," said Vera, still seated. "We seem to be getting along quite nicely. We might become friends. You do not really want to see me dead on your floor."

"No, but I probably will not be haunted by the image, and if I am, so be it. You will join the legion of the dead who invade my dreams."

Vera considered throwing the cup still half-full of tea at the head of Albina Babinski. It would almost certainly fail to save Vera, but there seemed to be nothing else to do. Albina raised the gun in a shaking hand and aimed it at Vera. The distance was but half a dozen feet.

"I cannot do it," Albina said, now cradling the gun as if it were a newborn baby.

It was at this point that the door to the apartment flew open, destroyed at the hinges and locks. Both women turned toward the noise and witnessed a giant filling the doorway. He strode in. Albina fired at him.

"Ivan, no," said Vera.

He pushed her to the side and advanced farther toward Albina Babinski.

Vera turned and leaped at the woman with the gun who was about to shoot again at Ivan Medivkin. Before Albina could fire off another round, Vera sank her teeth into the wrist of the arm with the gun. Both women tumbled backward, Vera on top, Albina letting out a scream of pain and dropping the gun.

Vera picked up the gun and turned to look at the Giant, who sat on the floor panting for air, blood pouring from a wound in his neck and another in his chest. She could see now that he was manacled.

"Are you all right?" asked Ivan.

"Yes, but you are not."

"I am sorry, so sorry," Albina said as she wept.

At that point, Iosef Rostnikov and Zelach thundered into the room. Iosef held a gun in his hand.

"Medivkin, you are a fool," said Iosef.

"We might have been too late," said Ivan.

Zelach stepped forward to put handcuffs on Albina Babinski, who held out her wrists dutifully and said, "My wrist is bleeding."

"We will fix it," said Zelach.

"I would not have shot her, you know, but when he came rushing at me—"

"No, I do not know," said Zelach, helping the woman to her feet.

Vera and Iosef knelt at Ivan's side. There was no point in trying to help him to his feet. He was far too big and solid.

Iosef had his cell phone out and called for an ambulance.

"Do not die," said Vera. "I will not forgive you if you die."

"I will not die," said Ivan.

Ivan, his eyelids now very heavy, considered the likelihood of his own demise and gave himself odds of five to two in favor of survival.

Iris Templeton was packed and ready to go less than an hour after the attack by the two men. Elena stood at the door watching her.

"You have what you need?" asked Elena.

"More than enough," said Iris, surveying her closed suitcase.

She had given her statement to two detectives, one in a leather jacket and the other in a zippered jacket that threatened to burst under the pressure of the man's distinct belly. Even before the two detectives, who were not from the Office of Special Investigations, released her, Iris had begun writing the story in her head. It would be in four parts. First, the prostitution ring in Moscow; second, the murders of the prostitutes and the pimp; third, the attack on her own life by Pavel Petrov's men; and fourth, the full exposé of Petrov himself.

The interviews with the prostitutes were on the miniature recorder that now rested in her suitcase, along with the recording of Pavel's confession of murder. She did not want it or the tape she had purchased from Tyrone to be confiscated at the airport. Most of all she did not want Petrov to make another attempt on her life.

"I am ready," she announced.

"You will wish to see Inspector Tkach?" asked Elena.

"Not necessarily."

"I see."

"Do you? I think you see a cold-hearted professional woman who has a great story and has used a handsome Russian policeman for fun and profit."

"Used?"

"As he used me for refuge from a past he chose not to disclose."

The door opened and the two detectives to whom Elena and

Iris had given their report on what had taken place reentered the hotel room.

The one in the leather jacket wore his thick dark hair brushed back. He wore a smile that suggested he found the world and its vagaries amusing.

"We will have to search your suitcase," the one in the leather jacket said.

"Why?"

"Orders," said the man as the other detective, the one with the belly, moved to the bed and began to go through it.

"Be careful with that please," said Iris.

Elena and Iris knew full well what the two men were looking for. Word had somehow gotten to them. Their orders were clear: find the tape.

They took only minutes to find the miniature tape recorder and the tape inside. They were tucked into the suitcase lining. The detective with the belly began to play the tape and immediately knew it was what he was looking for.

"We must take this," said the detective in the leather jacket. "It will be returned to you."

"I am sure it will," said Iris.

"We must also inspect your person," said leather jacket.

"I can do that," said Elena, stepping forward.

Leather jacket hesitated, a hand cupping his chin, and then said, "I will have to do that myself."

"I protest," said Iris.

"I understand," said the detective as his hands went over her body from neck to toes.

When he finished, he stood.

"Have a safe trip back to England," said leather jacket. "And come back soon."

"Thank you," said Iris, trying to control her anger as the men left the hotel room.

She checked her watch as she put her clothes back in the suitcases. "They were neater than I expected."

"They took your tape," said Elena.

"A copy rests uncomfortably wrapped in tissue between my legs, where I hoped that I would not be touched. There, I am ready to go."

Sasha had shaved hurriedly and managed to nick himself twice, small nicks, one just under his nose, the other on his neck. He was at Petrovka looking for Porfiry Petrovich Rostnikov. When Sasha reached the door of the space shared by the detectives of the Office of Special Investigations, he was startled to see Tyrone, Sergei Bresnechov, coming down the stairs.

Sasha and Elena's plan had been to find Rostnikov and suggest that he put the boy who called himself Tyrone into seclusion to protect him from Pavel Petrov. Sasha crossed the hall quickly to the Chief Inspector's office, knocked, got no reply, and entered to a sight that made his knees very weak and his stomach threaten to surrender.

There sat his mother and his wife.

"What?" he asked.

"We are here to see Porfiry Petrovich Rostnikov," said Lydia.

"Why?"

"To determine if you merit yet another chance," said Sasha's mother.

Maya sat, hands in her lap, looking up at him as if he were an unwelcome trespasser.

"Go away," said Lydia, sweeping him away with her arm.

A dazed Sasha Tkach backed out of the office unsure of whether he had witnessed reality or a hazy dream. He considered opening the door again but decided to go across the hall to his desk.

Could it be true? Has my mother pulled a plum from the pie?

14

Petrov and the Man Who Looks like Lenin

Pavel Petrov's office at Gasprom was impressive. It was meant to be. Colonel Igor Yaklovev, however, was unimpressed.

Both men wanted, lived for, power, but the Yak was content with a reserved power.

Petrov wanted those who came in contact with him and heard of him to think in terms of ruthless power. The Yak wanted few to hear of him and most to think of him not at all.

And finally, Pavel Petrov was a violent pimp and a murderer. Igor Yaklovev was definitely not violent, and if he had caused a death or two in his career, it was just part of the job.

Most visitors to Petrov's office were intimidated by its size, the awards on the walls, the massive antique desk, and the man behind it.

"Please sit," said Petrov.

It was not the Yak's wish to leave his office except on very rare occasions to dine, lunch or dinner, at a restaurant, seated at a quiet table to the side, from which he could watch the people at middle levels of power. This was sufficient public exposure.

The Yak sat, expressionless, across from the smiling, confident Petrov, who said, "You are admiring my desk."

"Yes."

"Following the Revolution the desk was taken from the office of the head of the personal guard of the Tsar himself. For sixty years it was forgotten in the office of a pompous notary. And then one day a collector of such pieces told an acquaintance of mine who owed me more than just a favor. And within a day, the son of the now-dead notary, after a very small payment and a few minutes of persuasion, sold the desk to me."

Petrov lovingly ran the palm of his left hand across the shining desk.

They were a study in contrasts. Pavel Petrov was tall, definitely handsome, with well-groomed black hair, almost perfect skin, and white teeth. He was a presence with which to be reckoned. Igor Yaklovev in mufti was a most unimpressive presence. He was five-foot-six, lean, pale. *Yes*, Petrov decided, *the man does look like Lenin.*

"It is yours," said Petrov, patting the table as if it were a favorite pet. "I give it to you."

"There is no room in my office for such a gift."

Pavel Petrov swiveled in his chair. His back was to the Yak.

"Then sell it. In one of the drawers you will find a very generous sum."

"How generous?"

"That depends on the evidence you have of certain indiscretions of mine."

Had Petrov sent someone to follow the Bresnechov boy?

"Like murder?" asked the Yak. "I am not interested in money. But I do have a counteroffer. I have a recording of a conversation between you and an English journalist named Iris Templeton."

Pavel Petrov spun around again to face his visitor. Petrov's fingers began to tap out a quite uneven beat.

"What does interest you in this fragile life?"

The Yak ignored the threat and told the powerful man across from him that he wanted only to let him know that he had the tape.

"I see," said Petrov. "And copies?"

"I expect to have all that exist in my hands before tomorrow ends."

"Am I to trust you, Colonel Yaklovev?"

"It does not matter if you trust me. It matters only that you know I have the tape."

"I think we understand each other," said Petrov, standing.

"No, we do not," said the Yak. "If you engage in any other criminal activity involving brutality or murder, if you hurt anyone, the tape gets released to the media and to all the members of your board of directors."

Petrov was up now pacing the floor, pausing here to touch some object or award, pausing there to look at a photograph of him with a famous person, including three with Vladimir Putin.

"Offer accepted," said Petrov.

"It was not just an offer. It is also a condition."

Petrov decided to probe the dour man's vulnerabilities. He would take his time. He would work slowly. He would find someone within the Office of Special Investigations to corrupt, someone who could find that tape and destroy it, as Petrov would then destroy this Colonel who reeked with the sweet smell of victory.

Pavel was brought to a halt in his pacing by the Yak, who said, "I am not vulnerable to intimidation. I have no living relatives that I care in the least for. I have no friends. I have never broken the law, not even when I was a child."

The policeman had kept up with him.

"I understand," said Petrov. "Now, if you please, I would like to get back to work and do my part in keeping the gas flowing for the people of Russia."

"And what is your work?"

"I am afraid I am not allowed to tell you that."

"Politburo."

"I cannot answer that."

The truth was that Petrov existed in the company as one of but several people who deflected attacks on the company with charm, half-truths, and lies.

The Yak nodded in understanding.

Petrov decided that Iris Templeton had to have a copy of the tape and it would have to be destroyed. How many copies of the tape were out there? How many people would he have to kill or have killed? It was his own doing, his own arrogance. He had lived long on the edge and felt he would never plummet. Even now, when disaster crawled toward him like a fat spider, Pavel Petrov felt a thrill.

The smug police bureaucrat sitting in his office might have to be disposed of and—

"The tape is safe," said the Yak. "If something happens to me it goes to someone who will immediately arrest you for murder. It will not matter if my death comes from a bullet in my brain or a fall down a flight of stairs."

This is the second time that Colonel Yaklovev has seemed to read my mind. Am I that obvious?

Petrov decided he would make a phone call the moment the Yak left the room.

"You want evidence of corruption within the corporation?" said Petrov.

"Yes."

"And you will overlook my . . . indiscretions?"

"No. Never, but I will not yet call them into the light as long as you continue to provide me with evidence that I can use."

"And you want this simply to uproot corruption?" said Petrov.

"I have other reasons you would not understand."

"An honest man. There are all too few of them. I do not like honest men."

The two men did not shake hands, nor did Petrov rise. Igor Yaklovev showed himself out, which was fine with Pavel. He had urgent business elsewhere. He picked up the telephone on his desk.

Paulinin took a plastic container from his desk drawer, popped it open, and put two yellow pills in his palm. He had been up for the past two days.

He had to speak to the dead.

Some of the dead had to be spoken to quickly, before they faded away. They did not stop yielding information, but they did deprive Paulinin of their company. The dead spoke only to him.

Porfiry Petrovich Rostnikov was accustomed to the darkness and smells in the laboratory below the surface of Petrovka. He was also accustomed to finding a corpse on one or both of the tables beyond the labyrinth of tables filled with books, beakers, poisons, and instruments whose function it was best to keep to himself.

"These two," said Paulinin, pushing his glasses up his nose with the back of his hand, which clutched a bloody scalpel. Paulinin preferred to work without latex gloves. He wanted to explore the nuanced corners, crannies, and protuberances that lay beneath the skull and inside the organs.

Paulinin, on rare occasions, admitted to himself that he might be mad.

"These two," Paulinin repeated, looking down at the pale naked corpses of a bearded old man and an older woman. "They are victims of yet another copycat."

The skull of the man was most recalcitrant. Paulinin picked at the cracked pieces as if they were parts of a coconut.

"Different hammer," the scientist continued. "Different power. Different hand. These two were struck by someone left-handed. Your others were all murdered by a right-handed killer, except for the two of which I told you already."

"He is even further from his goal than he thought," said Rostnikov.

"His goal?" asked Paulinin as he probed into the dead woman's stomach, which he had opened with a steel scalpel.

"To kill more people than any other Russian ever has."

"In that case, I will delve more deeply," said Paulinin, his fingers searching the cavity he had opened.

"Do that. And call me when you have something."

"You already have an idea," Paulinin said, using his free hand to turn the head of the man so it was facing straight up, eyes open.

"Perhaps," said Rostnikov.

There was no direct flight from Moscow to London. Iris would have to spend two hours in the Frankfurt airport. She had experienced such waits before. She had a book with her, *Notes on a Scandal*, but she was sure that she would be unable to read. She had begun writing her story before the plane took off.

Iris Templeton welcomed the distraction of her laptop even more than that of the book she was reading. Iris Templeton had a secret. She had a deadly fear of flying. Given the choice, she would never fly again, but she did not have the choice and she did not want anyone to know her fear was kept in control with pills, hypnosis, alcohol, and meditation. She always flew first-class and always sat in an aisle seat. She limited herself to one drink a flight, regardless of how long the flight. Her preferred drink was a premium straight brandy. She loved the taste of brandy.

Iris did not have to stand when the woman moved past her to the window seat. There was plenty of legroom. The woman was slightly heavyset, well-groomed, business suit and briefcase with laptop computer. The woman smiled. Good teeth.

"Elizabeth Croning," she said, reaching over to shake hands.

"Iris Templeton."

Iris was in no mood for new friends or idle conversation. She removed her novel from her briefcase, inserted the fragile airline plugs in her ears, and adjusted the volume. It was something classical, possibly German, and too sweet for her taste but all right for holding off conversation.

She removed her laptop from its sleeve and waited for the gate to open like a Thoroughbred and for the fear to be smothered by the bright light of ideas and music.

From where he sat, he could just see her arm resting.

He had almost missed the flight. The call had come when he was on his way home. He had immediately caught a cab, gone to the airport, showed his passport and his identification, and hurried to the gate at the final call for takeoff.

There had just been time to pick up a travel bag at the airport.

He had been told that he would be supplied with a very compact weapon in lockers when he got to Frankfurt and London. He would not have to carry a weapon onto the plane. He had been told that Iris Templeton had a two-hour layover in Frankfurt. He had been told what he had to do. He would do it.

He had an aisle seat next to a black man in a gray suit and matching tie. The black man gave the late-arriving passenger as much room as he could and concentrated on the notebook full of lists of numbers.

The man who had arrived late did not look away for more than a few seconds. There was reason to believe someone else was on this plane watching Iris Templeton. Before it was over, he fully expected to know who that was and what he should do.

"Well?"

"What do you want to do?"

Iosef shrugged. He had hoped Elena would answer the question, but it looked as if there was to be a stalemate.

They sat on the edge of the bed in front of the window. Iosef's apartment was small, hardly an apartment at all, one tiny room with a bed near the window and a sink in the corner with a single-burner stove top next to a small refrigerator with a microwave atop it. There was also the luxury of a toilet and shower right next to it with just enough room to stand.

Sara had done her best to make the room comfortable for her son, and she had done a good job.

It was the place where he and Elena could be alone.

It was the place where they now had to decide if they were to marry the next day.

"Do you really want to?" she asked.

"Yes, I wish to marry you. I wish to spend as many of my days as possible with you next to me laughing, frowning, humming, and I wish you to have a daughter with me, one who looks like you, and I wish to have a son with you, one who looks more like you than me, and I wish to begin this journey soon."

"Tomorrow? You are sure?" she asked, not looking at him.

"Everything is ready. It is as good a day as any and better than most."

"I sense," she said, "a lack of enthusiasm."

"You sense the nervousness of any normal bridegroom. And you? Are you not on less than sturdy legs?"

"Yes," she said with a smile, looking at him. "But I will not fall."

He leaned over, kissed her gently, and felt her arms tighten around his neck as they rolled back on the bed with Iosef on top.

"We had best call your mother and tell her," whispered Elena.

"We have something else to take care of first," he said, reaching down to unbutton her blouse.

Rostnikov did not hear the first knock at the door. He was asleep in the chair he had placed by the window from which he could cause unease in Aleksandr Chenko.

With the second knock, Rostnikov called out, "I am coming."

And come he did, rumbling to the door, urging his mechanical leg to cooperate with his good right one.

He went to the door, right hand in his pocket, where he had tucked in a small, efficient seven-shot Nagant revolver.

"I brought you something," said Aleksandr Chenko as the Chief Inspector opened the door.

Chenko held out a bottle.

"Nitin wine," said Rostnikov. "Perhaps we can have some later."

Then Aleksandr took a tarnished pocket watch from his pocket and handed it to Rostnikov, who held it in the palm of his left hand as he stepped back. Right hand still in his pocket, he motioned to the chair opposite the one he had been sitting in for the past two days. Chenko sat, a smile on his face, teeth showing.

Was this how the old couple sat night after night talking, reading, falling into a literary slumber?

Chenko was dressed in a pair of well-worn jeans and a black sweater. He sat awkwardly.

"I can offer you either tea or coffee the temperature of this room," said the policeman.

"Perhaps a glass of the wine I brought."

"Later."

"Yes," Chenko said, folding his hands in his lap and looking out the window at the darkened window of his own apartment.

"You look uncomfortable," said Rostnikov. "Would you prefer we go for a walk?"

"No, this is fine."

The younger man was not obviously armed. He had never used a gun in his compilation of the dead, and Rostnikov was reasonably certain he would not begin now. Nevertheless, Rostnikov sat in a position from which he could easily reach the revolver in his pocket.

"You know why I am here?" said Chenko, leaning forward.

"To confess," said Rostnikov, now examining the watch Chenko had handed him. On the back of the watch was some kind of badly scratched engraved writing that Rostnikov could not read.

"It says: '*S.M.K. TO E.L.P.*'"

"Who are they?" asked Rostnikov.

"I do not know. The man from whom I got it was named Taras Ignakov," said Chenko, still smiling. "You have questions. Go ahead. I will give you answers."

"Where did you get this watch?"

"From the pocket of a man with a dirty curly black beard, only one tooth, and yellow eyes."

"You took it," Rostnikov prompted him.

"From the pocket of a dead man."

"And . . . ?"

The deep breath was long and quite mournful before Chenko replied.

"Oh yes, I killed him. I think he was my sixty-first. You have not yet found his body?"

"No."

"When possible, I obtain their names and memorize them. And I always honor them by taking something from their pockets if there is anything to take. I have a hidden box filled with rings, watches, coins, even shoelaces."

"Why?"

"At first I did it to be recognized and feared. Then I realized that swinging the hammer and listening to a cracking skull and a final sigh gave me a sense of great power. It is better than sex."

At this point Chenko reached behind his back and lifted from his belt a claw hammer, which he placed in his lap.

"I was not asking why you kill. I asked why did you memorize their names? Why did you take souvenirs of your crimes? Do you want to remember what you did and who you did it to?"

Rostnikov shifted his weight to be better able to reach and retrieve the gun in his pocket.

"Yes," said Chenko. "That too."

"Normal people do not want to remember when they commit murder. Mafia members do not want to remember. Robbers who kill do not want to remember."

"And what is your point?" asked Chenko.

"You are sick."

"Can I be cured?" Chenko said with a smile.

"I do not think so," said Rostnikov.

"Nor do I. You want me to confess because I feel guilty? I feel no guilt. None at all."

"You like killing."

"Yes."

"And if you are not in prison you will kill again, and you may even do it in prison. You should be isolated in a cell for the remainder of your life. And I think you know I am right."

"You could just kill me. I know you have a gun in your pocket," said Chenko. "Or maybe I could kill you. I can leap from this chair and dig the claws of my hammer deep into your skull before you can get out your gun. Even if you manage to get it out and shoot me, I think with my lunge I could still watch my hammer strike."

"Let us hope the moment does not arrive when we must test your theory," said Rostnikov, looking almost sleepy. "Have you ever killed someone who was facing you?"

"No, but I will if I must. I wish to have a large and open trial at which I can tell what I have done. Can I have that, policeman, or do you plan to just kill me?"

"I have not yet decided," said Rostnikov. "I wanted to have this conversation first."

Chenko clicked his teeth together softly and said, "Look at my numbers. Am I not the maddest of all?"

"You are."

"Will I stun the psychologists and psychiatrists who examine me in prison?"

"Possibly."

"Yes, they will probe my life, ask questions about my child-hood, my mother and father, and discover nothing. Why do you want to help me?"

"What have I said that makes you think I want to help you?" Rostnikov said.

"Do you have handcuffs with you?"

"Yes."

"You will put them on my wrists and take me away."

"It will all end in a whisper."

"No," said Chenko, rising, hammer in his right hand.

"First place the hammer on the ground," Rostnikov said with a series of grunts as he rose with the revolver now aimed at the chest of Aleksandr Chenko.

Chenko ignored him and said, "People live with the constant fear of death. They, the old, fear its coming. With this hammer, I release them quickly so that they will fear no more. Do you fear death, policeman?"

He asked stepping forward, hammer now rising.

"I do," said Rostnikov. "But that does not matter. Put down the hammer, Aleksandr Chenko."

The door of the apartment flew open. There was a sudden storm of gunfire. Rostnikov distinctly heard a ping as a bullet hit a spot of metal on his leg. The bottle of Nitin wine exploded, its contents spraying upon the falling body of Aleksandr Chenko.

Rostnikov was certain that he felt one bullet hit him and then another one. He could see Aleksandr Chenko, spattered with wine and bullets, fall backward over the chair, the hammer spinning around in the air and breaking free through the window, sending a brief rain of shards of glass flying atop both the policeman and the serial killer.

Iris Templeton turned her head to the rear as if she were looking for the flight attendant. No one was looking at Iris. At least not at that moment. She considered the woman in a business suit in the window seat next to her. Then there was the dark, good-looking man in business class who spoke perfect Spanish on the airline phone. Perhaps it was the lean, pale man in a black suit whose eyes were turned toward the window. Even if someone was watching her, there was no point in worrying until they were on the ground, which would be very soon.

Of course she thought that the most likely truth was that no one was watching Iris Templeton. She changed her mind when the plane landed in Frankfurt and she was sitting in the coffee bar with a biscotto and a cup of coffee. She was certain she was being watched, though she recognized no one from the plane. Perhaps Petrov had called ahead, perhaps many things.

If someone was planning to get the tape of her and Pavel Petrov, they would have to wait until the plane landed in London and luggage had been picked up. Richard Neatly was supposed to meet her at the airport. She had called ahead. Richard was a very good man, but he was short, almost frail, fussy, and a few years past sixty years old and would be no good in a crisis. His heart was in a good place, but he sighed when news readers on the BBC made an error in grammar. She was certain that if he were here now he would, as he had done in the past, remind her that "biscotti" was plural and not singular, but she had never heard anyone order a "biscotto" and she did not intend to be the first.

Normally, Iris enjoyed nothing more than an almond biscotto.

Even a chocolate would do. Any biscotto would help compose her. But not today. She sat. She ate. She drank, but without the enthusiasm she usually savored.

She was certain the lean man would be on the plane to London. She looked at him. He looked away, not quickly but with the deliberation of someone who had seen enough this time.

The list of arrivals and departures above her clicked, and her flight to Gatwick appeared.

She had another hour with the dark man.

"The power of Christ has saved you, but why?"

Artyom Gorodeyov had brought his message to the bedside of Ivan Medivkin, who was in no condition to hear it. Vera Korstov at his bedside in the hospital thought it would have been more helpful had Christ intervened a little while earlier.

Vera was little interested in the question the man with the shaved head and no neck had posed. Though Marx and Lenin were not her gods, at least they were firmly rooted in reality.

"Why?" asked Vera over the rush of hallway noise through the slightly open door.

"You are famous," said Gorodeyov. "You are now a hero. You have the power to impel thousands, maybe even millions, to embrace the Union of the Return."

"Which is a political party calling for the return of Stalinist control," said Vera. "Stalin for Christ."

Ivan groaned and tried to roll into a more comfortable position, but the pain in his neck, arm, and shoulder was too much to bear.

Doctors, nurses, therapists had come, though Ivan was too groggy to fully understand what had happened. He did know that he was not expected to die. He did know that returning to the ring now was a distinct possibility. Only hours ago he had abandoned all hope of boxing again. Now he was a hero.

"Rest," Klaus Agrinkov had said. "No hurry. We have impressive offers from all over the world: Kuwait, the United States, Indonesia, everywhere."

Ivan reached for Vera's hand now as Gorodeyov leaned forward and continued his sermon.

"You owe it to Mother Russia," whispered Gorodeyov.

Ivan could smell the man's breath, an unpleasant combination of garlic and breath mint.

Vera was impressed by the man's ability to penetrate the imposing protection of the quite visible police in the hallways. The Union of the Return had more power than she had expected, to get through the gauntlet of uniforms.

"I am tired," Ivan said.

The bed was uncomfortable, at least half a foot too short. His feet dangled over just enough to disturb whatever comfort he might hope to find.

His unwanted visitor reminded Ivan of a soccer ball. He began to smile but failed. Even a smile brought pain.

"We will talk later," said Gorodeyov. "You can come to the compound to rest and recover. You will be protected, unbothered." The visitor's offer was very appealing to Ivan. He remembered the compound. Were the people that friendly? Was it really that beautiful?

"Consider it, Ivan Medivkin," said the man, patting Ivan on the arm.

The giant was now snoring fitfully.

The usual crowd at Gatwick stood waiting at the belt for their luggage to rumble by. Since it was just after midnight and many passengers had been traveling for as much as a full day or more from all over the world, the battle for a good space was less frantic than usual. There was almost a dreamy haze of shared understanding.

Iris had but one bag, green canvas, wheels, made for world

travel. She reached between the bustling woman and the lean man from the plane with a "pardon me." Someone bumped into her and the bustling woman's hand reached out to grasp the handle of the bag and start to pull it from the grinding belt.

Iris reached out to stop the woman. Before it was necessary to do battle, the woman loosened her grip and the canvas bag tumbled forward on the belt for another ride.

Iris turned toward the woman, heard an odd intake of breath, and saw a look of pale anguish on the face of the woman. She seemed about to fall. Iris reached out a hand, but the woman found sudden support from the pale man who immediately and calmly helped the woman to a seat. Many glanced; none moved; the woman seemed to be in safe hands. They all wished her well. They had apartments to get to with telephone messages, cats to feed, beds to drop onto.

On the belt came Iris Templeton's green bag once more, but somehow it had lost the thin blue ribbon attached to the pull-up handle. She pulled it down. There was no longer a name tag on it.

She took it down and wheeled it out in search of Richard Neatly's minuscule blue German car, and as she did so she walked within a few feet of the reclining woman and the pale man.

When Iris was out of sight, the pale man leaned close to the woman and in Russian said, "You are not seriously injured, Christiana Davidonya."

Christiana, Pavel Petrov's assistant, had felt a sudden sharp jab to her kidney just as she had the handle of the green canvas bag in her hand. The jab had taken her breath. She had managed to glance at the pale man who supported her to the bank of aluminum and leather.

Her assignment had been simple: switch the bags. She had failed. Christiana had watched in pain as Iris Templeton wheeled past her, the tape deep inside the canvas bag.

There would be no follow-up attempt. It was too late. Even

now Christiana anticipated Pavel Petrov's rage and imagined that it might be taken out on her.

"We go back on the same flight," Karpo said. "Perhaps we can sit together."

Christiana gasped from the pain in her lower back and decided she would be in Moscow just long enough to pack, get to the money she had saved, pick up the passport in another name hidden in the bottom of a double boiler in her apartment, and make the next airplane connection to Brazil.

The planned attack on the English journalist in the Frankfurt airport had been called off by Christiana because it had proved to be too dangerous. She was sure Pavel would have tried it, probably would have succeeded in killing Iris Templeton, but Pavel had not been there. Christiana had decided it would be better to face his extreme displeasure than to be caught by the German police. Pavel liked taking chances. She did not.

Pavel Petrov was not going to survive.

She was.

On the flight to São Paulo, after a nap she would study Portuguese.

The pale black-suited man who now reminded her of a vampire guided her firmly in the direction of the ticket counter. She went quite willingly.

As soon as Neatly dropped her at her apartment, Iris locked the door behind her, put her bag on the bed, opened it, and found the small tape where she had placed it inside a stocking.

She pulled out her tape recorder, inserted the tape, and hit the "play" button. She let it run and then hit the "fast forward" button.

The tape was empty, nothing but the rush of ambient air. She turned the tape over. The other side yielded no voices.

Iris sat on the bed for about thirty seconds before she allowed herself a smile. Sergei Bresnechov, Tyrone, had fooled her. He had made a deal with another, perhaps several others, buyers, perhaps Pavel Petrov. It was too late and she was too tired to work it out now. She would sleep on it. In the morning it was sure to make more sense.

Just before she fell asleep it came to her. Tyrone would not make a deal with Petrov, the man who was responsible for the destruction of his apartment, the beating he had endured, and all that had been taken from him. No, Tyrone would want to cause maximum pain to the murderous Petrov. Tyrone would turn the tape over to the police or, better yet, make a deal with someone in the police to help him torment Petrov.

And just as she was dozing, at the very moment when thoughts and dreams are forgotten, Iris came up with a name: Colonel Igor Yaklovev. And then she was asleep.

15

A Power Play over Borscht

General Misovenski sat red faced and in full uniform to impress Colonel Igor Yaklovev, who was dressed in a gray suit and matching tie. The General wanted to remind the Colonel who the superior officer was at this table. The General had already pressed home his superiority by indicating where he and Yaklovev would lunch.

Now they sat over brandy after a meal of cold borscht with cucumbers, beets and sour cream, and chicken *tabak*.

"A satisfactory conclusion to the Maniac murders now that he has been identified?" asked the General.

"Yes," said the Yak. "The Maniac taken out of the picture, no trial, which might suggest a lack of investigation by your office, your team presented to the world as coming to the rescue of my chief investigator. Your highly efficient team came into the room and almost killed my Chief Investigator."

"It could not be helped," said General Misovenski. How is your man—Rostnikov, right?"

"He was shot in the shoulder and leg," said the Yak. "Fortunately, it was his artificial one. It resulted in only cosmetic damage."

"You were clearly and emphatically in support of the elimination of the Maniac."

"I was."

A look of sudden concern passed over the General's face.

"You are not wearing a wire, are you, Colonel? I should not take it kindly if you are."

"I assure you I am not," said the Yak, sipping the amber drink. "However, I was the last time we met."

"You are joking."

"No."

The General sat back and adjusted his collar. His medals jingled oh, so quietly.

"This seriously challenges our friendship."

"We are not friends," said the Yak. "We are business associates."

"I am your superior officer."

"Yes."

"And if I were to order you to turn over your recording?"

"I would gladly give you a copy."

"But there would be more. You are treading on dangerous ground, Igor Yaklovev. What do you want?"

"For you to continue to protect my office and provide assistance as we need it. And, in the future, be very careful when you have your men fire guns when my inspectors are present."

"Yes, what else?"

"Chief Inspector Rostnikov wants your Major Aloyosha Tarasov to be punished."

"For what?"

"You and I know full well that he murdered his wife, pushed her from a window."

"Why does this interest your Inspector Rostnikov?"

"He wants justice."

The General shook his head.

"He is my best officer."

"Yes."

"I will take care of it. Anything else?"

"No."

General Misovenski finished his brandy and considered himself most fortunate to have gotten away with so much and to have paid so little for it. Of course the Colonel had the tape, which could be brought forth at any time. There was no use searching for the tape. There were probably half a dozen copies well hidden anyplace in the world.

"I should like you to consider becoming my deputy," said the General.

"I would prefer not."

"I could order you."

"We could take the decision to a higher authority."

The General was well aware of a supposed direct connection between Yaklovev and the Prime Minister. He was not prepared to challenge it.

"Well," said the General. "I can do one more thing."

"Yes."

"I can pay for this marvelous lunch."

"Thank you."

The General motioned to the waiter to come over with the check.

"Coffee and a light fruit compote?" asked the waiter.

"Yaklovev?"

"No, thank you."

The Yak had not mentioned the other tape in his possession, the one that would damn Pavel Petrov. He might never mention it.

The General waved the waiter away, placed his hands on the table palms down, and, with a smile, said, "You are a devious man. Take care of yourself, Yaklovev. Take very good care."

16

Whispers at a Wedding

Without looking up, Zelach knew his mother was at the top of the stairs. He even knew what she was wearing, but that was not a prescient knowledge. She always wore the same thing, a dull dark smock with bright flowers. She had three of them of variously minimal hues.

"You are all right?" she said softly.

"I am all right," he said, trudging up the stairs, trying not to bother Mr. and Mrs. Gornick in the apartment next to theirs or the Volstoys right below them.

"A giant attacked you," his mother said.

"Yes," he said. "But I am fine."

He was not surprised by her observation. She had extra-sensory powers, which had been tested and tested, checked and rechecked, at the Moscow Institute of Paranormal Research. He too had been tested, examined, prodded, and punctured and found to have abilities that did not match those of his mother.

He was at the top of the stairs now. She reached out and touched his left cheek.

"You are hungry," she said. "I have sausage and cabbage for you."

The sweet smell of sausage and cabbage filled the stairway.

"I am hungry," he said.

She put up her right hand to hold the smock closed against her pendulous breasts. She was overweight and had a heart problem. She ate carefully, but both mother and son knew the battle with heart disease would soon end.

He followed her into the apartment, took off his jacket, and deposited it on the chair near the door with a heavy thump.

He sat and she poured him a small glass of white wine. She joined him. He did not ask how she knew when he would be home so that she could have his dinner on the table. That was one of the things he would miss, one of many things, when she was gone.

"You have a question, Akardy," she said, picking up her fork.

He ate slowly and considered his response, though he knew he was about to ask his question. The only issue was how he would couch it.

"Do you believe in an almost instant deep attraction of one person to another?"

"You mean love," she said.

He said nothing for a moment, forkful of sausage on the way to his mouth, and then, "What if your affection is addressed toward someone with great problems?"

"Akardy, there are some things I cannot penetrate that require normal conversation."

"Love," he said. "I think I am in love."

"The problem?"

"She murdered her husband and tried to kill an innocent woman."

"And you love her?"

"Her rage at her husband was well justified. Her life has been one of misfortune."

"Sometimes one cannot help being attracted to or falling in love with the wrong person."

He shrugged and went on eating. Then he sensed a sudden stiffening of his mother's body, a catching of breath. At first he thought it might be her heart, but then she sat upright and said, "She will not go to jail."

He believed his mother.

"I think you will help her. I think you may regret it."

"You are certain?"

"No," she said. "Never, but as close to certainty as one can get. One more thing."

"What?"

"Do you not know?"

It came to him.

"For dessert you have plum pudding."

"Yes," she said. "Tell me more about this woman you love who murdered her husband."

Yuri Platkov sat at the end of the bench gnawing at a bright orange carrot. In the middle of the bench sat the one-legged policeman. Both the boy, who was on his way home from school, and Porfiry Petrovich Rostnikov watched the afternoon traffic go by.

Over the last two days, the temperature had risen again, and a wet snow that turned to slush formed a thin, shoe-penetrating lake of dirty water.

Finally, Rostnikov, without looking at the boy, said, "We have switched from less-than-nutritious candy to healthy vegetables."

Yuri looked at what was left of his carrot, which was not much, and answered, "The school."

The boy, fair skinned, thin, with dark hair sticking out around the earflaps of his woolen shirt, crunched loudly on his carrot.

Rostnikov nodded in understanding.

"Carrots are not bad."

Rostnikov, hands folded in his lap, nodded.

"Would you like one? I have two more."

"Yes."

The boy dug a plastic Baggie from his book bag, unzipped it, and handed Rostnikov a carrot.

"You got him, the Maniac."

Rostnikov took a bite of carrot.

"He was eternally detained."

The boy nodded as he pulled his legs back to avoid the splash of a group of hurrying men and women anxious to get home.

"Shot when he was going to try to kill you. A SWAT team."

"Would you believe me if I told you I was never in any danger from the Maniac, that I could have brought him in if men firing automatic weapons had not appeared?"

"Yes, I believe."

"However, I was shot."

"How? Where?"

Yuri was looking at the policeman with great interest.

"In my leg and shoulder. Fortunately, one bullet hit my artificial leg, where it was removed without pain. The other bullet went through my arm and scraped a bone."

"Does it hurt?"

"A bit."

"May I see the bullet holes?" asked Yuri.

Rostnikov awkwardly leaned forward, pulled up the leg of his pants, and pushed down his sock. The sight of the washtub of a man displaying his artificial leg for the boy in the slushy cold caused usually weary commuters to hesitate, look, and continue. A few considered informing the police. More simply averted their eyes and walked on.

The boy looked at the dent on the artificial leg, which the policeman pointed out.

"To show you the wound in my shoulder would require me

removing my coat, shirt, and undershirt and you would see only a white bandage. I am sorry."

"Do not be. You found him, for which I am pleased."

Rostnikov pulled up his sock, dropped his trouser leg, and sat back.

"My grandfather, who has been known to stumble around the park and on the street, might have been next."

"And you have great affection for your grandfather?"

"No. Maybe. Sometimes. You are telling me a great deal about your case. Do you usually go about telling boys in the park what you are doing?"

"No, I do not. I suppose I like you."

"I like you too. Another carrot?"

Rostnikov looked down at his hand. The carrot was gone. He had not even noted its passing.

"I think not," said Rostnikov.

"Then it is over. No reason to return to this bench, the park."

Rostnikov let out a small grunt as he watched a young woman make a dangerous crossing of the street. She held a large purse in one hand and kept her small hat in place with the other.

There were still the copycats to deal with. He was not prepared to share that information with the boy on the bench.

"Perhaps I will find myself back here from time to time," said Rostnikov. "It is a pleasant place to watch pretty girls, to think, to find stimulating conversation."

"You like superheroes?" said Yuri.

"*X-Files*. My son gave me an 'I Want to Believe' T-shirt some years ago. I frequently sleep in it."

"Your son?"

"He is a policeman too and probably older than your mother and father."

"Then you are old?"

"As old as Moscow itself."

"I am going to be a policeman," said the boy. "Of course I am only eleven, so I may change my mind."

"Return to this bench and keep me informed of your various changes of mind."

"I should go home now."

"We should both go home now."

The boy bounced up. Rostnikov positioned his nonexistent leg and pushed himself up slowly with a hand on either side of him.

Yuri Platkov held out a thin right hand and Rostnikov took it lightly with respect.

"It is nice to see you again. My name is Yuri Sergievich Platkov."

"And mine is Porfiry Petrovich Rostnikov."

"That sounds like a very old-fashioned name."

"I am a very old-fashioned man."

The sun had begun to rise by the time Emil Karpo reached the street on which he lived. He had traveled without luggage and had not slept going or coming back from London.

One block away, he could see a gathering in an alcove near the entrance to his building. As he moved quietly closer, he could see that it was a group of six boys, *bezprizorniki,* children of the streets, homeless, dangerous. They were all bent over, looking down at something he could not see, calling out encouraging words.

Karpo touched the shoulders of two of the boys in his way. They looked up at him and parted. In the doorway was a boy with a stick. He was perhaps fifteen years old. He was dirty, as were they all, and their clothes were odd in size and they were obviously not slaves to fashion. The older boy was jabbing a black cat trapped against the door. With nowhere to go, the cat sat back and waved a paw at the prodding stick.

The boys called out, "Get him, Borka. Kill him. Let's eat him."

Karpo leaned over, took the stick from the boy called Borka, broke it, and dropped it on the pavement.

Borka, whose face was lopsided to the left, stood up in anger. He was almost half a foot shorter than Karpo, who knelt to pick up the cat, which did not resist.

Karpo tucked the cat under his right arm and faced the boy as he rose.

The boy could not decide whether to search for a way to back down or attack the intruder. There were six of them and only one of him. Every boy in the group had been through fights over food or shelter in which their lives were at stake. They would win, though something about the man's pale, expressionless face made Borka hesitate.

"Give us your money and we will let you pass," said Borka, moving to block the entrance.

"I cannot do that," said Karpo.

"Why not?" asked one boy to his left.

"Because I am a police officer."

Karpo pulled his badge from his back pocket and held it up.

Borka glanced at it and said, "We have faced policemen before."

"Then," said Karpo, returning his wallet to his pocket. "We shall have to see how you manage with this one."

A caw of insults came from the mouths of those surrounding him as he moved to the door and removed the key from his pocket.

"*Meduk*, asshole."

"*Govniuk*, shit head."

Karpo could sense one of the boys, not Borka, step behind his back. He turned and faced a boy of no more than ten with a six-inch piece of pipe in his right hand.

The insults stopped. There was a mad look in the eyes of the boy and Borka stood at his shoulder.

"Bash him, Nicki," a boy in the semicircle called.

As the boy was about to strike, Emil Karpo softly said, "No," and the boy lowered his weapon. Karpo entered his apartment building and with his free hand made sure the door was locked behind him.

"We know where you live," called Borka.

The threat meant little to Karpo. They would not want to do battle with a policeman, a policeman who would certainly have a hidden gun. There was nothing to be gained from confronting this unblinking ghost. The gang would almost certainly not return.

After climbing the stairs, he checked the door for the telltale hair that would inform him whether he had had company. There were no signs of company. He entered and put the cat down. The room was cold. The window was open. Nothing had been moved. Nothing had been touched. The narrow bed was hunched in one corner. The chest of drawers stood against one wall, with the freestanding closet at its side. Under the window stood a small, round wooden table with two chairs, and at the foot of the bed against the wall was a small sink and counter, with minimal dishes and utensils and a microwave. A few groceries, most conspicuously a large box of instant oatmeal, were lined up next to the microwave.

The entire remaining wall was covered with notebooks dealing with the investigations of all cases with which Karpo had been involved. The unresolved ones, the ones he worked on in the evenings and on his days off, were neatly labeled to the left on plain wooden shelves he had built.

He removed his clothes and placed them all neatly on a chair after removing something from his pocket. He held it up, looked at it, and brought the ocarina that Porfiry Petrovich had given to him to his lips. He blew into it gently, one note only. The cat's ears turned to him and twitched. He placed the ocarina on his desk.

After two hours of rest on his bed in the nude and cold, he would rise and report to Chief Inspector Rostnikov.

Completely nude, Emil Karpo lay back atop the tautly tucked rough khaki military blanket on his bed and closed his eyes. Seconds later he was aware of a gentle movement on the bed to his left. The cat nestled down against his hip. Emil Karpo's fingers touched smooth, silky hair. Then cat and man fell asleep.

Iosef knew that Elena was as uncomfortable as he as they stood before the desk of the ZAGS officer.

ZAGS (Zapis Aktov Grazhdanskogo Sostoyaniya), the official bureau that handled Russia's weddings, had to grant permission for every wedding, and once a request was denied, little or no recourse existed in the Russian bureaucracy.

ZAGS, an unimposing two-story half-block-long building, sat on the Butyrsky Ulitsa. In front of the shoe-box building, traffic ran heavily down the wide street and horns blared.

The mandatory thirty-second day after they had applied for their wedding license had come to an end. This was the final chance for either of them to back out of the *brakosochetanie*, the minimal but official service in the sparse office in which a fluorescent light twinkled and pinged.

Behind them stood the witnesses, Iosef's mother and father and Elena's aunt and cousin Edith. Iosef thought his father, two days out of the hospital, should not be there. Elena thought her aunt Anna, who awaited her probably inevitable fourth heart attack, should not be there. Elena and Iosef had no luck in convincing either one of them. Both Porfiry Petrovich and Anna Timofeyeva stood a few paces back, with Anna Timofeyeva between Porfiry Petrovich and Sara. Once Elena's aunt had been a robust and often-uniformed procurator in the Soviet Union with Rostnikov as her chief investigator. But then both Anna Timofeyeva and the Soviet Union had collapsed.

According to tradition, Iosef had been picked up at his apartment by his parents, and Elena had come with her aunt and cousin. An unmarked police car, a black ZiL, had been provided by Porfiry Petrovich to transport Elena.

They had all met in the stark lobby that carried a nervous echo. Iosef wore his only suit, heavy and navy blue, with a white shirt and a blue-and-red-striped tie. Elena wore a white dress that Iosef had not seen before. She also wore a touch of makeup. To Iosef she looked healthy and beautiful.

Papers had been signed. The ZAGS officer, a lean, smiling man of about sixty, bore an uncanny resemblance to the American actor John Carradine. Iosef remembered an old movie in which Carradine, a consumptive prisoner in an Australian hellhole, saved the life of Brian Aherne by killing an oppressive guard by throwing sheep shears into the guard's back. Iosef imagined the ZAGS officer reaching into his desk, pulling out scissors, and hurling them toward someone in the room.

The officer spoke, but Iosef, on the one hand, did not hear from his hiding place in the Australian outback. Elena, on the other hand, struggled to keep her attention on the words.

Abruptly the officer stopped and looked at both of them, waiting. Neither knew what to say or do. They looked at each other and smiled broadly, sharing a thought about the officer and the ceremony.

Iosef was instantly happy and Elena's look conveyed that she was too. They embraced, kissed. Iosef took in the distinct scent of Elena mixed with an unfamiliar perfume while Elena was aware of his smell of bath soap and the familiar touch of perspiration.

Porfiry Petrovich handed his son two plain gold marriage bands. Iosef placed one ring on the ring finger of his right hand. He then placed the other band on the same finger of Elena's right hand.

Then on to the party, which began with a toast from Porfiry Petrovich, who raised his glass and said, "*Za molodykh*, to the newlyweds."

A Russian wedding traditionally takes at least two days. Elena and Iosef had decided theirs would take one afternoon. Traditionally, the guests drank vodka and got drunk. Elena and Iosef had decided that vodka would be poured freely, but the length of the party would minimize drunkenness. Traditionally, the groom's friends would block his way to the waiting bride. They would demand answers to embarrassing questions and, if not satisfied, would reject passage, forcing him to find another way into her room, possibly through a window. Elena and Iosef would skip that too, though they had both laughed one afternoon while at Petrovka imagining Karpo, Tkach, and Zelach blocking a stairwell. They added Paulinin, the Yak, and Pankov for more broken-up laughter.

The party, held in the small third-story corner apartment of Sara and Porfiry Petrovich, quickly spilled into the hallway, where several neighbors joined in. Elena and Iosef stood in the living room greeting guests who brought white envelopes containing traditional gifts of money. The envelopes were handed to Porfiry Petrovich, who handed them to his wife.

A twig of an old man from the second floor congratulated Iosef and Elena saying, "Your father fixed my toilet."

"Good," said Iosef.

"It was full of shit and wouldn't flush. The man is a great plumber."

"Thank you for sharing that," said Elena with a straight face.

Iosef couldn't hold back. He turned and pretended to cough.

On the stairwell, Galina's granddaughters, Laura and Nina, had come upstairs tentatively but had soon met Pulcharia Tkach, who took them under her wing along with her four-year-old brother. The four of them played on the stairs with squeals and shouts.

In the crowded living room sat a table continually being re-stocked with glasses, knives, forks, and plates. New rounds of table-ware and empty trays were constantly being gathered and washed in the small kitchen by Galina and Lydia, whose shrill voice could be heard chattering above the rumble of conversations around her. Having left her hearing aids in her apartment, she was barely aware that anyone was speaking.

In addition to vodka, bowls and platters piled high with food crowded together, some threatening to topple to the floor. The food included *pelmeny*, small balls of minced meat covered with pastry; *vareniky*, pastry filled with berries; *soleniye ogurscy*, cucumbers prepared for two weeks in salt water with spices; *vinegret*, pieces of herring, chopped beef, beets, cucumber, carrot, potato, and oil; and *yazyk*, slices of boiled beef tongue with horseradish.

On the sofa with a glass of Pepsi-Cola in hand sat Anna Timofeyeva, who was keeping a secret that weighed upon her; she had promised to keep it, and keep it she would. Next to her sat Maya Tkach, who looked no happier than Anna Timofeyeva or the other person on the couch of gloom, Sasha Tkach. Sasha held a plate that had been piled high with food and handed to him by his mother. With the plate in one hand and a fork in the other, he ate dutifully.

A man laughed, more the sound of a horse than a human. A man whom Porfiry Petrovich did not recognize called out, "Has anyone seen Victor?" A glass broke. The party went on.

In the middle of the room with Pankov dutifully at his side, Igor Yaklovev, in a perfectly fitted blue suit and red tie, checked the time on his gold pocket watch. The watch was rumored to be a gift from Vladimir Putin. The Yak and Pankov were given room by the guests, who either knew who they were or recognized the presence of persons of power. It did not hurt this aura that the Yak looked very much like Lenin.

Against the wall leaned Emil Karpo and Akardy Zelach. Hands folded in front of him, Karpo looked like a sentry before a secret conclave. An unbidden thought came to Emil Karpo, the flash of the face of Mathilde Verson, killed in the cross fire between a Chechen and a Russian gang. Mathilde, the only woman he had ever been involved with, had been a prostitute. That did not matter to either of them. She found him amusing and worried about him, but it was she who had been flung back against the window of a restaurant, her waves of red hair flowing as she flew.

"Can I get you anything?" asked Zelach.

The image was gone. Mathilde was gone.

"No, nothing."

Zelach leaned back against the wall again and caught a glimpse of Sasha Tkach.

Zelach knew that Maya had agreed to come to the wedding reception, where she would decide whether or not to return to Moscow. Sasha had told him this. Zelach had given him sympathy but no advice.

Akardy Zelach slouched forward, face close to his plate of *yazyk* and *vinegret*, his eyes on his food, his thoughts with his mother at home too ill to come to the party. Zelach longed for a way to leave, and then Porfiry Petrovich appeared before him and said, "How is your mother?"

"Poorly."

"You should be with her."

"Yes."

"Go. Bring her some food. Tell her I hope that she will get well soon. Go."

Porfiry Petrovich smiled and touched Zelach's arm and then repeated, "Go."

"Thank you. I will just finish this quickly."

"And you, Emil Karpo, are you well?" asked Rostnikov.

"Perfectly," said Karpo.

Rostnikov decided not to press the issue, not at his son's wedding reception, but knew that something was troubling the gaunt detective. Karpo's emotionless façade had been showing subtle signs of distress, which Rostnikov was reasonably sure that no one but he would notice.

"Good," said Rostnikov, turning to make his way back through the crowd.

Anna Timofeyeva left first. Escorted by Elena's cousin. Porfiry Petrovich guided them through the crowd and down the stairs. At the curb stood an unmarked police car for which Rostnikov had arranged.

Just before Anna got into the car, she did something she had never done before. She touched and then kissed the cheek of her former chief investigator and said, "*Rad za tebya*, I am happy for you."

After two hours of pressing bodies, loud and shrill voices that created an unpleasant cacophony, Colonel Igor Yaklovev looked at his pocket watch. Time to leave. He had given the couple a suitable gift of cash and had wished them the best. Iosef sensed a slight tension in the Yak's good-bye to him. Iosef had long shown signs of often-sullen disagreement with some of the work he had been assigned to do and some of the lies he was forced to tell. His father had kept him in line, and Iosef had performed with distinction.

The Yak had met with Porfiry Petrovich while he was in the hospital. They had agreed that when Iosef and Elena returned they would no longer be teamed on an investigation. Porfiry Petrovich, however, took issue with the Yak's wish that Rostnikov not team with either his son or new daughter-in-law.

Colonel Yaklovev reconsidered. The decision that Porfiry Petrovich not work with Elena or Iosef had been a wish, not an order. Had it been an order, the Colonel was sure his Chief Inspector would have acquiesced.

Pankov left the party with Colonel Yaklovev. He felt that he may have given a greater cash gift than necessary. He had asked his highly unreliable neighbor Mrs. Olga Ferinova how much he should give. Olga Ferinova, a huge woman who supervised two street-cleaning crews, was certain about everything. She had told him what was proper, and he had done it.

On the way out, the Yak almost bumped into eleven-year-old Laura, who looked up at him and stopped laughing. Once outside, the Yak climbed into the waiting black police car at the curb. Pankov followed. The Yak had work to do.

With the departure of Colonel Yaklovev, the party got even louder and the vodka began to flow even more freely.

Zelach was next to leave, with a bag of food Lydia Tkach had prepared for his mother. He shook the hands of bride and groom. Iosef held Zelach's hand a bit longer than he would hold others. Iosef smiled and Akardy returned the smile. When he touched Elena's hand, he felt again that she held something back. She seemed to sense that he knew her secret. She gave him a reassuring touch on the arm.

Emil Karpo stepped through the dwindling crowd, shook the hands of Porfiry Petrovich, Sara, Elena, and Iosef, and left without a word. The departure of the ghostly figure in black further emboldened the remaining guests to consume even more vodka. More bottles were brought out. The empty ones were carried clinking to the cartons from which they had come.

A few of the now-drunken neighbors had to be politely urged to return to their apartments by Sara and Porfiry Petrovich. That left only Maya, Sasha, their children, and Lydia, in addition to Galina and her granddaughters. Maya had risen from the sofa to join her mother-in-law, Galina, and Sara in cleaning up, which they did with efficiency. Sasha watched his wife for signs of her intent to stay or go back to Kiev. He could detect nothing. He prided himself on his ability to see the small signs of intent in suspects. It was an ability he could not exercise on his wife. The children, a plate of food in each lap, sat on the floor of the now nearly empty living room.

The bride and groom moved to the bedroom to be alone before leaving for a four-day honeymoon in Yalta.

"Sit," she said, gently ordering Iosef to his parents' bed.

He obeyed and she paced nervously, touching the unfamiliar ring on her finger.

"I have to tell you something," she said. "I should have told you this before we were married."

"You mean about the baby?" he said, looking up at her.

She stopped fidgeting and pacing and met his eyes.

"You know."

"I am a detective," he said with a grin.

"And?"

"A girl would be nice. So would a boy."

"My aunt knows," she said.

"Do you want to tell your parents?"

"Certainly."

He stood now. She moved into his arms with a sigh of great relief.

"I love you," she said.

"I know," he said.

The couple thanked Iosef's mother and father when there was no one else in the apartment and the door finally closed. At that point, Elena told Sara and Porfiry Petrovich that they were going to be grandparents.

17
Talking to the Dead, He Misses the Wedding

Only one invited guest did not show up for the wedding party.

On the night before the wedding, Paulinin slept on the cot in his laboratory within a dozen feet of the two corpses laid out gently on two slabs. One was a male. The other a female. Both were covered by gray-blue sheets, the man's just above his waist, the woman's up to her neck. They were two corpses seemingly unrelated except for their means of death. She was forty-two, well dressed, well proportioned, decidedly handsome, and decidedly peaceful in death. He was an alcoholic of perhaps sixty years of age, underweight, ill clothed. If the killer had not selected him, he would have been destined to die within the year from a final rebellion of his organs.

Paulinin had slept five hours. When he rose, he had completely forgotten the wedding. Buoyed by hot coffee and the ever-present laboratory smells, he was prepared to talk to the dead. The white mug had blue printing on the side saying: "Police Target Champion 1987."

Paulinin fired at no targets. The mug had been given to him

years ago, though he could not remember by whom. He chose to ignore the three dark brown ring stains inside the mug as he drank.

And then he made his phone call.

"Paulinin," answered Porfiry Petrovich after the third ring. "Do you know what time it is?"

"No."

"And you do not care?"

"No. I have information."

"I am listening."

"I dreamt that my two latest guests told me something," he said.

Rostnikov could hear Vivaldi playing in the background.

"Both of them have deep trauma to the back of the head caused probably by a hammer, a clean new one, which gave up tiny shining metal chips," Paulinin said. "The wounds are not as deep as any caused by the Maniac. The corpses were simply dropped in the woods off of a pathway. All the other corpses were laid out in repose, on their sides with hands as pillows. Two hairs from atop the body of the man were DNA tested. They belonged to you. However, another bitten-off fingernail proved not to be from the dead Aleksandr Chenko."

Paulinin was unable to resist the urge to gently touch the cheek of the dead woman.

"Get some sleep, Paulinin."

"I have. Stop by in the morning with Karpo for pastries, coffee, and to discuss the situation. You bring the pastries."

"We will be there," said Rostnikov, although he could, if pressed, make a list of perhaps one hundred places he would rather be. His hope was that the scientist would make some effort to clean the autopsy tables and wash whatever dishes, cups, and forks they might be using. Rostnikov knew, however, that his wishes would be in vain. It might well be better to bring paper plates and napkins.

"Who?" asked Sara at his side dreamily.

"Paulinin," answered Rostnikov, reaching for his pants.

"Not those," she said. "They have a bullet hole in the leg."

He grunted, rose, and reached for his artificial leg.

"Time?" she asked.

"After dawn," he said, continuing to dress.

"Your shoulder?"

"Feels fine."

"Porfiry Petrovich, you could have, should have, died."

He had talked his way out of the hospital with the promise of seeing Sara's cousin the next day. There was the wedding of his only child, his only son, to attend. Leon had rewarded him with large round yellow pain pills, which he had been using generously.

"Yes," he said. "But . . ."

" 'Yes, but,' " she said. "Be careful."

"I am only going to visit the dead and talk to Paulinin."

"That does not reassure me," said Sara, starting to rise.

"Sleep," he said, now standing and buttoning a clean white shirt.

"I cannot," she said. "Wait. I will get you something to eat. Kasha and some of the pork from last night."

"Why not? I must call Emil Karpo."

"You really think the wedding went well?"

"Yes," he said. "Very well.

"We are going to have grandchildren," he said, now heading for the cubbyhole bathroom/shower.

"Yes," she said. "Yes."

There was something in that final "yes" that made Rostnikov pause and turn to look at his wife, whose eyes were fixed on a slipper in her hand halfway to her foot, hovering in wait as if for some great something she knew would never come.

As he shaved, Porfiry Petrovich Rostnikov vowed to buy his wife colorful flowers, to take her out to dinner at her favorite restaurant, and to hold her for a very long time in his arms before they went to sleep that night.

They would talk about babies.

As it turned out, two of the copycat killers were a husband and wife working together, he to hold, she to strike. She was a night supervisor at a supermarket not unlike the one at which Aleksandr Chenko had worked. The husband was the head of the meat department. They had been married two years, and the tales of violent serial murder had entered their imaginations and moved them sexually. Murder together proved to be a powerful aphrodisiac.

And then one night in Bitsevsky Park, a few days after Aleksandr Chenko had been torn to pieces by bullets and Rostnikov had fallen wounded, the couple encountered a hulking man with an unsteady gait. They attacked. The hulking man turned out to be not nearly as old or as drunk as they had assumed.

His name was Andrei Anronkovich. He was the former middleweight wrestling champion of Moscow. He had fought back, but the woman had cracked his skull from behind. Responding to loud voices in the bushes, a policeman named Julian Ivanovich made his way to a secluded spot where the husband and wife stood over the dead Anronkovich.

The end of the Maniac murders had come, and if the victims of the young couple were to be counted, the sixty-four spaces on the chessboard had been filled. That still left two more copycats to catch.

It was one of those unpredictably pleasant mornings in Moscow. The temperature had climbed to almost forty degrees Fahrenheit. The trees in Bitsevsky Park swayed gently and whispered to Porfiry Petrovich, who almost dozed on the bench.

He recognized perhaps two dozen people who hurried to the Metro station in the morning and emerged from it at night. There was little reason for Porfiry Petrovich to return here, but here he found himself waiting with the few remaining pastries after his visit to Paulinin.

Then the boy appeared. He was on time for school but would be late if he stopped to talk to the policeman. Yuri could not resist. This time he sat almost at the policeman's side.

"Why are you here? The Maniac is dead."

"I came to say good-bye to you."

Yuri nodded in understanding and accepted a pastry from the bag the policeman extended to him. The one he picked was very sticky but most delicious, with dark berries and brown sugar. He planned to down it quickly, lick his fingers, and hurry off.

"We are moving," the boy said as he ate.

"Where are you moving?"

"To Tiblisi. We are Georgians. My father and mother say we are no longer welcome in Russia. Some other kids have made remarks. I know little of what is happening or why, and my grandfather is now cursing a great deal."

"I am sorry," said Rostnikov.

"That is all right. We have family in Tiblisi. A job awaits my father."

Yuri paused for almost half a minute, looked at the last of his pastry, and quietly said, "I do not want to go."

"Yes," Rostnikov said. "Yes."

The boy rose from the bench and extended his hand. Porfiry Petrovich Rostnikov took it. The boy waved and was off.

Moments later Rostnikov rose and walked slowly into the park toward the swaying trees.

He shrugged his bandaged shoulder. Then he realized he wanted to weep.

But he did not weep.

CPSIA information can be obtained at www.ICGtesting.com
Printed in the USA
LVOW12s1737181214

419464LV00004B/281/P